3

He'd never be a fool for any woman's soft lies again.

Keegan sucked in a harsh breath and felt heat escalate throughout his body. Besides his twin brother, Elizabeth Ralston was the only person he knew who could make him furious with very little effort. She touched a raw place in him that was better left alone.

When she continued to study him, his fury with life . . . fate . . . whatever . . . went into high gear.

"Look who's here," he drawled. "The last known living member of the legendary Ralston clan."

Beth flinched. She'd wondered what Keegan's reaction would be to her return. Now she knew.

She raked up a careless smile. "Well, if it isn't Keegan McPherson of the fightin' McPhersons. Hello, Keegan. Do we shake hands—or just come out swinging?"

Dear Reader,

Welcome to Silhouette **Special Edition** . . . welcome to romance.

Last year, I requested that you send me your opinions on the books that we publish, and on romances in general. Thank you so much for the many thoughtful letters. For the next couple of months, I'd like to share some quotes from these letters with you. This seemed very appropriate now while we are in the midst of the THAT SPECIAL WOMAN! promotion. Each one of our readers is a special woman, as heroic as the heroines in our books.

This September has some wonderful stories coming your way. *A Husband to Remember* by Lisa Jackson is our THAT SPECIAL WOMAN! selection for this month.

This month also has other special treats. For one, we've got *Bride Wanted* by Debbie Macomber coming your way. This is the second book in her FROM THIS DAY FORWARD series. *Night Jasmine* by Erica Spindler—one of the BLOSSOMS OF THE SOUTH series—is also on its way to happy readers, as is Laurie Paige's *A Place for Eagles,* the second tale in her WILD RIVER TRILOGY. And September brings more books from favorite authors Patricia Coughlin and Natalie Bishop.

I hope you enjoy this book, and all of the stories to come!

Sincerely,

Tara Gavin
Senior Editor
Silhouette Books

Quote of the Month: "All the Silhouettes I've read have believable characters and are easy to identify with. The pace of the story line is good, the books hold my interest. When I start a Silhouette, I know I'm in for a good time."
—P. Digney,
New Jersey

LAURIE PAIGE

reports that life after a certain age (thirty-something and then some) keeps getting rosier. She was recently presented with the *Affaire de Coeur* Readers' Choice Silver Pen award for favorite contemporary author. Laurie gives the credit—and thanks!—to her romance readers, who are the most wonderful, loyal people in the world. She's also just had another super event—the birth of her first grandchild, a boy. ''Definitely hero material!''

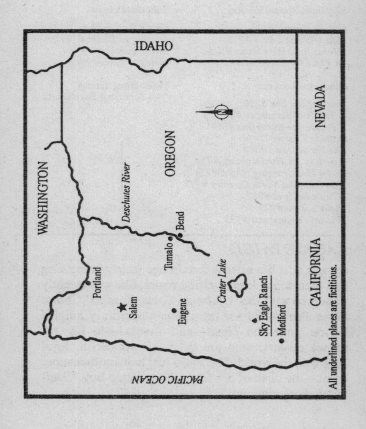

All underlined places are fictitious.

Chapter One

Elizabeth Ralston gave up trying to restart the rental car. Its demise had been quick—one minute the vehicle had been purring along the road, the next it wasn't.

She climbed out and raised the hood, then leaned against the fender and scrutinized the landscape.

A sparse meadow of sage and manzanita skirted the road to the south. Beyond that, hills thickly coated with fir trees notched the skyline in a sweeping arc. The sky was clear. Not even a jet trail marred the pale blue tint.

While standing on this particular stretch of road, she could see no other living person. Only the fences indicated human habitation. A chill of unease chased over her. For a brief second she felt alien, an intruder in this primal setting.

Home, she thought, as if to remind herself. *Home.*

A dust devil rose to the east of her, swirled by a miniature cyclone of hot, dry wind. The whirlwind subsided abruptly, its energy spent, and the debris settled, leaving a cloud of dun-colored powder on the hot August air.

Beth watched the haze of dust until it disappeared, then raised her sights to an eagle riding a thermal high overhead. Her uneasiness changed, becoming pensive.

Two hours ago she'd flown in from San Francisco. Observing the land from the lofty height of the plane, she'd wondered for the thousandth time if she was doing the right thing.

With a great deal of trepidation, she'd convinced herself that she was. After all, she had every right to be here. It was just that she was unsure about her future . . . which she had chosen with her eyes wide open and her feet on terra firma.

That thought produced a brief smile. She'd best remember that the earth could be treacherous and not firm at all. This area had once been a gigantic volcano that had blown apart aeons ago. Its tormented past was visible at Crater Lake and in the lava flows and granite upheavals throughout this section of southern Oregon.

The land could be unforgiving to the foolish.

Life on the ranches that nestled within its rugged contours was hard. She knew just how hard. She'd been born and raised less than fifteen miles from where she now waited for someone to come along and rescue her.

"Calling all knights in shining armor!" she said aloud, her patience with her predicament wearing thin.

Her errant knight might arrive on horseback, but more likely he would be driving a four-wheel-drive pickup with a rifle slung across the back window. His armor would consist of boots, jeans and a work shirt with snaps instead of buttons. Cowboys didn't like to waste time getting out of their clothes.

Yes, she knew this land. And the men who lived there.

A shiver ran down her spine in spite of the heat. Perhaps she was making a mistake...had already made it, she corrected, knowing she wouldn't turn back. She had sold her car and leased the flower shop she owned, her condo and all her furniture. She was now on an extended leave from her normal life...perhaps from her senses.

The West had a reputation for being rough on anyone too weak to stand up to its demands. It was a place for dust devils, for eagles and for hard-minded men determined to follow their dreams no matter what the cost.

It was hell on the women who loved them.

She watched the eagle another moment before turning toward the sound of a vehicle coming around the bend, headed for town. She pushed her sunglasses on top of her head.

Oh, no, she protested when the pickup braked to a stop across the road. *Any knight but this one.*

Keegan McPherson stopped the truck and turned off the engine. In the resonant silence, he stared at the woman who stood utterly still at the side of the road, staring back at him.

He surveyed her peach-colored slacks, her yellow and peach blouse, and high-heeled white sandals. Now *those* were really practical to wear out here, he scoffed. She'd break an ankle if she stepped on a piece of gravel.

A gust of wind swirled her hair into her face. She brushed the short curls back with a quick, familiar gesture.

A painful sensation tore at him. He'd once run his hands through those glossy strands that were so dark, so shiny, they'd reminded him of a blackbird's wing. Her hair was pure black, without a trace of other tints...black and shiny...all over.

He sucked in a harsh breath of hot, dusty air and felt the heat escalate throughout his body. With a curse he climbed out of the truck and started toward her, half expecting her to disappear from sight like a chimera sent to haunt him by some vengeful god.

She didn't move.

Instead she watched his approach without one shred of welcome on her face. Noting her expression, he thought she'd rather have met up with a timber rattler than him. Well, that was just too damned bad.

A smile pursed her mouth and was instantly gone.

It wasn't one of humor, he observed, catching the whiplash of irony in it. He felt the same. Given a choice, she was the last person he'd have wanted to meet on a deserted road, or anywhere else for that matter.

For a second his attention wandered as the wind toyed with her blouse, alternately outlining and obscuring the finely wrought curves of her breasts. The heat turned into a fire in his gut.

Three years ago he'd have lifted her into his truck, driven off the road to a secluded glen and made love to her until they were both sated.... He swore furiously to himself. He would never be a fool for any woman's soft lies again.

She still didn't speak as he came nearer. His temper kicked like a half-wild bronco. He clamped down on it. She was the only person he knew, besides his twin brother, who could make him furious with very little effort. She touched a raw place in him that was better left alone.

He stopped four feet away. She continued to study him as if he were some strange specimen she'd happened upon, and his fury with life...fate...whatever...went into high gear.

"Look who's here," he drawled. "The last-known living member of the legendary Ralston clan."

Beth mentally flinched at the verbal attack. She'd wondered what his reaction would be to her return. Now she knew.

She raked up a careless smile. "Well, if it isn't Keegan McPherson of the Fightin' McPhersons. Hello, Keegan. Should we shake hands or just come out swinging?"

She hoped he wouldn't take up the offer to shake hands. Hers were probably trembling. She kept her smile intact. No way would she give him the satisfaction of knowing that he upset her. She could be as cold as the wind off Jackass Mountain, too, and as mulish as any McPherson.

"I've learned not to fight with women. You hit below the belt," he said in the same laconic tone as before.

His words struck a vulnerable spot in her. If she'd thought they could meet on some kind of neutral ground and perhaps learn to coexist, this encounter dispelled that notion.

With the McPhersons a person was either their friend or their enemy. There was no middle ground.

"You grow more like your grandfather every day," she goaded, wanting to hurt him, knowing how he'd felt about the old man who'd grudgingly taken him and his brother in, orphans of only ten, then worked them harder than pack mules in a gold rush.

Even behind his sunglasses, she could detect the fury that smoldered in his winter gray eyes. So, she could still strike a sore spot in him, too. The victory felt hollow.

"Maybe. You have to give the old man credit. He never forgot who his enemies were. You can bet I never will again." A smile spread over Keegan's face, hard and lethal and unforgiving.

Her heart contracted. He was incredibly handsome, with his dark, wavy hair and light gray eyes with a touch of blue, his teeth dazzling white against his tanned skin. He had the dead-level gaze of a man who stood his ground and never backed down. Her personal experience with him proved that point beyond a doubt.

In *his* eyes, she'd done him wrong, and he would never forgive her.

That worked two ways. He'd misjudged her, and she would never forgive him for that, either.

Check, as they said in chess. An impasse. Neither could make a move without conceding the game.

And so they'd both lost.

Regret ricocheted deep within her, mingling with the pain of their remembered past. Once she'd thought they would join forces and be finished with the bitterness between their families.

So much for dreams.

"It seems we've both learned some valuable lessons." She shrugged as if amused, but suddenly she felt like crying, just plunking herself down on the side of the lonely road and letting it all out—the hurt and worry and sadness of life.

"So why are you standing out here in the middle of nowhere?" he asked, his gaze going to the raised hood behind her.

She waved a weary hand toward the crippled car. "I have a slight problem with the engine."

Actually, the vehicle was the least of her worries, but it was the most urgent at the moment. She had to get to the ranch before she could delve into her troubles there.

"What's wrong with it?"

She saw his quick survey of the interior of the compact car. The trunk and rear seat were packed with her belongings.

"It quit running."

He gave an impatient snort.

"If I knew what was wrong, I'd fix it myself," she elaborated, keeping her tone bland despite the rush of anger caused by his unrelenting attitude. "It was running, then it quit."

"Let's check the gas," was his first brilliant suggestion.

"Be my guest. The keys are in it." She moved away from the door so he could climb in.

"Seems to have plenty of fuel," he concluded after checking the gages. He tried to start the engine. The starter clicked but the engine wouldn't crank. He tried several times.

Beth permitted herself one tight smile.

Keegan scowled through the window at her. He climbed out and poked around inside the engine.

While he was intent on the chore, she dropped her pretense of indifference and let herself look at him. The curve of his body as he leaned over the fender was lean and powerful. She wanted to run her hands along his shoulders and absorb some of his strength.

She noted the taut slenderness of his hips through jeans that covered him like a second skin. Cowboys didn't like wrinkles in their clothes. He'd told her wrinkles in the cloth could cause blisters, so the pants had to fit just right.

Under the denim, his flesh was lashed just as smoothly over the sinews and bones of his legs. There was a scar on his inner thigh, a reminder of his days as a rodeo champion. The injury he'd received from a maddened bull had come close to ensuring he led a celibate life.

Not that it had. She could vouch for his prowess as a lover. When she'd first seen the scar, she'd touched it. Later, becoming bolder, she'd kissed it, anguished that he'd been hurt.

She took off her sunglasses, found a tissue in her purse and wiped the moisture from her brow and cheeks.

When Keegan straightened and turned toward her, her gaze was drawn to the juncture of his thighs where his robust masculinity threatened the confinement of the cloth.

"Everything is still there," he said softly, with an edge of danger in his voice. "And in working order."

A flood of heat hit her face when she realized he'd known exactly where her thoughts had flown. She forced her gaze upward, but not before she'd seen the hardening of his body into frank arousal. Deep within, she felt an answering flicker of desire.

She slipped her sunglasses back on and stuck the tissue in her pocket. "I'm sure it is." She returned his gaze stoically.

He wouldn't intimidate her, not with his blatant masculinity nor with his obvious fury at her presence. He acted as if she'd invaded his personal turf.

But the ranch was her home, and after all, it was a free country. What could he do if she decided to stay?

Nothing, she told herself. Except make her life miserable.

She stood her ground for a tense minute, the world around them silent, as if waiting for the outbreak of hostilities. A crow broke the silence with its hoarse call.

Keegan spun and stalked across the road toward his truck.

"What about the car?" she called to his back, suddenly fearing he was going to drive off and leave her. Stifling her panic, she added imperiously, "I'd like to get to the ranch before lunch."

"Good luck," he mocked. "That particular car is known to be a lemon. The computer goes, and that's it." He shrugged.

He was giving up? Just like that? Keegan McPherson? She couldn't hide her shock. "You mean . . . you can't fix it?"

"Sorry," he said sarcastically. "I don't carry spare parts for other people's cars around with me." He reached into his truck and wiped his hands on a rag he scrounged from under the seat.

Beth followed him, walking on the rough pavement, aware that her ankles wobbled precariously on her spiky heels.

He climbed into the truck.

She put her hand on the door and looked up at him incredulously. "You can't leave me out here. I have to get to the ranch. It's only fifteen miles—"

"I've got business in town. I need to go by the bank before it closes. It's Wednesday, you know."

The bank closed at noon on Wednesdays and stayed open late on Fridays so cowboys and people from the lumber mill could cash their payroll checks. This latter had been instituted only recently, she understood. Welcome to modern times.

He gave her a feral smile. Two lines appeared at each side of his mouth, almost dimples but not quite. Her heart skittered around in her chest.

At their first meeting his smile had completely captivated her. At their third, they'd made love . . . in the water . . . on the sandy bank . . . with moonlight pouring over them like liquid silver. It had been so beautiful, she'd wept.

"Well, get in," he finally said.

She came out of her daze with a jerk. "Get in?"

"If you want a ride to town."

"I just came from town. I want to go home."

"So call your ranch and have someone come out for you. If you can raise anyone over there."

"What do I do—climb a telephone pole?" she demanded.

The next thing she knew, he'd picked up a phone—obviously one of those cellular phones connected by satellite to almost anywhere in the world—dialed and thrust the receiver into her hand.

She listened to the faraway sound of the ring and imagined the emptiness of the ranch house where no one answered. After twenty rings she handed the phone back to Keegan.

He replaced it and gave her an impatient look.

Another thought came to her. "Call the service station in town. Harry can come out and get me."

"Harry's not there anymore. He sold out. Some new people are running the place. They don't make road calls."

Again she had a sense of being an alien, of not knowing her place in the scheme of things. In the spring, when she'd come home after her father had suffered a massive heart attack, she'd spent most of the time at the hospital in Medford. Then there had been the funeral to get through....

Keegan had attended the memorial service, but he hadn't said anything to her, not "I'm sorry," or "Is there anything I can do to help?" or "Do you need me?"

Her father had been buried next to her mother in the family cemetery. Beth had stood alone at the grave. As Keegan had said—she was the last living member of her family.

She'd put her father's foreman in charge and fled back to the city, leaving the lawyer to handle the details of the will while she wrestled with her desire to return home and her vow never to see Keegan McPherson again.

Naturally he was the first person she would run into. Fate liked to play nasty little tricks like that.

"Do you want a ride or not?" he demanded.

She couldn't stand by the side of the road forever. From town maybe she could get hold of the rental car company. "I'll get my purse," she said and headed back to the car.

She didn't need to hear laughter to know he was mockingly amused at her situation. She could tell by the tingling on the back of her neck.

The cool air coming from the truck's air conditioner felt wonderful after the blistering heat. The radio was tuned to a pop-country station. Beth thought the music was designed to forestall conversation, but she didn't have anything to say.

Everything had been said between them three years ago, when they'd parted with angry words . . . words that could never be unspoken and never forgotten.

Old, painful memories condensed in a hard ball in her chest. She'd come home when her father had had a mild heart attack. Her first meeting with Keegan had been over a fight between his ranch hands and her father's men, regarding grazing rights in the Rogue River National Forest. She'd gone in her father's place to the forest service office to solve it. Keegan had been there.

Of course, she'd known of the McPhersons all her life. Their grandfather's spread had joined the back acres of her ranch. After the old man died and the twins had made their fortunes on the rodeo circuit, they'd increased their holdings until they were one of the largest ranches in the state.

"So," he said as they neared the outskirts of the small town that served the lumber mill and the ranches thereabouts, "I guess your lawyer called you."

She looked at him, confused.

He scowled at her. "About the offer."

"What offer?"

"My brother and I want to buy your spread."

"No," she said without thinking.

Keegan stopped, then pulled onto the main road to town. He gave her a calculating glance. "You won't get a better deal," he told her. "I'd advise you to take it now while we're willing to be generous. We'll pay less when you go bankrupt."

She felt as if the breath had been knocked out of her at his low, threatening tone. She set her jaw at a lofty angle. "What makes you think the Triple R will go bankrupt?"

"I've watched your place go downhill for several years." He rested his arm on the back of the seat, keeping one hand on the steering wheel. "Going into the fifth year of drought, your land is overgrazed, overstocked and mismanaged."

She'd already figured that out from the attorney's reports of the past few months. Her father had done a terrible job. Tears filmed her eyes. She had to open her mouth and take several slow breaths to relieve the tightness.

"How long do you think you can go on abusing it like that?" he demanded.

"I don't know," she managed to say, but her voice wobbled.

Stupid, useless emotion. She wouldn't give in to it. In order to survive in this world she was going to have to be as tough as the McPherson twins.

He gave a disgusted snort. "For God's sake, are you going to cry?"

"No," she whispered. "And, no, my attorney hasn't talked to me about any offers. I have an appointment with him on Friday."

"He'll probably tell you about it then."

"I'll ask," she said.

He wanted her gone. When she left, *if* she decided to sell out, the Ralstons, who'd come across the country in covered wagons, survivors of the ill-fated Donner party, would be no more.

He was silent for a couple of miles. "There're drinks in the cooler," he finally said. He pointed over his shoulder.

Looking over the seat, she spied the cooler. One of the first rules of survival in the West—never go off without water and a gun. She glanced at the rifle in its rack before reaching behind her and opening the cooler. She also caught sight of the blanket tucked behind his seat.

Smart cowboys were prepared for every situation, Keegan had once told her. A blizzard, a chance to make love...

"I'll take iced tea," he said.

She found a can, opened it and handed it to him.

"Thanks." He took the drink.

Selecting a fruit juice for herself, she settled back in the seat and bent the tab forward, then back to open it. They sipped their drinks in silence, each lost in thought. She wondered what he was thinking. If he was remembering...

Keegan gulped down the cold tea, but it didn't help put out the fires that blazed deep inside him.

Beth's perfume filled the cab of the oversize pickup, the aromatic oils enhanced by the heat of her skin and the time spent waiting in the blazing August sun for someone to come along.

His imagination supplied the rest. The way she would feel if he ran his hands over her—hot and smooth all over, moist and welcoming in those secret places he'd delighted in exploring. The taste of her—sweet and tempting as forbidden fruit. The way it had felt to merge his swollen, aching flesh with hers and know that bliss would come, for both of them, with one swift thrust, but holding back, wanting the pleasure to go on forever.

He shifted on the seat, but couldn't find a comfortable position. The only thing that would give him relief was...

Damnation!

No way was he going to get embroiled in her clutches again. He'd learned the hard way that Ralstons would use any method to reach their goals. Lies, passion, whatever it took to turn a man's weakness into their gain. Yeah, he'd learned.

Then he made the mistake of glancing over at her.

Her gaze was on his face...his lips. She was staring at his lips. A muscle suddenly jerked at the side of his mouth. He pressed his lips together hard to stop the reaction. For a second he saw the desire in her eyes before she turned away.

"Watch it," he said, fighting the surge in his blood.

"I beg your pardon?"

"So polite," he taunted. "You always asked so nicely to be kissed. Your seduction technique was perfect."

Keegan... kiss me... please... now... yes...

He whipped his head around and glared at her. He realized she hadn't spoken. She was still looking out the window at the passing scenery, her face so still it could have been a portrait.

The voice had been in his mind, dredged from his memories of the two of them and summer nights so filled with pleasure he'd thought he would die from it. Hunger gnawed at him. Around her a man could easily go off the deep end. He would watch himself from now on.

"Poor innocent," she said. "To be taken in by a woman."

"Yeah," he agreed with a harsh laugh. "You did take me in. The sex was great, but the price was too high."

Chapter Two

"I suppose a gentleman wouldn't mention such a thing," Keegan snarled into the shocked silence between them.

He heard her exhale slowly, carefully, as if she were glass and would shatter at his touch. He knew she wouldn't.

When they'd first made love, she'd startled him by holding her breath when she was very close to the final pleasure. He'd learned it was a trait of hers when she was under stress . . . or greatly excited.

He frowned as memories formed in his mind, one scene giving way to another, until all his thoughts were on the nights they'd met at the creek. They had come together with an explosive hunger that had driven out every other concern.

She hadn't faked that. . . . *Damn*.

He had to quit thinking of the past. It had no place in the dealings between them. Back then, he'd blindly believed in her. But, as they say, the truth will out.

"I wouldn't expect you to be anything but your natural self," she finally said.

He didn't like the flicker of irony in her tone. "I suppose your pin-striped stockbroker in San Francisco would never be so impolite as to mention sex in broad daylight."

That got her attention.

"What do you know about him?" she demanded.

"Your father let it be known that you were dating some rich dude. He seemed to think your fiancé would pull the ranch out of the doldrums." He glanced at her ringless hand. "What happened? Did he figure out the cost and skedaddle?"

Beth realized she was holding her breath again and forced herself to breathe deeply and calmly. She hadn't expected to return home and, on her first day back, become tangled in the old web of hurt and accusation. And desire.

Oh, yes, she was as aware of the undercurrents between them as he obviously was. She glanced at his lean body and then she turned away. He still wanted her—she knew him too well not to recognize that fact—and he hated her for it.

"We decided what we felt for each other was friendship, not a . . . grand passion." A stupid choice of words, she realized, hoping he wouldn't notice the slight falter in her voice.

She'd felt a grand passion for only one man. A sharp pain tore through her chest. Cowboys were hell on hearts.

To her surprise he didn't respond, but was quiet as they drove into the small town. He stopped at the farm store that carried everything from feed and seed to spare tractor parts.

"I'm going over to the bank first," he said, stepping down to the dusty pavement. "Then I have some things to pick up here." He looked at her with a question in his cold, stormy eyes.

She pushed the mop of curls off her forehead. "I think I'll go to the diner. I haven't eaten since dawn."

He nodded, slammed the door and walked off.

Beth got out and looked around. The diner had started out as a hot-dog stand, but it had been added to over the years by various owners. Now it was a small restaurant, saloon, poolroom, dance hall and general gathering place for the locals.

The town looked prosperous. The tourist trade was increasing as more people discovered the area. The new dude ranch and ski resort attracted the sports crowd. Hikers liked the Pacific Crest Trail and the solitude of the forest.

The Rogue River had been declared a wild and scenic river—no dams could be built on it, other than the one that had formed Lost Creek Reservoir. The salmon fishing was supposed to be good in season. In the lakes, trout and catfish were the big draw.

Beth used the pay telephone before she went inside. The rental agency was very apologetic when she told them she'd been stranded out on a country road until a rancher had come along. They said they'd send someone to take care of the car. She gave directions, hung up and went into the diner.

The place was full. She waited for an empty table.

"Beth Ralston," a voice called out, attracting attention to her. A woman came out from behind the counter.

Beth recognized the manager of the diner, who had been a couple of years ahead of her in school. "Hello, Sita. Looks like business is booming."

Sita rolled her eyes. "The tourists are taking over. The loggers are mad as hornets about them invading the diner. We'll have a table for you in a jiffy. Are you alone?"

"Uh, yes."

"Ah, here you are," Sita said when the waitress indicated a clean table was ready. She led Beth to it. "I've got to get the cash register. We're short of help today." She rushed off after handing Beth a menu.

Beth chose a chair facing the door and looked over the lunch specials. A shadow loomed beside her. She glanced up, startled.

Keegan pulled out the chair opposite her and sat down. The waitress, who was maybe eighteen and dressed in skintight jeans and a knit shirt, rushed over.

"I'll take the chicken-fried steak, green beans and tomatoes, salad, ranch dressing, apple pie, a large milk and coffee," he ordered. He looped an arm over the back of the chair and looked across the table at Beth.

"The grilled chicken salad for me," she decided. "Iced tea."

The waitress looked at Keegan and giggled before taking Beth's menu and rushing off. A laconic grin spread over Keegan's face.

"She has a crush on me," he explained.

"Do tell," Beth commented dryly.

She glanced up and saw Sita watching them. The woman smiled, then went back to counting out change to a customer. A survey of the busy room produced a flurry of shifting glances. The residents of the town were certainly interested in the two of them, Beth realized.

She wondered if everyone knew of their affair three years ago. She and Keegan had dropped by for dinner and dancing a few times after her father had improved.

The waitress placed Keegan's salad in front of him. Again she giggled before she hurried off. Beth clamped her teeth together.

When the girl returned, she brought his milk and coffee.

"The lady would like her tea now," he said, nodding toward Beth. He picked up the milk and took a drink, watching her over the rim of the glass, his eyes unreadable.

After the waitress served the tea, Beth sat there in silence. The lack of conversation didn't seem to bother her uninvited companion. After several tense minutes, Sita came over.

"Are you just visiting, or are you planning to stay this time?" she asked with a friendly smile.

Beth was acutely aware of Keegan's narrow-eyed attention as she chose her answer. "Visiting for now. I may change my mind later. It's according to how things go."

"What things?" Keegan snapped, sitting up in the chair.

The tension zoomed upward like a kite out of control.

"I'll discuss them with my attorney," she replied coolly.

"It would be nice to have you back," Sita broke in, apparently unaware of the electricity in the air. "Things wouldn't be the same without a Ralston around. They were the first settlers... Oh, excuse me." She dashed back to the cash register.

Keegan put down his fork. "What things?" he repeated, his tone low and dangerous.

Beth thrust her chin out. "That's my business."

"I'm making it mine," he said. "If you have an offer, I'll top it. The McPhersons deal fair."

"I haven't decided what I want to do yet."

"If you think you'll win that lawsuit, think again." He resumed eating.

That had been another surprise when she'd inherited the ranch. Her father hadn't thought it necessary to inform her that he'd brought a lawsuit against the McPhersons over land and water rights that had been in dispute for more than twenty years.

The sooner that was settled, the better. Her father hadn't believed *his* father had sold that valuable acreage to Keegan's grandfather. Neither did she.

Samuel Ralston had been determined to get back that land and the creek that flowed through it by fair means or foul. The status of the suit was one of several topics she needed to discuss with the family lawyer.

"That land had belonged to my family for almost a hundred and fifty years. My grandfather would never have sold it."

"He would if he was desperate for money to pay his taxes."

"He'd have sold off some cattle. That creek is the only year-round source of water on the ranch. No one in his right mind would sell it," she said, negating his argument.

"My grandfather said he bought it. He put up the fence."

"Fences can be removed."

"Try it," he invited.

She returned his harsh gaze without blinking. The giggly waitress interrupted the developing quarrel with their meal.

Beth had to force the tender slices of grilled chicken down her throat. Resentment grew in her as Keegan ate every bite of steak smothered in gravy with no difficulty whatsoever.

He had turned into the epitome of the hard-nosed rancher, ruthless and without a shred of compassion in his soul. It was good she'd found out before—before what?

In truth she couldn't remember that he'd mentioned marriage at any of their meetings. She'd realized, after their passionate interlude had ended and she'd assessed every conversation they'd ever had, that she had assumed marriage would follow.

She put her fork aside when he finished the apple pie down to the last crumb of flaky crust. Nothing bothered his appetite, she saw. He pulled out his wallet and took out a bill. Their waitress rushed over with the check.

Beth tossed a dollar on the table for her share of the tip and handed Keegan the money for her food.

"I'll get it," he said. A grin played at the corners of his mouth while his gaze swept down her when they stood. "You were always a cheap date to feed. I used to think about fattening you up a bit. Wondered how you'd look..." His voice trailed off.

Blood pounded through Beth, in fury or passion, she couldn't tell. He'd teased her about her slenderness, his hands running over her, making her weak and restless with need.

The way she felt right this minute.

"I can pay my own way." She followed him to the cash register and plunked her bills on the counter, then walked out.

The heat settled over her like a dusty cloak. She went to the pay phone and tried the ranch. Still no answer. The men were out, rounding up the cattle for the fall sales, but Skully should have been at the house. He was too old to be working the herd.

What should she do now?

Ah, her old school chum, Susannah...what was her married name? Hunter. Susannah Hunter. Perhaps Susannah could loan her a car for a couple of hours, long enough for her to remove her things from the rental car.

Keegan came out of the diner. "Let's go."

She raised her brows slightly in question.

"I'll drop you by your place." He looked as thrilled at the prospect as finding a scorpion in his boot.

"No, thanks. I can manage."

He snorted. "How? Was anyone home at your place?"
He waited three seconds for her answer. "I thought not,"
he continued when she didn't bother with a reply. He
stepped off the sidewalk and turned to her, waiting for her
to accept the inevitable, his face without expression.

After ten painful heartbeats, she gave up. "Thanks. I'll
do something for you someday."

He opened the door of the truck and steadied her with a
hand on her elbow when she climbed in. "Lady, you did
enough the first time," he said softly, for her ears only, as
a noisy group of tourists went into the diner. He slammed
the truck's door closed.

While he eased into the flow of traffic on the busy main
street, she regretted her decision to accept his ride. It was
war all the way as far as he was concerned. She drew a deep
breath and held it, wishing the air would absorb all the
misery in her so she could breathe it out and be done with
her regrets. If only...

She let the breath out silently so he wouldn't notice. She
kept her eyes on the passing scenery. There were a lot of
new houses in town.

His icy gaze flicked to her. "You used to do that," he
said, speeding up when they reached the outskirts of town.

"What?"

"Hold your breath when we made love."

She jerked around and stared at him. There was no
mockery in his eyes, only a freezing wall of indifference.

Where was the passionate man who had trembled in her
arms, desperate with his need for her? Where was the man
who'd groaned and even cried out with the depth of pleasure he'd found with her? Where was the man who'd spoken of children to inherit their land, the man who'd
believed in her love until she'd made one simple request,
asked one simple favor of his love?

He'd turned against her in the blink of an eye.

Keegan had refused to believe she hadn't used his passion for gain, that she hadn't planned all along to ask for the return of the meadow on one side of the creek . . . just as soon as she softened him up "for the kill." The memory still hurt.

Looking back, she knew she shouldn't have been surprised at his attitude. As boys, Keegan and his brother had acquired a reputation for being tough and single-minded. Perhaps too many people had failed his love, for him to trust easily, his father inadvertently by getting killed on an oil rig, his mother by letting herself sink into grief and alcoholism.

Beth didn't know much about Keegan's grandfather, except that he'd been a grim old man with no kindness in him for the two young boys who'd been given into his care.

"Your brother," she said. "I understand he and his wife have a child."

Keegan flicked her a harsh glance before concentrating on the road once more. "A boy. Kelly McPherson."

"Kelly," she repeated, a knife twist of envy in her heart. She'd thought by now she would have a child, perhaps two.

"Yeah. My heir," Keegan said on a note of satisfaction. "Now I won't have to fool with finding a woman and taking a chance that she'll try to carry off half our holdings in a divorce."

"What about your brother's wife? Don't you worry about her?"

"No," he said promptly. "She's rich. And she loves him."

What about you? Beth wanted to ask. *Don't you need a woman who loves you?*

She had wanted to be that woman . . . once. Not anymore. She looked up to find his cool, unfathomable gaze on her. For a second she thought he could read her thoughts.

When he turned off the state highway onto the country road, she continued to study the hard set of his features. The McPherson twins had been the best-looking guys in high school and as friendly as spring rattlers just out of their winter dens and famished. Keegan was still the handsomest man she'd ever seen.

A rush of desire had her clenching her hands together. Her dreams had been filled with him for the past two weeks. Present longing mingled with past memories. He'd known just how to please her with his slow, gentle touch....

"Stop it," he ground out suddenly, startling her.

"What?" she asked, her voice a hoarse whisper.

He pulled off the road behind the rental car. After turning off the engine, he sat still, staring straight ahead, his mouth an angry slash in his face, his hands gripping the steering wheel.

"Stop looking at me like you're asking to be kissed," he growled. He opened the door and leapt from the truck. "Let's get your stuff loaded."

Beth's hands shook uncontrollably as she got out. "I can come back in one of the ranch trucks. We don't have to bother—"

"What if the rental agency comes and tows it to Medford before you get back? Or somebody steals your clothes? Life isn't as simple around here as it once was."

"It isn't simple anywhere."

He shot her a warning look and gestured toward the car. She retrieved the keys from her purse and opened the doors and trunk. Keegan looked the suitcase and boxes over, then started loading the pickup with orderly precision, fitting everything in like pieces of a jigsaw puzzle. When he came to her art portfolio, he lifted it out carefully.

"Still drawing, I see."

"Some," she replied. She saw the string had come untied and instinctively reached for the smoother leather. "Be careful. It's coming open."

She got her hands on it just as some papers slipped out the edge. His grip tightened. For a ridiculous second they played tug-of-war, then he dropped his hand.

The unexpected release of pressure rocked her backward, and she cracked her elbow on the fender, sending a numbing pain up her arm. She lost her hold.

The loose sheets fluttered and scattered when the portfolio flew through the air and landed in the dust by the side of the road. Embarrassed, she stooped and began gathering the drawings.

"This is good," Keegan said. "Really good."

Beth resisted the urge to tear it out of his hands. She stacked the sketches into a neat pile and leaned toward him to see which one he held. A sigh of relief escaped her when she saw it was a landscape.

"Thank you." She stretched out her hands for it.

"It's the warm springs, isn't it?"

"Yes."

"Let me see the rest."

"No." She realized she sounded too abrupt. "They're nothing, just pencil drawings from memory."

His hand whipped out and took them from her before she could stop him. He partially turned his back to keep her from getting them. Without thinking, she lunged at him, reaching around him and trying to grab the sketches.

"Keegan, don't," she ordered sharply. "They're mine. Give them here." She sounded like a possessive child, but she didn't care. Too much was revealed in those drawings, things she didn't want him to see.

Without a word he placed the one he had picked up on top of the others and gave them back to her. With trembling hands, she took the sheets and placed them inside the pocket of the portfolio and tied it securely. She placed the package of artwork behind the seat in the truck cab.

He looked the rental car over, then, satisfied that they'd gotten everything, he closed the trunk and rear doors. She put the keys in the glove compartment as instructed and locked the doors.

"I'm ready," she announced.

With a nod, he climbed in the truck, waited until she was in and the seat belt fastened, then eased onto the road once more.

Beth sagged against the hot seat, exhausted from the long day, the car trouble and the tension of seeing Keegan.

"Kerrigan is doing sculptures as well as carvings now. You and he have talent," Keegan informed her. "Rachel wants to take his work to a gallery in D.C., but he hasn't agreed, not yet."

"Sometimes it's hard to share your work with others." Maybe he'd accept shyness as a reason for her overreaction, she hoped.

"Your drawing of the cowboy was . . . good."

She tensed. She knew which picture he'd seen. The cowboy had his back turned to the viewer while he watched his cattle. Had Keegan caught the loneliness in the picture as well as the richness of the landscape? "It was a quick draw . . . from memory."

"You've a good eye for detail." He was silent for a minute, the low murmur of the radio and the wind noises against the truck the only sounds. "Was that me?"

"Such conceit," she said, on the defensive.

"Is it?" He laughed briefly, a cynical sound. "That horse had the markings of the stallion I usually ride, right down to the scar on his rump."

"Did you see identifying marks on the cowboy, too?" she demanded and immediately wished she hadn't.

"No. He had his pants on," he said in a soft drawl. "Now if I'd been able to examine the sketch of the cowboy in the next picture, the one bathing in the springs—"

"He doesn't have a scar," she interrupted, heat rising to her face. When she'd first drawn it, he had. She'd erased it when she'd realized what she'd done.

Keegan gave her a cool smile, his feelings hidden behind the mocking, sardonic mood he'd adopted earlier. He turned up the radio and let the music fill the silence.

The ranch yard was empty when they drove across the cattle guard. Keegan pulled up next to the house under the shade of an old cottonwood and immediately set to work, lifting a large box in his arms and looking at her.

Beth got out and grabbed a suit bag. "In my room," she said.

The wood frame house was in need of repairs and paint. She noted a rotten plank in the front porch, which wrapped around the side of the house, giving access to her bedroom through double doors. She tried the knobs and found them unlocked.

After opening both doors, she led the way inside. "Just put it down anywhere," she advised. "Hello?" she called into the hall.

No one answered. The house had the feel of emptiness.

"Well, I guess Skully is out somewhere," she said. Brilliant deduction, she thought. "Let's get your truck unloaded so you can leave."

"Before I get shot," he added sardonically.

She didn't answer. Surveying her room, she realized how girlish it looked with its peach and green color scheme, a high school pennant still on the wall. The bleached pine furniture seemed too innocent for her now.

Had she really been that young once?

An ache started inside, and a dam that she'd erected long ago threatened to spill over. She'd trusted the two men in her life. She'd loved them—her father and Keegan—and they'd torn her heart to pieces, one with demands, the other with distrust.

Keegan came in with another armload of her belongings. He gave her a quizzical glance as she stood immobile in the middle of her bedroom. She went out and brought her toiletries case in, then a box of dishes.

"Let me get the heavy stuff," Keegan said with a frown. He took the box from her.

She wondered if he realized she'd bought the set with their household in mind. She'd thought they would share a life as well as lovemaking. Emotions rose in her, harsh and hurting. It was the oddest thing, but she suddenly wished she could lean into him and have him hold her and comfort her. She needed comforting.

"Do you want these in the closet?" Keegan asked.

She jerked her gaze from the dishes to him. She couldn't speak. Her throat had closed. Nodding, she hurried past him to the truck. In a few minutes they were finished.

Keegan took out his handkerchief and wiped sweat from his face. "That's it."

The code of the West demanded hospitality. "Would you like something to drink before you go?"

"I have drinks in the truck."

"Oh, yes, I remember." She spoke much too brightly. She held her eyes wide as the tears, ridiculous and inexplicable, pressed against her control. "Well, thanks for your help." She held out her hand. Her fingers trembled ever so slightly.

"Damnation," he said and clutched her by the shoulders.

She stared up at him, at his mouth so near her own. His lips were so finely molded, so mobile and skilled in giving pleasure. She moaned and caught her breath, trying to hold back the flood of need that was overpowering her will for survival.

Crazy. This was *crazy!*

He muttered a curse, then his mouth slammed down on hers. She met the kiss with equal passion—with anger and despair and hunger so great it wiped out every shred of common sense either of them possessed. The floodgates opened, and she was lost . . . lost.

He touched her lips with his tongue, as if testing his memory against the actual taste of her. She opened her mouth and invited him in, wanting his hot, thrusting moistness inside.

The kiss was endless, with a thousand different ways of touching in the simple yet complex meeting of lips.

She felt his hands leave her shoulders and glide over her back, his caress kneading her flesh as he moved lower and lower. Finally he cupped her hips and pulled her against him, into the warm space between his legs.

The hard staff of his desire fitted against the soft ache the kiss had created in her. She arched against him, then moved with mindless need.

Her heart was pounding now, her body and its responses beyond her control. At some level, she knew his were, too. A wild exultation raged in her.

He wanted her. He wanted her still.

Keegan swore savagely even as he ruthlessly ground his lips against the softness of hers. She'd been staring at his mouth since he'd stopped to help her at the side of the road. Hell, he'd been just as captivated by hers. When they'd met as adults three years ago, in the forest service office to settle a dispute, he'd been taken with her lips.

Like the rest of her, they tended to the slender side. Nor was her mouth very wide, but it had an engaging lift at the corners, as if she harbored a secret smile just waiting to leap out at a man. And when she *had* smiled at him at that meeting, well, it had lunged right down the middle of his chest, leaving him wounded in some way. He'd never recovered.

Not even after he learned the real reason. Even betrayal couldn't stop the hunger and the need. He was hard and aching and quickly giving in to the urge to lay her on that frilly bed he'd only dreamed of sharing with her three years ago.

With trembling hands, he held her and slowly stroked back and forth against her, knowing he was driving her wild . . . which was just the way he felt, too.

With a last effort at control, he wrenched himself away from her. She opened her eyes and stared at him, her eyes reflecting the smoky haze of sensual fire.

He had to do something before he gave in, before he was lost in her lies again. He summoned up a cynical smile. "Well," he said, "nice try, but I'm older and a hell of a lot wiser than I was three years ago. A kiss doesn't soften me up like it once did."

She blinked, then frowned. He saw the exact instance his words hit home. Her eyes—dark green eyes inherited from her Irish father—widened slightly, then changed abruptly.

As if a door had slammed shut behind them, he thought, feeling a strange jab of regret for the loss.

"I didn't start that kiss, Keegan," she said, her tone quiet, almost sad, instead of angry as he'd expected.

He leaned over her. "You didn't stop it, either, honey."

She visibly flinched at the brittle endearment. Keegan knew she didn't like it. She'd told him so one time.

"Cowboys call everyone that," she'd complained. "As if it's a generic term for women."

"Not all women," he'd teased, "only the ones we want to do this to." And he'd shown her what he'd meant.

With a little shake of her head, she stepped away from him. He felt the emptiness invade his soul. Oh, hell, no need to get poetic about a simple thing like sex, he snarled at himself.

"I think you'd better go," she said with a dignity that tugged at his admiration.

She wasn't a woman who used tears against a man. He had to give her credit. "Yeah," he agreed. He was much too aware of that bed no more than three steps away.

He strode out the door without a backward glance, went to the truck and climbed in. The scent of her perfume filled the cab, overriding normal ranching smells of leather and horses and a man's honest, working sweat.

Before he put the truck into gear, he saw her come out the door and stand on the worn planking of the old porch. An ache, whose cause he couldn't fathom, started up in him.

He rolled down the window. "Oh, I forgot," he said, flashing her a mocking grin, "welcome home, neighbor."

Feeling he'd gotten in the last word, he drove off. Through the rearview mirror, he saw her lips move. Then she simply stood there, not smiling, not moving. All the way to his place, he wondered what she'd said.

Beth kept seeing that last mocking smile before Keegan departed. She wondered if he'd understood her last silly taunt. "Home is where the heart is," she'd said. "Where's yours?"

His heart or his home? She wasn't sure herself what she'd meant by the question. It didn't matter. She had work to do.

The house showed signs of obvious deterioration, worse than last year, much worse than three years ago. She'd been shocked at the appearance of the fences and barns when she'd arrived. Nothing had been repaired, at least not properly.

Worry ate at her. What had happened to her home since she'd moved to San Francisco right after high school ten years ago?

She knew something about running an enterprise. She'd taken business classes at the university. She'd happened upon a Help Needed sign at a tiny flower shop and on impulse had gone in. She'd ended up buying the place from the owner, a widow who wanted to retire, and had turned it into a very successful business. There was a different atmosphere about a place going downhill and one that was rising on a wave of prosperity. The ranch wasn't the latter.

Maybe she'd better start on the books while she waited for Skully or the foreman to show up.

Going into the ranch office behind the kitchen, she couldn't help noting how dusty and littered the house was. Lass, the woman who'd kept house for her father, had left with her husband, the former ramrod before a local man named Cawe had taken over last year.

She couldn't imagine the homestead without Lass and her husband, who was as quiet as cowboys were reputed to be but who could play the fiddle and make a person want to dance a jig, his playing was so lively and jolly.

In the office Beth touched the furniture as she passed, needing contact with solid, familiar things. She stood by the window and listened to the wind in the cottonwoods that lined the creek that the McPhersons had fenced off from Ralston property.

When the lawsuit was settled, she would take great pleasure in tearing that fence out, post by post.

She opened the desk and started checking the ledgers. An hour later she looked up. She thought she'd heard a sound. After a few seconds she realized it was only the house creaking. The sound of loneliness, she thought, an empty house without love and laughter and children to brighten it.

How long had her home been like that?

It was dark before she put the ranch accounts aside. She rubbed her eyes wearily. There were bills due to the vet, the feed and seed stores and to the tax assessor's office. She'd have to check with the attorney to see which ones had been paid. And how much money was left in the ranch account.

The ledgers hadn't been posted since she left. Why wasn't the foreman keeping up? Money flow was vital to any business. Without a balance sheet update, a person couldn't judge profits.

Leaving the desk, she went into the kitchen, flipping on the lights as she did. After peering into the refrigerator and chest freezer, she selected a ripe tomato off the windowsill and fixed a BLT sandwich. At least Skully had planted a garden.

Just as she finished her lonely meal, she heard a truck drive into the yard. She saw Skully, as thin and wizened as a piece of rawhide string left in the sun, climb out. Come to think of it, Skully had been baking in the Oregon sun for almost seventy years.

"Skully," she called from the door and ran out to meet him.

He opened his arms and took her in, much the way he had when she'd been thirteen and had come to him for comfort after her mother had died.

"Oh, Skully," she whispered brokenly.

"Well, gal," he said, "you're home at last."

His voice was the same bear growl of affection and gruff kindness he'd always used with her. His rough hands patted her head as if she were still a child instead of a grown woman. When she looked at him through tears, his eyes were watery, too.

"How'd you get in?" he wanted to know. His deep blue eyes scanned the yard. "Thought you'd let me know when to pick you up."

"I rented a car. I shipped some things by air, too. I thought I'd take a truck and get them on Friday."

He looked puzzled at her chatter. "Where's the car?"

"It broke down on the road about fifteen miles from here." She paused. "Keegan McPherson came along and gave me a ride into town, then back to the ranch."

"McPherson, huh?" His expression darkened. She'd gone to Skully three years ago and poured out her grief to him.

"It was okay," she said quickly. "He helped me bring my things home. I...oh, Skully, it's so good to see you again."

He nodded, and strands of white, wiry hair that had escaped the rubber band at the back of his neck wafted around his thin, lined face. He briefly touched her shoulder. "The land needs you, gal. Don't leave it again."

"I don't know how long I'll stay." She gazed at the far hills as a sadness, remote yet touching, tugged at her.

"You're needed," he said again. "Well, the horses have been fed, and I smell like a pile of manure."

"Where have you been?" she asked on the way to the house. "I thought everyone had deserted the place when I arrived. It was so...lonesome."

"I've been working with the cattle, doing some late branding."

"Skully, you shouldn't," she scolded. "Your rheumatiz will start acting up again."

"Someone had to help. We're short of hands."

She detected a warning in the exhausted look he gave her. They stopped at the back steps. "Shall I make you a sandwich while you clean up?"

He nodded and headed for the tiny cabin next to the big house that had been his for fifty years.

"Then we'll talk," she called after him. There were things about the ranch that she had to know. She went inside, got out the bacon and heated the skillet.

The house seemed much more cheerful now that she had company. She and Skully loved this place. They'd both been born on it. So had Skully's older brother, Ted. And Jeff, Ted's grandson. They'd all been part of this ranch for years.

But everyone else was gone, she reflected, putting bacon in the skillet. A premonition caressed her neck with cold fingers, and she shivered. In its wake came sadness, a mourning for the time when she would be gone....

Chapter Three

Beth walked into the lawyer's office on Friday morning on the dot of nine. She was glad the appointment was early. That way she could worry all day and be too frazzled at night to stay awake.

"Hello," Jack Norton said when his secretary admitted Beth to the inner sanctum. He leapt from his chair and waited until she was seated beside his desk before taking his chair again.

His dark eyes gleamed with approval when he looked her over. She'd worn a simple white sheath and medium-high pumps for the trip, with a jade necklace and earrings to set off her eyes. She knew white was dramatic with her black hair, inherited from her Hispanic mother, combined with the rosy complexion and brilliant eyes which came from her redheaded Irish ancestors.

"Nice," she said, glancing around, then back at him with a smile. Jack's father had been the ranch attorney for years. It was natural that his son would take over.

He grinned. "I had to pay for it out of my own pocket, but I always wanted an impressive office."

The chairs and small sofa were of the chesterfield type, the desk and conference table of mahogany. Glass-fronted bookcases, filled with law texts, lined one wall, and a lighted curio cabinet held pride of place beside a collection of framed diplomas.

"You succeeded. It reminds me of an old gentleman's club in England or someplace like that." She leaned forward in her chair. "Tell me where I stand in the lawsuit against the McPhersons."

His beaming smile disappeared. "Well, it's funny. The land is recorded on both deeds. Your claim is the oldest, but they've had the land for over twenty years. There's a question about why your grandfather didn't do something if he owned it."

She felt a sinking within. They needed access to that creek so badly. "Grandfather died that year. My father was running things when the fence was put up."

"And the courthouse burned, so the record of the transaction was lost. There's only the evidence of the deeds. Contradictory evidence." Jack paused, thinking. "And they have possession. Why didn't your father bring the suit before last year?"

Beth had considered that question. "I think he knew he wasn't going to be around much longer. From some things he said the last time we talked, I think he wanted to leave the ranch intact as it had been in the past—his legacy to future generations."

Jack gave her a sympathetic smile. "Yes, that sounds like a Ralston. Well, we'll do the best we can. It's your word against theirs, after all."

And the Ralston name still counted for something in these parts, she added to herself. She wouldn't let Keegan run her off without a fight.

After discussing the case and its schedule, Jack laid the balance sheets, from a computer printout, in front of her.

"Here's what's been paid," he pointed out. "Your expenses are outrunning income by about ten percent right now. You should try to consolidate and refinance this loan since the rates have dropped. The interest is eating you alive."

She looked at him blankly. "What loan?" she asked.

Jack pulled some papers from the file folder and laid them in front of her. He didn't need to explain. Her father had been taking out short-term loans to make payroll and operating expenses, paying them off or extending them into the next year. The ranch was now running a three-year deficit.

"Well," she joked ruefully, "debt doesn't seem to be a problem for the federal government."

"They don't have anybody to foreclose on them," Jack reminded her. "You do. Have you done a cattle count and tallied your hard assets yet?"

She shook her head.

"You'd better see into it."

"Things are that bad?"

"Yeah." He tossed the papers back in the folder. "Here, you can have these printouts. They'll help you get your accounts in order since everything's up-to-date as of yesterday."

"Thanks. I tried to go through the books, but nothing's been posted for months. Well, I guess I'd better go—"

"There's one more thing," he broke in. "I have a couple of offers for the ranch. The buyers will take it as is."

"Offers?"

"One from the ranch next to you. The McPhersons. If you sold to them, that would solve the problem of the water rights. The other is from a foreign conglomerate looking for recreational and residential property to develop."

"A resort and housing development?" She considered it from a personal angle. "I can see the neighbors getting together a lynching party if I sold out. There's already resentment over the influx of tourists in the area."

Jack shrugged. "Times change. I'd advise you to sell."

"I'm not ready to throw in the towel... yet."

"Hold on to these offers for a month or so," he said. "Let me know if you need any more information."

Beth stood and held out her hand. "Thanks, Jack. You've done a good job for the ranch without much input from me these past months. I'm sorry about that. I'll take over the books. Would you have all bills sent to me in the future?"

"Sure." He glanced at his watch. "Do you have time for coffee? Or perhaps you could meet me for lunch? Dinner?" he added when she smiled regretfully.

"I really have to get back. Medford is a long drive, and I have things to pick up at the airport. But thanks, anyway."

"A rain check," he said with an air of friendly aggression. "I'll call you."

"That would be nice," she agreed when she saw he wouldn't be deterred. They shook hands, and he walked her to the door.

Once on the street, driving the ranch pickup to the airport to collect the best of her boxes, she contemplated the attorney's interest. Jack was really sweet.

Right. Sweet. That sounded insipid even to her. He deserved someone whose heart would race when she thought of him. Hers didn't. She'd have to discourage him . . . but gently.

After finding and claiming the rest of her belongings, she started back to the ranch. As much as she hated to admit it, Keegan had been right. The ranch was on the verge of bankruptcy. She had to figure out how to stop the flow of red ink or she'd have to sell the place. If she sold, she could go back to San Francisco and take over her shop. *Get a life,* as the current saying went.

She frowned, realizing she was already thinking of leaving. Tightening her grip on the steering wheel, she reminded herself she was a Ralston. Ralstons didn't give up at the first setback.

With the money from the lease of her business and condo, plus the rest of her inheritance from her maternal grandparents, she had some resources Keegan didn't know about. She would close out her money-market account and pay off the debt first thing. Then she'd have a talk with the new foreman, a man she'd met only once.

On the long drive back to the ranch, she made several plans. She'd discarded most of them by the time she arrived at the house. Skully met her and helped unload her personal goods.

"The men will be bringing the cattle in tonight," he told her. "Did you get the groceries?"

"Yes. I'll change, and we'll start cooking."

One thing she'd forgotten—how much food it took to feed eight hungry men . . . five of whom were strangers to her. That was another thing she needed to look into. What had happened to the cowhands who'd been there for years?

Skully hadn't told her much, just who was working the cattle at present. He'd shrugged when she asked about men she remembered being there three years ago.

"Your dad let a bunch go," he said. "Times are hard."

"Times are always hard for ranchers," she said. "But we always had enough money to make it before."

If the old cowboy suspected skulduggery, he wouldn't say. "The land needs you," was his refrain, again.

The sun was setting when she heard a truck in the yard. Beth dampened a paper towel and went out onto the porch. She and Skully had hung the old porch swing that afternoon. She'd sat in it and broken a panful of fresh pole beans for dinner earlier.

Wiping the perspiration off her face with the towel, she leaned against the support post while Keegan parked and climbed out of his flashy red truck. It was new, not the one he'd had while they were dating...where they'd made love.

She was acutely conscious that he had recently taken a shower and put on clean jeans and a white shirt, the sleeves rolled back on his tanned forearms. He looked wonderfully fresh and masculine, like a man going on a date.

A whimsical thought popped into her mind. If she were eighteen and he were twenty-two, they might be going to a dance. The excitement of being with each other would build all evening. When he brought her home, they might park next to the creek, in the dark, whispery shadows under the cottonwoods. There, they would kiss and explore the boundaries of love.

The blood rushed madly through her. For a second, she felt dizzy. If she'd been eighteen, if they'd been in love, she'd have launched herself from the porch and flown into his arms, ready for his kiss....

But it wasn't ten years ago and the visit wasn't a date. This was now, and life, she'd found, could be merciless.

The scent of his cologne wafted to her on the evening breeze. She glanced at her own disheveled self. After a morning of running business errands and an afternoon of working in the garden and helping prepare a huge meal, she was anything but fresh.

Her cutoff jeans were full of holes, her blouse had spots where hot grease had splattered when she put the chicken pieces in to fry, and her hair clung to her temples in damp spikes. The makeup she'd put on that morning was long gone.

She was too tired to care.

"Hello, Keegan," she said when he paused beside his truck, his gaze dark and moody on her. "Lost?"

He reached behind the seat and brought out her art portfolio. She realized she'd forgotten it on Wednesday. Too many exciting things had been happening, she mocked.

He crossed the lawn, which was now a rectangle of dried grass. "I came to talk to you." He handed her the art case, then stood at the bottom of the steps.

Nodding her assent, she watched warily as his gaze took in her attire. Her heart beat a little faster when he paused on her bare legs, the ragged edges of her cutoffs tickling her thighs. When she moved back, he climbed the steps.

She set the portfolio on the porch. Had he looked inside? She hoped not. Her drawings were not for public consumption. They revealed too much of her soul. She should have destroyed them.

"Did you see Jack Norton?" Keegan asked.

"Yes."

"Well?"

She bristled at his impatience. "You're awfully eager to see the last of us Ralstons," she said in a considering drawl. "Is there gold on the property that I don't know about?"

He arched one brow and made a dismissive gesture. "I wish." His grin was startling in his clean-shaven, deeply tanned face.

A reluctant smile pushed its way to her lips. He could be so heartbreakingly charming when he set his mind to it. "Me, too," she admitted, thinking of her problems.

"Are you going to sell?" he demanded bluntly.

"Not this minute." She returned his icy glare with a cool glance of her own. "You needn't try to intimidate me with your dark scowls. It won't work."

He opened his mouth, thought better of his argument and decided to sit in the swing instead. Beth frowned as he sat down and invited her to join him with a sweep of his large, callused hand, as if *he* owned the place.

"Got any tea? I was out working with the herd all day. It's so dusty, my throat still feels parched."

After a moment's hesitation—when she thought of telling him where the cattle trough was located—she turned and went inside. She heard his chuckle just before the screen door slammed.

"Here," Skully said when she stomped into the kitchen. He handed her a tray with two tall glasses of iced tea and a plate of fresh baked brownies. "Don't let him run you off, gal. Show him your backbone." He went back to tending the meal.

She looked anxiously across the pasture when she returned to the porch. Twilight was descending and still no sign of the men. Had there been trouble moving the herd?

Keegan took the tray and placed it on a rough pine table beside the swing and waited until she was seated before resuming his place. "Tell Skully I said thanks. And that I've seen plenty of your stubbornness, if that's what he calls backbone.''

''Do you make it a habit to listen in on other people's conversations?'' she exclaimed in annoyance, knowing how voices carried through the open windows and doors.

''No.'' Keegan bit into a chewy brownie and closed his eyes in ecstasy. He quickly finished it. ''Now that was worth facing a pride of mountain lions. Or one enraged lioness,'' he added. His glance skimmed her. ''Did you go to town like that today?''

Beth took a cooling drink of tea, then rubbed the glass over her forehead before answering. ''Of course not. I dressed like a lady, not a tourist, just as my mom taught me. Besides, I had to go all the way to Medford to see my lawyer.''

''Better snap up my deal before I change my mind.''

She waved a brownie airily. ''I have another offer.''

Black eyebrows bunched into a furious line over cold gray eyes. Then Keegan settled back in the swing. He let his gaze run over the length of her legs. ''What kind of offer?''

''For the ranch.''

''How much?''

Silence.

''Not as good as mine, I'll bet.''

Not nearly, but she wasn't going to tell him that.

''Who was it from, if you don't mind my asking?''

''A conglomerate. They want to develop a resort and build some vacation homes—''

His low curse stopped her. ''Over my dead body!'' he said.

''That can be arranged.'' She kept her expression solemn as she returned his glare.

"Don't play games with me, Beth," he warned with a razor edge to his voice. "I won't let anybody come in here and destroy this land." Then he looked thoughtful.

"How can you stop them?"

A triumphant smile appeared on his lean, handsome face. "You don't have enough water to wet a frog's gullet, much less to service the needs of a whole community. Your conglomerate had better think twice before they come in here. If they try anything with the natural watershed or ground water, I'll have them in federal court so fast they won't know what hit them."

"Money can buy a lot of things...."

He stood and ambled over to the steps. "Neither you nor your conglomerate have enough to buy the land next to the creek."

She stood and followed him to the edge of the porch when he stepped down and headed for his truck. "Maybe I won't have to worry about buying it. Maybe the judge will give it back to the Triple R, where it belongs."

"Not a chance," he said over his shoulder. "Possession is nine-tenths of the law. Didn't Jack tell you?"

Biting back a retort, Beth kept her temper in control... and her discouragement at bay. She hadn't decided to sell, but she might have to. She made a slow survey of the land.

Her roots went back a hundred and fifty years into this soil. Ralstons had given their lifeblood for it. They'd watered it with their sweat and with their tears. It would be hard to give it up.

Picking up her drawings, she went into her bedroom and tucked them in the closet, out of sight. They were pictures of dreams that could never be.

Rolly Cawe was a big man, fairly tall with a large build. She'd looked at his personnel record and been surprised to find he was thirty-two, the same age as Keegan. He looked older, like a man going to seed.

He slouched down in the armchair next to the desk without waiting for her to invite him to be seated. That didn't bother her—cowboys didn't stand on ceremony—but his obvious glance over her figure did.

She ignored an instinctive uneasiness. Keegan had looked her over much more blatantly the evening before.

"Coffee?" she asked. "I just made a fresh pot."

"Thanks, I'd appreciate it." Cawe's voice had a caressive quality that she disliked. She sensed he was trying to charm her, to score points and get in her good graces.

After serving them coffee, she got down to business. "I've been going over the ranch accounts, trying to bring them up to date." She shot him a questioning look.

He frowned thoughtfully. "Glad to hear it. I've been worried about that lawyer down in Medford handling the finances. Always thought the money should go through the ranch manager. Of course, I'm sure your father thought he was doing right when he appointed the man as executor."

Beth bristled at the implied criticism. If Cawe thought he could do better, then why was the ranch in such poor shape?

She realized she wasn't being fair to the foreman. He'd only taken over a little more than a year ago.

"I need to get the figures on the stock count this year. What's the size of our breeding herd? How many yearlings do we have? How many two-year-olds? How many fall calves?" She waited pen poised over the livestock ledger, for the numbers.

Cawe's face changed from the serious demeanor meant to impress the new lady boss to one of irritation. It was gone in a flash. He spoke defensively. "With all this work and being shorthanded, I haven't had time to do a count."

Beth nodded. His complaint reminded her of another worry. "That's another thing, the lack of ranch hands. What happened to the men who'd been here for years? We've never had so much turnover as in the past year."

The foreman shook his head, seemingly as puzzled as she was. "Some of them quit, and I had to let some of them go. They worked too slow, seemed to think they were on a vacation instead of a working ranch. I soon put an end to that notion." He rolled his beefy shoulders and gave a self-satisfied grin.

She couldn't help but notice the paunch that lolled over his belt and the overfed heaviness of his body compared to Keegan's muscular leanness. She forced herself to stop judging her foreman. He kept coming up on the short end.

"Well," she said, "I think the first thing we need to do is get that head count so we know exactly where we stand. We'll start on that Monday morning. Unless you have something else that needs to be done?"

He fingered his chin as he thought his answer over. Beth suppressed the impatience that rose in her. She was sure the McPherson twins knew, down to the last cow, what needed to be done at their place and in what order. Not that she cared, except she wanted the Triple R to be in as good shape as the ranch next door before she made the decision to sell or not.

"Well, we need to start the roundup in the outlands—"

"You haven't done that yet?" Anger rose in her. It was getting late in the season to be rounding up stray cattle in the national forest land they leased from the federal government.

"The main herd needed moving," he explained, his gaze sliding from her hard look. "Without rain, the grass is thin. We have to move 'em around more often and keep fewer head in each pasture."

"I understand." She sighed.

In some places in the West, it required many acres per cow to feed a herd, the grazing was so poor. Some ranchers in this area trucked their cattle to southern pastures for the winter.

"You want me to have two men start a head count?" Cawe asked.

"No. I'll have Ted and Jeff handle it. Skully and I will work with them and cull the breeding herd here at the home place." Skully and his brother were too old to go out on the range. Jeff had school coming up. She thought over the options. "Take the other men with you for the roundup. I'll try to hire four more."

Cawe flashed her a look of surprise. She realized she'd taken charge. If it bothered him to have a lady boss, he'd have to get used to it. She intended to give out a lot more orders before the year was over.

"There aren't any more men to be had," he said, a slight whine in his tone. "The McPhersons have taken on every spare man in the county this year."

"Good for them," she said without emotion, feeling her heart sink. Blast Keegan McPherson. Every which way she turned, he stood in her path.

Pulling out a map of the ranch and surrounding forest, she discussed each area, checking on usage and water levels in each pond and reservoir. Four hours later she concluded the business meeting. A line of sweat circled the foreman's shirt under his collar by the time she'd finished asking questions.

After he left to assign the men to their various tasks, she leaned back in the ancient desk chair and watched him cross the creek gravel that covered the driveway to the stable. She didn't like him much, she realized. He wasn't a "go-getter" like the McPherson twins, who'd worked their way from a debt-ridden ranch to one of the best outfits around.

Keegan and his brother had made their fortune in the fast-paced world of the rodeo circuit. They'd earned it the hard way, willing to take enormous risks. Keegan had the scars to prove it.

She figured the outlay needed to bring the ranch to an even keel financially. It would eat up most of her trust fund to bail the place out of debt and make the payroll. Maybe she should take to the road and earn her money riding bulls and broncos.

A sudden pain jolted through her. Keegan had gotten gored by a bull. He could have been killed. She closed her eyes and remembered the first time she'd seen the scar on his inner thigh.

Bending over him, she'd been exploring his body, so in love that when she'd seen the evidence of the wound, she'd nearly wept. Leaning down, she'd kissed the white, jagged line . . . then she'd moved slightly upward and kissed him again . . . and he'd come apart in her hands. It had been exciting—the discovery of her power over him.

Remnants of old, useless anger surged through her, slowing her heart and bringing her back to reality. Keegan had accused her of using that power for her own gain. *That* still had the power to hurt, she realized.

She glanced at the calendar. Saturday, August fifteenth. A shiver of fear touched her. Time was the enemy. If she ran out of money before she got the ranch going again, she'd have to sell.

Sighing, she stuck the ledgers in the drawer and rubbed her eyes. She'd need another week to finish going over the accounts. There were other things she had to do in the meantime.

Skully tramped into the office with his bow-legged gait. He carried a tray with a glass of milk, two cups of coffee and a plate of brownies.

"You're spoiling me," she scolded.

Only Skully, Ted and Jeff had made her feel truly at home. They'd been glad to see her back. The other four men were cowboys, unknown to her, hired by Rolly Cawe. They'd eyed her suspiciously when Cawe had introduced them Friday night, although they had spoken respectfully enough. It was almost as if they resented her as an intrusion into their lives.

Some men thought of women that way. They liked the solitary life of a cowboy or a sailor because it took them away from the demands of society and women in particular.

Some men had the intelligence of a panicked herd, she tacked on waspishly, picking up a brownie.

"You think me, you, Ted and Jeff can start a cattle count Monday?" she asked.

Skully sat in the chair vacated by the foreman. He gave her a happy grin. "I knew you'd take hold and get things going again."

A wave of misgiving swept over her. He had a lot of faith in her ability to get the ranch back on its feet. She was suddenly scared and aware that she was a woman and very much on her own in a world of men.

Beth felt the horse bunch and jump to the right. The cow lowered its head as if she would charge at them. The cow pony stood its ground as it had been trained. The cow gave up trying to go with her calf and bellowed her rage instead.

With a nudge of her heels, Beth spun the horse in the opposite direction and headed another cow toward the chute where Ted was toting up the numbers as she ran the cows by him. Skully did the same with the calves that Jeff herded past him.

They were killing two birds with one stone, so to speak—getting a count on the active breeding herd, weeding out the older cows and culling the rest of the herd for the fall market.

At six o'clock, they called it a day.

The men set up camp near the stock pens. They'd sleep in the RV and the pickup tonight. Beth called out goodnight and headed for the house on horseback.

Going along the narrow trail through a patch of woods, she yawned and stretched wearily. It had been years since she'd been on a horse for more than a couple of hours. A full day in the saddle had taken its toll on her. She thought of the hot bath that awaited her at the house.

There was a warm spring less than a quarter mile from where she was.

She knew it well. She and Keegan used to meet there. At the end of the day, when he could get back to his house after bedding down the herd, he used to come to the edge of the woods and call to her, mimicking the *who-o-o who who-o* of the brown-spotted owl. She'd rushed to his arms...

Like a love-struck adolescent, she admitted. Those days were long gone. However, the aches and pains in her body weren't.

Too tired to dwell on the consequences, she turned her mount and rode to the fence that separated her property from the McPherson ranch. She tied the horse to the post and ducked between the strands of barbed wire.

The warm springs were just as she remembered—three steaming pools of clear water welling up from an underground source into a rocky slab of granite strewn with car-sized boulders. She laid her clothes on a boulder and slid into the nearest pool.

Closing her eyes, she rested against a warm rock and let her body soak in the heat. Fatigue radiated outward from every pore in her skin. After a while, she opened her eyes and watched the light in the sky deepen into shades of rose and lavender.

Her horse threw up its head and whinnied. Another horse answered from behind the trees.

Beth tensed. She measured the distance to her clothes and decided to go for it. Pushing straight up, she took a flying leap toward a flat rock. When the rock wobbled, making her lose her balance, she fell back into the pool with a loud splash.

When she came to the surface and flicked her hair out of her eyes, Keegan sat on his horse, watching her. She wrapped her arms across her chest and stared back at him.

"Strange," he murmured. "I keep seeing a fence over there next to that tree. Must be a mirage."

She stuck her bottom lip out and blew water off the end of her nose. "Very funny," she said in a cutting tone.

"The lady's angry," he commented to his horse while he dismounted. "Could she be embarrassed because she's caught—" he paused and let his gaze run over her "—in the flesh, one might say, on my property?"

"Turn your back," she ordered, keeping her arms folded over her chest. She'd need at least one hand free in order to pull herself out.

"I like the view from this angle." He cocked his head to one side and studied her intently.

Ripples of sensation rushed headlong over her nerves. Every part of her tingled with longing and renewed energy. "Keegan—"

"You're still as slender as a willow twig," he said, staring at her arms where they crossed over her breasts.

A flush settled in her cheeks. She had once been embarrassed because her figure was so slender. She'd never thought of her body as particularly feminine...until one man had shown her it was.

Keegan had taught her to see herself through his eyes, as a woman of irresistible allure. He'd made her feel voluptuous and beautiful and fulfilled. Then he'd taken it all away with his doubts and distrust.

She decided to fight fire with fire. Raking her gaze down his body, she saw he was blatantly aroused. Before she could soften at the thought of making love with him...here, in this place where they'd first made love...she gave him a mocking smile. "And you're the same, too, I see."

"Not quite," he drawled. "That first time we made love, my hands were shaking, I was so eager for you. Since then, I've found there are plenty of women around to satisfy a man's appetite."

His words were meant to hurt, equating what they'd shared to a casual affair. She raised her chin, determined to answer in kind.

Chapter Four

"Where? At Pete's?" Beth scoffed.

Pete's Place was a fishing camp whose owner didn't ask questions of the couples who came in late and left early. Supposedly there were women available for men who showed up alone.

Keegan tied his stallion to a tree near her horse. The two animals touched noses as if kissing.

"Nah," Keegan said with a careless wave of his hand. "Haven't you heard? Everyone loves a champion."

She hated the cynical smile that flashed over his mouth. She wanted him the way he used to be—demanding and eager for her and yet so very gentle. It had been from Keegan that she had truly experienced the tender side of a man toward a woman.

Before she could respond, Keegan's hands went to his shirt. He gave a yank. The snaps popped open, revealing a whorl of dark hair on a chest of well-developed muscles. To her consternation, he removed his shirt and tossed it on the boulder next to her clothing. He sat down and took hold of one boot.

Her chest felt as if a cow had landed in the middle of it. "What are you doing?" she demanded in a breathless wheeze.

"Taking my clothes off." He tugged one boot off, then the other. Glancing up, he gave her a sardonic grin. "I knew you'd be here."

"How?"

"I saw you working the cattle." His gaze slid slowly over her shoulders and the arms she clutched protectively over her chest. "It seemed unlikely you'd get much of a chance to ride a cow pony in San Francisco with your pin-striped stockbroker."

"Stopping here was an impulse," she said. "I never thought you'd show up." She lifted her chin. If he wasn't enough of a gentleman to leave, then she would have to gather her dignity around her and depart under his mocking gaze.

She rose, holding one arm over her chest. Keeping a wary eye on her uninvited companion, she picked her way carefully over the rocky bottom of the pool. The water was slightly over waist level.

Keegan stood, too. He unfastened his jeans and shucked them off. She couldn't stop the gasp that tore from her throat.

He grinned at her. Underneath his pants, he wore bathing trunks...form-fitting ones, but a cover nonetheless.

"You louse," she said.

His satisfied smile irked her. He'd deliberately provoked her, making her think he was stripping completely.

"Why, Miss Ralston, did you think I'd go buck naked in front of a lady such as yourself? Heaven forbid."

"Very funny." She stopped, uncertain what to do. She hated for him to see her in a vulnerable state. She felt so defenseless without the armor of clothing.

And there was the feeling she didn't want to acknowledge. Seeing his strong, masculine figure did things to her that she'd repressed for three years. Life suddenly seemed very unfair. A violent tremor raced over her.

"Take it easy, Beth," he said, his voice deeper, softer. "I'm not here to hurt you."

She looked at him. "You do that just by breathing."

The muscles in his forearms tensed, then relaxed. "Well, I'm sure as hell not going to quit breathing as a favor to you."

"I wouldn't expect it." She tried to sail past him. If she could just grab her clothes and slip behind the boulder...

He scooped her up into his arms.

For a split second, she was stunned. Then she was outraged. "Put me down this instant. Keegan, put me down!"

She pushed against his chest, angry and humiliated. He stepped forward and jumped into the pool. Instinctively she threw her arms around his neck and hung on. When her head broke the surface of the water, she was furious.

"What do you think you're doing? I'll have you arrested—"

"For catching a trespasser on my own land?" he broke in, lifting one dark eyebrow in wicked amusement. His gaze dropped downward and lingered.

She glanced down and gasped. Her breasts were solidly pressed against his chest. She released her hold on his neck and thrust her arms between them, covering herself.

"You're still as light as a feather," he murmured, his voice dropping to dangerously sexy levels.

When he sat on the boulder she'd vacated, she felt his blatant hardness against her thigh. Before she could recover her voice, he turned her back to him and began kneading the muscles of her neck and shoulders.

She knew she should stop him, that it was more than foolish to allow him this liberty, but, oh, his hands felt so good.

"Tired?"

"Exhausted," she admitted, dropping her head forward while he rubbed her neck and scalp.

"Was this what you were thinking of when you did the sketch of the couple here in the pool?"

She stiffened. "So...you looked."

"How could I help it?" There was a tinge of self-mockery in his brief laugh.

"The drawings didn't mean anything."

"But you kept them."

"To remind me of how stupid it is to trust a cowboy."

His hands stopped caressing and tightened on her shoulders. "*My* honesty wasn't in question."

She twisted out of his grasp and splashed into the middle of the pool where the water was over her chest. She bit back the angry words that choked her as she faced him. "Neither was mine. I was young and stupid three years ago. I thought I could bring peace between the two men in my life."

"You thought you could bribe me with your body. You almost did. I was that far under your spell."

The horrible memory of his accusation hit her again. He'd thought she'd prostituted herself for access to that damned water. He still did.

All the hurt, all the anger, all the buried frustration burst forth in her. She doubled her fist and swung at him.

Her wild jab took him by surprise, and she connected with his mouth. Blood appeared on her cut knuckles as flesh tore against the edge of his teeth.

She stared at him, shocked by her action. He raised one hand to his mouth. She couldn't believe she'd hit him. She'd never struck another person in her life.

"I'm sorry," she murmured hoarsely. "I'm really sorry."

He grabbed her hand and pulled her against him, crushing her in his powerful embrace. "You drive a man crazy," he muttered.

His mouth covered hers in a kiss that seethed with anger and control. That much hadn't changed. He would never hurt her with his brute strength that could wrestle a steer to the ground.

She tasted blood when his tongue invaded her mouth and realized his lip had been cut by her wild punch. Then all thought disappeared when he slid one hand down her back and scooped her against him, holding her between his thighs.

His arousal was hard and demanding against her. She felt his heat and realized only the thin material of his swimsuit separated their total joining.

Hunger erupted like a sleeping volcano. She wrapped her arms around him and returned his rapacious kisses, her need matching his, both of them refusing to be denied any longer.

His hands touched her waist; then he was lifting her, tearing his lips from hers to settle on her breast, taking her nipple into his mouth and running his tongue around and around the sensitive tip. He groaned as he wrapped his arms around her hips and held her captive to his wild embrace.

She closed her eyes and held on to his shoulders. He was the only stable thing in a world gone completely out of her control.

"No, no, no," she whimpered, but something stronger than her sense of self-preservation said *yes, yes, yes*. She didn't fight it. She couldn't.

Keegan feasted upon her. It was as if he'd been starving for years, only he hadn't known it. She was so incredibly sweet and supple in his hands, her back arching delicately as she gave herself fully to him.

She was so slender, her breasts no bigger than those of a girl just budding into womanhood, yet no woman turned him on quicker than this one. She made him forget his wise intentions.

All he wanted was to bury himself in her, to find the warm welcome of her body, to release his hot seed into that moist, secret chamber and know fulfillment.

He groaned again, the need so great, it was like being burned alive from the inside out. He suckled and laved her nipple, being careful with the tender sweetness of it. A tremor racked through her, and she pushed her fingers into his hair and held him closer, letting him see her need.

Without thought to the consequences, he rose and placed her on a boulder jutting out of the water. Another rocky ledge rose behind it at an angle. He laid her back against the ledge so she was partially reclining.

Carefully, he bent and lowered himself to her. She opened her legs and wrapped them around his hips, wringing another moan of need from him. He reached between them and caressed her, feeling her warm honey moisten his fingers.

"I haven't slept in three nights," he whispered against her lips. "All I've thought of is . . . this."

He dipped inside and explored the smooth feminine space. Her hips arched against him, inviting . . . demanding . . . that he come to her. He wouldn't last a second.

"I know," she whispered on a half sob. "I didn't know it would still be like this, so hot and wild and demanding."

"Yes."

He moved from her lips to her throat. He sampled the tiny hollows of her neck, then swept down her chest, selecting first one, then the other breast, to taste. She writhed against him.

The roar of blood through his body drowned out all other sense and sound. He had to have her. *Now.*

Quickly he pulled back and pushed at the clinging nylon that separated them. He stepped out of the bathing trunks and flung them toward the boulder where he'd tossed his clothes. Then he moved back within her embrace.

Her eyes opened and met his. They were as green as jade, as bewitching as a spell and sexier than any movie star he'd ever seen. He leaned close. Their flesh touched. Gently, he rubbed against her, stretching out the moment, letting the madness build.

''Keegan...oh, yes, please,'' she said, her voice a tremor of sound in the deepening twilight.

He pressed forward.

Suddenly the stallion rent the air with a piercing scream. The other horse reared against the tied reins and stamped its feet. With a curse, Keegan straightened. He looked at the animals and followed their nervous gazes.

A cougar stood like a statue in a half crouch across the sandy clearing beyond the other, smaller pools of the spring. The big tawny cat stared at them without blinking. Then she was gone.

''A mountain lion,'' Beth said, sounding like a person coming out of a daze.

He felt the same. He looked at the woman he'd so very nearly made love to, realization dawning on him. He'd fallen into her clutches again. Anger over his lack of control infused him.

"It's a damned good thing we were interrupted," he snarled. "I'd have taken you right here, without any protection...."

Beth saw Keegan's eyes narrow and knew the direction of his thoughts. She braced herself.

"Did you plan this?" he demanded, stepping back from her into the deeper part of the pool. "If you're counting on me getting you pregnant, then forcing marriage, think again."

"I'd never—"

"I'd take the kid, though."

"Would you trust a child of mine?" she asked. Fatigue made her voice husky, she told herself, not desire.

"Babies are innocent. They don't inherit the mother's sins." He climbed out of the pool and started pulling on his clothing, not caring that he got them wet.

Beth did the same. "What about the father's?"

She walked to the barbed wire fence before looking back at Keegan. He leapt from one boulder to another and dropped to the ground beside her. She felt intimidated by his greater height and width, but she didn't flinch from his hard stare.

"I trusted you," he ground out. "I thought we'd marry."

"So did I." She held her ground. "Trust is a two-way street, you know. So is forgiveness."

"Forgiveness? I didn't try to extract any rash promises from you. Or use my body to gain your trust."

Neither said anything for a long moment. She thought she saw regret in those icy gray depths for a second, then it was gone.

All the tender moments long ago haunted her with dreams of the life they could have shared. Until she'd tried to reconcile her father and her lover. That was a lesson she'd never forget.

Now that the excitement of passion had drained from her, she was more exhausted than before. The air was turning cold, chilling her damp clothing. Her legs shook under her weight.

Keegan muttered a savage oath and lifted her into his arms before she fell. Stepping on a fallen tree, he raised her over the fence and plunked her into the saddle. He untied her mount and handed the reins to her.

"Don't come back on my land," he ordered.

She clutched the saddle horn. "You didn't have to come down here," she said defiantly. "Since you knew I was in the pool, you could have ridden on."

"Yeah, I could have." He thrust his hands into his pockets. "I wanted to scare you—"

"Scare me!"

He shrugged. "Don't expect an apology. I thought it would help you make up your mind about leaving." He gave her a cynical smile. "Only it backfired on me. I was the one who got the scare. That was a close call."

Beth swallowed the knot of misery that formed in her. Everyone wanted to get rid of her, it seemed. Except Skully, Ted and Jeff. Two old men and a fourteen-year-old boy—her allies.

"I'll never forgive you," she whispered.

The harsh smile left his face. "For what? Not falling for your scheme? You'd do best to accept my offer. Your place won't make it another year."

She turned the horse toward the trail home. "I'll think about it," she said coolly. "There's certainly nothing to hold me here." She hoped the slight emphasis she put on the word *nothing* would get across to him. It did.

His expression changed with the suddenness of the weather, becoming furious at her relegating the attraction between them to an unimportant event in her life.

"Come back on this land again, and that could change," he promised softly.

She rode off without looking back.

At the house she took a quick shower and put on a cotton-knit pajama set. Unable to sleep, she sat on the porch swing and watched the night. There was no moon yet, and the sky seemed overwhelmed with stars.

Her fierce anger gave way to the emptiness she often felt inside. Something had disappeared from her life when Keegan had accused her of using the feelings between them for gain. She'd thought only of ending the feud, of having the two men she loved be friends, maybe work together.

But she hadn't succeeded. The land and its water had been more important to them than her. She'd always known that was true of her father; with Keegan... well, she'd thought she was first.

Live and learn.

She had.

"Up ahead," Jeff said, lightly jumping down from the knoll of rock and mounting his gelding again. His light blue eyes gleamed with excitement at being allowed to guide his boss.

"Good," Beth said.

She and Jeff had been trying to locate the main herd in order to drive the cattle down to the home range for counting and sorting. She hoped their help would speed up the fall roundup since the foreman and his men were taking forever.

Both she and her attorney had tried to find extra men, but to no avail. It irked her to admit Cawe had been right.

Here it was, Wednesday, the third of September, and they weren't finished with their cattle drive in the wild country.

A storm was hurdling in over the mountains from the northwest.

Rain, which was desperately needed, would slow down the roundup. Snow could make it impossible to get a cattle truck over the logging road to pick up the beeves. If the storm dumped a real blizzard on them, she might lose part of the herd.

Worry gave her a sick feeling inside. She needed the money the cattle would bring in.

Finances were much worse than she'd thought. After she'd prepared a balance sheet and a list of upcoming expenses, she had realized how tenuous her hold on the land was. Taxes were due in November, and the cash flow was a sea of red ink.

One thing at a time. First she needed to light a fire under her foreman and get him to work faster.

"Yo!" she yelled as she and Jeff rode out of the woods.

Rolly Cawe and three men leapt up from their bedrolls around the glowing fire.

"It's just us," she called. She smiled, relieved at having found them. "Jeff and I thought we'd come give you men a hand. We finished the count at the homeplace. Are you about through?"

"Uh . . . just about," Cawe answered, striding forward.

She dismounted before he could help her. "Glad your fire is still going. We haven't had supper yet."

"We didn't expect company," Cawe said with just a smidgen of irritation. "There isn't any grub left."

"That's okay. Jeff and I brought our own."

Cawe unsaddled the mare and made a space for her bedroll close to his. Jeff squeezed in beside her as his grandfather had ordered him to do. Beth smiled slightly, then set about heating two cans of beef stew. With crackers, cheese and peaches, it was a filling meal.

While they ate, she asked her foreman about the roundup. "Where are you holding the herd? Jeff and I thought you'd be at the Sky Creek pasture."

"We're separating the calves in temporary stock pens down in the draw over the ridge," Cawe explained, adding that the fourth cowboy was staying with the cattle.

She frowned. "Why do it now? Let's take them to the ranch and then do the sorting."

The foreman grunted, which she took as agreement.

"How many head do you have?"

"We haven't taken a count yet."

Beth found her foreman's answer unsatisfactory. The man never knew how many beeves they had. He didn't know their distribution on the ranch nor here on the national forest land. As soon as she had time, she'd pay him off and find someone else.

Later, listening to the snores of the cowboys and the night sounds, she fretted on the hard fall and winter that lay ahead of her. There was no hay for winter feed. She'd have to buy it.

With what?

Good question. Too bad she didn't have an answer. If she put all her assets into the ranch and still failed, she'd have no money to start a new life.

She woke at first light with a gun in her face.

"Jus' ease up nice and quiet," a man with a thick drawl told her. He stepped back and waited.

Beth rose from her sleeping bag and looked around. Jeff slept soundly beside her. Cawe's eyes flickered under his closed eyelids, but he pretended to be sleeping.

She glanced around the clearing. There were three other men with the one who'd ordered her up. They were all mounted, and they all carried rifles on their saddles.

"Get up," Beth ordered. She shook Jeff's shoulder. "Rise and shine, boys. We have company from the Sky Eagle ranch, it seems."

Her men climbed out of their warm bedrolls. They tentatively raised their arms. Beth wasn't sure of the protocol of being held under a loaded rifle, either, but she wasn't going to stick her hands in the air like a character in an old Western movie.

Cawe cursed violently. "I'll have the law on you for this," he threatened. "You better have a permit for toting a gun, and a damned good reason for pulling it on a sleeping man."

Beth shot her foreman a glance that silenced him. "Is it okay if we put our boots on?" she asked.

The oldest man, the one who held his rifle on her, nodded. "One at a time, you first, then the boy."

Beth shook out her boots and pulled them on. She slipped into her jacket and zipped it against the morning chill.

"Mind telling me what this is all about?" she asked as Jeff took his turn.

The old cowboy curled his lip as if he didn't believe she needed an explanation of her sin. "The boss'll tell you when he gits here."

"Keegan?"

The cowboy nodded.

"Where is he?"

"At the house. One of the boys has gone to fetch him."

"Great," she said with false cheer. "In the meantime, I want breakfast. Have you men eaten?" she politely asked her captors.

"Jus' don't make no sudden moves," the cowpoke advised.

Beth smiled at Jeff. "You heard the man," she joked with him to relieve the fear he hid behind an impassive expression. "Let's get the bacon on. You get the skillet. I'll start the coffee."

They had eaten and digested the meal by the time Keegan rode up with another cowboy. She recognized Hank, whose guitar was strapped behind him. The singing cowboy nodded to her shyly.

Keegan ignored her. He and the old cowpoke talked quietly to one side; then he came over to her.

"Saddle up."

"Where are we going?" she asked.

"Down the ridge to the herd."

"Do the condemned get to know their crime before they're executed?" she inquired.

"Rustling."

The word bounced through her skull in a shock wave. She grabbed Keegan's arm when he turned to remount his stallion.

"Just a darned minute. Are you accusing Ralston men of stealing cattle?" She was incredulous.

He smiled coldly. "Mount up, and I'll show you." He swung into the saddle.

Jeff had already tossed her saddle on the mare. She cinched it while he and the other men broke their camp. In a few minutes they were on their way in single file along the ridge trail.

Beth looked the herd over while they descended to the tiny valley where maybe a hundred head of cattle milled and grazed. The cattle were a sorry-looking lot—the lack of grass and water showing up in their tired stance and bony backs.

Separated by a pole fence, calves bawled for their mothers, and the cows crowded each other aside in an effort to reach their young. This was the part of ranching she found hard to take.

"Over here." Keegan rode up beside her. "We use ear tags and notches to mark our cattle," he informed her, his face chiseled in granite. "Do you see any like that?"

She did.

In one of the stock pens, twenty, twenty-five cattle milled restlessly. They had no access to water and looked dusty and thirsty. There were no calves with them, she noted.

"Cawe," she called, ignoring Keegan's sarcastic question. "Release the Sky Eagle cattle and turn them over to the McPherson men." She returned Keegan's hard gaze. "This is our range. In the future, keep your cattle off it."

"Cattle wander where they will. We drive yours back over the ridge when they try to join up with ours." He raised one thick dark eyebrow. "I can understand why your beeves head over our way. What surprises me is why ours would come over here."

Looking at his cattle and hers, she had to agree. His were obviously bigger and better fed than the rest of the herd.

"I wonder if the forest service realizes what the Triple R is doing to the public range," he continued. "It's so overgrazed, the cattle eat anything that sticks a shoot out of the dirt."

She'd already noticed that. She hardly needed a lecture from him to see that there wasn't a blade of grass in sight and that the sage was chewed to a nub.

"With five years of drought behind us, you should have been decreasing the herd each year. Your cattle look like hell."

"Thank you for your helpful advice," she managed to say with a mendacious smile. After paying the taxes and bills, the Triple R might not have any cattle left to graze the land. "Don't let us detain you."

"I want the calves," he said in a flat tone.

A flush rose to her face. Her men had to have known they were taking McPherson cattle when they separated the cows from the calves. "Open the gates," she ordered Cawe. "All of them."

She shot him a dangerous look when he looked as if he would argue with her order. Damn him for putting her in this position.

She watched without saying a word while the cows and calves sorted themselves out. At a nod from Keegan, his men expertly cut their cattle out of the herd and headed them down the east trail toward their ranch.

Nearly every Sky Eagle cow had a calf. Only about half the Triple R cows did. She rejected the depression that kept trying to steal over her. After three weeks of hard work and restless nights, it was harder to do.

When Keegan and his men were out of sight, she turned to her ranch hands. "Let's move'em out."

Jeff grinned and swung a short whip. It cracked in the air. The cattle nearest him startled and began moving. That set the stringy herd in motion. She did a quick head count as they milled past her position on a small rise.

Well, she reasoned, what they lacked in pounds, they made up for in numbers. Keegan was right. The Triple R was running way too many cows for the available range.

She glanced at the foreman when he charged by after a group of cows heading for the trees and wondered what his intention had been toward the McPherson cattle. Would he have freed them after moving the herd out? Or would he have left them to die of thirst?

Uneasiness crept over her. Here she was, out in the wilds with five grown men she hardly knew and didn't trust, with only a fourteen-year-old to guard her. Unwilling to admit that she, a woman, couldn't handle the situation, she stayed with the herd.

When they made camp that night, she decided to take the first watch on the cattle. She checked her rifle and made sure the men saw that she was familiar with its operation.

Jeff wanted to ride herd with her.

"Get some sleep now," she told him. "I'll call you to relieve me around midnight or so." She turned to Cawe. "The rest of you will be able to get a good night's sleep. I want to get to the home pastures tomorrow."

For the next few hours, she rode in slow circles around the herd, keeping a sharp lookout for predators. At two o'clock, she was too sleepy to stay in the saddle. She turned her horse toward the sleeping camp.

Suddenly, nearing a copse of oaks, her mare lifted its head and tested the air, then snorted softly. A tremor ran over her smooth hide. Beth tensed.

The cougar?

She eased the rifle out of the scabbard and brought it to her shoulder. She didn't want to hurt the animal, but she might have to scare it off. A human form separated itself from the shadows.

"Don't shoot. I give up," a sardonic male voice said.

A spasm of surprise threw her aim high as she jerked on the rifle. "Keegan!"

He bowed from the waist.

After her fright, anger flooded her. "It's a good thing I didn't have my finger on the trigger. I might have shot you," she snapped at him. "On second thought, that might be a good idea."

"Never think second thoughts." His soft laughter floated out of the darkness.

Mysterious, wholly male and strangely intimate, it seemed to caress her senses. Longing flared in her before she could control the impulse. She realized how vulnerable she was.

One kind word and she would fling herself into his arms.

"You're on Triple R land, not leased range," she reminded him, holding tight to her emotions. She was too tired for another confrontation with him.

"When is someone going to relieve you?" he asked.

"I was going to wake Jeff when you appeared. I thought you were the cougar," she added. She slipped on the safety and put the rifle back in the scabbard. "Where's your horse?"

"Back in the trees. I saw you take up guard duty from the ridge. You need more men."

Her laughter was brief. "That's rich. You've hired all the men who used to work for us, the good ones, that is. Tell me where to find more."

He didn't answer.

She drew a deep breath, held it, then let it out slowly. "I've got to get Jeff. I'm dead tired. And I don't feel like arguing with you all night." She turned the mare.

Keegan stepped forward and caught the bridle. "There are other things to do in the night," he suggested, his voice husky.

Her nerves danced at the possibilities. The mare shifted in reaction. Tension arced like invisible lightning between them.

"Get Jeff," he ordered. "Then bring your bedroll over here. There's a sheltered place under a ledge in case it rains."

She looked at the sky. "Not a cloud in sight."

"The storm is supposed to be here by tomorrow. It may rain before dawn. Did you bring a tent?"

"I brought a tarp."

"That's not good enough if we get a real storm. Tell Jeff to keep his rain gear handy."

"How neighborly of you to be so concerned."

"Yeah," he said.

She wished she could see his face. The moon had come up, but its light only outlined his stern features. She hadn't a clue as to what he was thinking. Or feeling.

He let go of the mare. Beth moved the reins, and the horse headed off toward the campsite after whinnying softly. An answer came from the stallion hidden in the trees.

After waking Jeff and seeing that he ate a snack and had a couple of candy bars in his pockets, she told him where she would sleep and sent him out to the herd. "Stay alert. I saw a cougar near our land the other day."

He positively glowed with excitement as he rode out. Beth smiled. He'd be all right. Ted and Skully had taught him well.

She turned her gaze to the camp. The other men slept without stirring. She watched them for a few seconds, then climbed back onto her mount.

When she reached the trees, Keegan stepped out and lifted her from the horse. His hands were large and warm on her waist. "Back here." He took the reins and led the way.

Sure enough, there was a shallow alcove under a ledge of rock. She found it was deep enough for her saddle and sleeping bag.

Keegan rigged her tarp over the opening in case the storm brought a blowing rain. She'd be snug for the night.

"Why?" she asked.

He didn't pretend not to understand. "I didn't think you were safe at your camp."

She spread her bedroll out with an irritated gesture. "Do you think my own men would hurt me?"

Keegan didn't respond in anger. "It was a . . . gut feeling." He sat back on his heels, his head under the tarp, and watched her preparations for bed.

His admission did things to her that she didn't want to acknowledge. His concern was real. And it disturbed her.

Did he still have feelings for her?

"My camp is near here," he murmured. "If you call, I'll hear you. Don't take on trouble on your own."

"What kind of trouble?"

"One of my men spotted cat tracks over at the creek a while ago." He paused. "I also saw tire tracks on the logging road."

"I haven't called in the cattle trucks yet."

"Neither have I."

In the dim, barely discernible light of the moon, their eyes met. Rustlers weren't merely the bad guys in cowboy movies. They were for real, and they were dangerous men who carried guns.

A softness stole into her. She wanted to melt into his arms and renew the passion they'd once shared. She gasped at the errant thought. Rustlers weren't the only dangerous men around.

Beth forced her gaze from Keegan's. She tugged off her boots. "Thanks for the warning. I'll sleep with Winnie here." She patted her Winchester repeating rifle.

Keegan stroked one finger down her cheek and across her mouth. "I'd rather you slept with me."

She went as still as a rabbit, not moving, not even breathing. Then she laughed. "Nice try, Keegan," she said, turning the words he'd used after that kiss in her bedroom against him. "But I'm also older and wiser than I was three years ago. I'm not available for a fling. I have a ranch to run."

He withdrew abruptly. She felt cold without his touch. He rose to his feet, the tarp still in his hand.

"So do I," he growled at her. "But I don't think you'll hold out much longer on yours. Taxes are due in two months."

He strode off, letting the rain sheet fall.

Beth pushed it aside so she could see the sky. The stars were so thick it seemed she could reach up and grab a handful.

Dreams, like stars, sometimes seemed close, too. But she knew they were impossibly far away. It was time to think of her future in practical terms. She had no choice. Before next spring she would run out of money. Unless the calving went well, she would have to sell. Next time when she left, she would never come back.

Chapter Five

"Did you remember to put beans on the list?" Skully asked.

Beth checked. "Yes. Are you sure you don't want to go to town? You and Jeff can go in. Ted and I will stay here and keep an eye on the ranch."

Skully shook his head and flicked his hair over his shoulder. It reached to his waist now and was fastened at the back of his neck with a rubber band, as usual. He wore a gold stud in one ear and reminded her of Willie Nelson—rough around the edges, with an appeal that had to do with the heart rather than looks.

"Jeff's too young for Saturday night in town. You ought to stay and dance awhile."

"Who with?" she asked with resigned patience. He'd been goading her about "getting out" for a month.

"Bound to be some young bucks at the saloon."

She thought of Keegan. He wasn't exactly a young buck. Not that he was ancient, but he wasn't like the cowboys who went into town on weekends, to dance with the young girls, mostly tourists thrilled to meet a real live cowboy.

"Cawe said he and the men were going into town."

Skully grimaced. "Don't get mixed up with them."

Beth bit at a split cuticle on her thumbnail. Her nails needed attention. So did her hair. She and Skully had put up apples from the gnarled old trees in the orchard for two days, freezing some for pies plus making jelly and apple butter.

"I don't like him, either," she admitted.

"Something sneaky about him."

Skully so rarely ventured an opinion about a person that Beth was surprised. It meant Skully more than disliked the man; he was suspicious of the foreman. She had no time to dwell on it.

"Well, I'd better get a shower and hit the road if I want to be back before dark."

"I'll load the coolers in the truck," Skully volunteered.

"Thanks."

Beth dashed to her room, flung off her clothes and headed into the bathroom. A few minutes later she dried off and wrapped a towel around her hair. She needed a haircut if she was going to keep her hair in the short, carefree curls she preferred.

Stopping in front of her closet, she paused before opening the door. The mirror reflected her figure, faithfully outlining the curves of her hips and legs. She weighed less than she had when she'd graduated from high school and moved to San Francisco.

What did Keegan see that set him on fire for her?

She swallowed as long-suppressed thoughts erupted into her mind. The night she'd slept in the alcove, knowing he was within calling distance, had been the last she'd seen of him.

His warning about rustlers, his concern for her safety... had those been for her as a person or for her as a neighboring rancher?

A rancher, she decided. The only thing personal between them was lust and hate. A powerful combination, she acknowledged.

After pulling on her robe, she gave herself a manicure and painted her nails for the first time in weeks. Using the blow dryer, she brushed her hair into order, flipping the ends under on one side and up on the other.

She liked the effect—sort of saucy, a little defiant, as if she thumbed her nose at her troubles... and at those who thought she couldn't handle them.

For several minutes she hesitated over her clothes. Vanity urged her toward a dress she'd bought shortly before leaving the city. Of teal green silk, it made her eyes glow like jewels. Its short length was definitely flirty.

With her favorite high-heeled sandals, her legs would look long and graceful. They were her best feature, so her friend, Tina, had told her. "With your hair and eyes, you have great color," Tina had declared. "And super legs. Make the most of your assets, kid."

The silk dress did just that, Beth thought.

She reached for the dress. Hesitated. Then dropped her hand. Who was she trying to impress?

Not a stubborn, hard-hearted rancher who wouldn't recognize the truth if it bit him on his backside!

Grabbing a pair of white slacks and a red cotton-knit sweater, instead, she jerked them on, put on a smidgen of makeup, then paused over her shoes. Resolutely she pulled on red sling-backed flats that were nice and also practical.

She picked up her purse, found the keys and left for town.

There was only one parking space to be found. It was in front of the old livery stable that hadn't been used in two generations. The streets of the small town teemed with the usual mob of loggers, cowboys and travelers.

Beth headed for the grocery. With her list in hand, she pushed a cart up and down the aisles and loaded it with the items she and Skully had decided they needed.

Stopping by the dairy case, she hefted two gallons of skim milk and made a place for them on top of the canned goods.

Behind the seven-foot shelving of the next section, she heard a woman greet a friend. She recognized Sita's voice. A man replied, his voice low, but Beth recognized it, too.

"Have you bought the Ralston spread?" Sita asked.

"Not yet," Keegan answered. He laughed. "But we're working on it. If Plan A doesn't succeed, we'll go to Plan B."

Beth saw red. She abandoned her cart and stalked around the end of the table. "You can forget your plans!" she said coldly. "I'll see you in hell before . . . Oh."

The man who faced her wasn't Keegan.

She stared at him in stunned surprise. "You're not Keegan," she said, then realized how foolish she must appear. Heat flared in her face. She lifted her chin.

"I'm Kerrigan." He touched the brim of his hat and nodded to her. He studied her for a second; then he grinned. "Beth Ralston—all grown up. Glad to see you again."

She nodded, confused by his attitude. He truly seemed pleased to see her, which was strange in light of the lawsuit and all the other contretemps that had occurred between her family and his.

Sita grinned at Beth, then moved off down the row in search of an item. She stopped several feet away.

Beth glanced back at Keegan's brother.

Kerrigan McPherson apparently wasn't a man to hold a grudge. The next thing she knew, he was apologizing to her for his careless words. "I was joking earlier. There isn't any plan at all. I hope I didn't hurt your feelings."

He looked so much like his twin in height, breadth and general features that it was like looking at a familiar picture that had been subtly altered, but she wasn't sure how. He was watching her, his expression solemn, as if he really cared about her feelings.

"Your eyes are blue," she said inanely.

"Yeah. Big brother's are gray." His grin was exactly like his twin's, with the attractive slashes and the faint crinkles at the corners of his eyes. His hair was just as dark.

Her heart quivered in her chest like a spent pendulum. "I'm sorry I...uh...reacted so strongly."

He pushed his hat back, then stuck his thumbs in his pockets. "I'd be mad as hell, too, if I heard someone plotting to take over my spread." He stuck out a hand. "Friends?"

She hesitated, then shook hands. Managing a smile, she gave him fair warning of the situation between her and his twin. "I'm not sure we can be friends, but I suppose we can be peaceful enemies."

He laughed at her wry remark. His merriment was a pleasant, rumbling sound that rolled over her senses. Once, she'd heard Keegan laugh like that. A long time ago, it seemed.

"My wife is at the beauty shop, getting her hair fixed. She's dying to meet you. Will you join us for supper in the diner in about an hour?"

The invitation surprised her.

"I'll save y'all a table when I take over," Sita volunteered. She dropped several articles in her basket. "See you later." She smiled and hurried toward the cash register.

"I'm not sure I'll have time." Beth was sure she shouldn't get any more involved with the McPherson family. One of them was all she could handle.

"If you do, join us. This is Rachel's first time out without the baby. She's nervous about it. Another woman might make her feel better." He tipped his hat and walked off with his basket of groceries and a package of diapers.

Beth stared after him. For just a second she thought of Keegan, of the children she'd thought they would have. She could see him shopping for them, buying diapers and baby food. She tried to smile, but it wouldn't come.

Lifting the list, she blinked the sudden mist from her eyes and gathered the rest of the groceries. No way was she going to eat at the diner. She'd starve first.

An hour later, her staples stored in the coolers in the back of the pickup and the feed ordered at the farm and ranch store, she stood on the sidewalk and dithered. She was hungry. She had almost an hour's drive ahead of her to the ranch. Maybe no one she knew was in the diner at this moment.

Ha. She'd been known in this town all her life.

If Kerrigan McPherson and his wife were there, she'd have to sit with them. She couldn't be rude and ignore them. Her stomach growled. Slinging her purse strap over her shoulder, she took a deep breath and went in.

The McPhersons were there. So were the Hunters. Susannah and her husband Tom were sitting with Kerrigan and his wife.

Beth sighed in relief. She could take a corner table by herself, eat and leave before they noticed her.

"Over here," Sita called across the room. "There's a place for you."

Several pairs of eyes turned to her, including the two couples. Kerrigan stood. So did Tom Hunter. And Susannah.

"Beth, come on over," Susannah yelled, a big smile on her face. She stood and gave Beth a bear hug when Beth made her way through the crowded diner to their table.

"Glad you could come," Kerrigan said. "This is my wife, Rachel. The nervous mother," he added with a teasing smile.

"This is the first time I've left him for more than an hour with anyone else," Rachel McPherson explained. "Do sit down. I've been dying to meet you. Our house is only a quarter mile from yours, you know, through the woods and over the creek."

"Uh, yes, I know," Beth answered. "It was being built when Keegan...when I..." She licked her lips. "When my father was ill a few years ago," she finished lamely.

"I'm sorry about your loss," Rachel said so naturally that it didn't seem awkward to accept her sympathy.

"Thank you," Beth said, taking the seat Tom Hunter held for her. She sat between him and an empty chair at a round table that could seat six comfortably. She noticed there were water glasses at each place setting. Six of them.

She darted a glance around the diner as a nervous premonition rushed along her back. Keegan wasn't in sight. Maybe he was home baby-sitting or tending a sick cow or something.

Forcing herself to relax—she wasn't in enemy territory, for heaven's sake; this was the diner where she'd spent as much time as her father would allow her while growing up—she sipped her water and answered a hundred questions Susannah shot at her for the next few minutes.

"She was with the Inquisition in a prior life," Tom finally broke in, drawing an indignant "Oh!" from his wife.

Everyone laughed as Susannah poked him on the jaw, then leaned over to kiss the fake blow away.

At that moment there was a commotion at the door. Beth, still laughing, looked up.

Keegan stared at her from the doorway.

Her first impulse was to make a dash for it. Her next was to stand her ground. Why should he put her to flight? Ralstons had loaned the money for the first general store at this crossroads.

"Don't let him scare you off," Kerrigan advised.

Beth jerked her gaze from Keegan, who was making his way to them amid much handshaking and greetings, to his brother. Kerrigan and his wife smiled at her sympathetically. She didn't understand anything about this family. *They* seemed to be on *her* side.

Keegan reached them and stood behind the vacant seat next to Beth. "I didn't know we were going to have company."

If his intent was to make her feel the outsider, he succeeded. She could sense his animosity coming at her in waves like heat radiating from a branding iron.

"We met at the store. I invited her to join us."

Kerrigan's voice carried a subtle warning. Keegan raised his eyebrows but said nothing. He pulled the chair out.

His knee brushed her thigh in the tight space between the chairs as he sat down. A jolt of sensation went up her leg. She shifted her legs away from his.

His gaze mocked her movement. She met his eyes, then glanced away. Looking around the table, she saw the other four watching them. They all smiled at her as if in approval. She felt confused by their attitude and by her own feelings.

"Did you get your cattle counted?" Rachel asked.

"Yes."

"Keegan said he saw you up near Eagle Ridge."

"Uh, yes, we were moving the cattle and getting a count on the breeding stock. Keegan warned us about a cougar in the area."

Beth saw Rachel and Kerrigan exchange glances, then smiles.

"So, the cougar is back," he said with an amused drawl.

"It may not be the female," his wife said, a worried line nicking the space between her eyes.

For some reason Beth thought the cougar meant more to the couple than was obvious. Husband and wife secrets, she thought. Even her parents had had them, although her father's true love had been the ranch. Beth crumpled her napkin in a clenched hand. How did a person ever reach a rancher's heart?

"Rachel is a naturalist," Keegan said. "She came up here last year to study a pair of eagles."

"And fell in love with the Sky Eagle ranch," Susannah declared with a sly smile. "Of course she had to marry a McPherson in order to stay...."

"It was the smartest move she ever made," her husband informed them with an endearing arrogance. "McPhersons are prime catches." He looked directly at Beth and Keegan.

Beth felt a flush build up her neck and into her face. Keegan gave his brother a hard glance, then went back to studying his place setting. Conversation stopped while the waitress took their orders. Beth noticed that the young woman stood between her and Keegan and leaned against him each time she took a menu.

It was dark by the time they finished eating. The band was warming up in the saloon. She could see the five young men through the archway between the rooms. They, like the waitress, looked to be in their late teens or early twenties.

The passage of time became an ominous internal ticking. At their age, she'd been struggling with classes in accounting and flower arranging, trying to learn to run a business while actually doing it. She wondered about their dreams.

She glanced at the other two couples at the table. Rachel and Susannah were discussing their children. If she and Keegan had married three years ago, perhaps they would have had a child by now. She could join in, telling the latest exploit of their son or daughter with that droll exasperation and loving pride that all parents seemed to have.

"The music is starting," Susannah exclaimed. "Does anyone want dessert?" It was obvious she was dying to dance.

Her husband threw back his head and laughed at her eagerness. He patted his wife's hand. "Only at peril of their lives."

"Not me," Beth quickly said. "I think I'd better go. It's a long drive to the ranch."

"Oh, no, you have to stay for the music. This band is the best we've had in months."

"Yes, please stay," Rachel added to Susannah's protest of her leaving.

Beth didn't know what to do. She was torn by her desire to escape and an equally strong impulse to stay. It had been a long time since she'd been with people she enjoyed this much.

She mustn't get used to it, she thought. She was going to leave when she sold the calves and got the ranch on its feet.

An impatient movement caused her to look at Keegan. He turned an icy gaze on her. "Beth has probably had enough of the yokels for the evening."

"The company has been delightful," she contradicted him. "Most of it."

"Meaning I haven't," he concluded.

"I'm sure you've had many charming thoughts this evening."

"But I haven't shared them?"

She shrugged and rose to her feet. The others stood. "Well," she said, preparing to say her farewells.

Keegan clamped his hand around her elbow. "It wouldn't be neighborly to run off so early. Stay for an hour, then I'll follow you home to make sure you don't have car trouble again."

"The truck runs fine—" She stopped, realizing four people looked at her with differing degrees of friendliness and curiosity.

Keegan expected her to run, she realized, looking at the challenge in his eyes. He dropped her arm.

"For an hour," she said, unwilling to run from him.

Rachel and Susannah exclaimed with pleasure. The men consulted on the check. Beth opened her purse.

"I'll get it," Keegan said in a low growl.

Again there was a duel between them. She gave in as graciously as she could. As a group, they moved from the dining room into the saloon. The band was already playing the first tune, a lively country rock and roll number.

Tom and Susannah were the first on the floor. Others flocked to join them. She and Keegan sat alone at the cocktail table they'd chosen. Keegan ordered beers for the men, wine for the women. He didn't say a word to her.

Well, she decided, she didn't have to stay the full hour. She could leave at any time. She let a breath out slowly.

Keegan stood all at once. "Come on."

He held out his hand for her. She rose and put her hand in his. They went to the crowded floor and faced each other. He let her hand go and began moving to the music.

She had to admit he was a wonderful dancer. So was his twin. Whereas Tom moved rather stiffly to the beat, obviously dancing to please his wife, the McPherson twins moved with a natural grace.

Keegan felt the beat echo through him. His pulse kept time with the fast tempo of the music. Each pluck of the bass fiddle strings set off a resonant hum inside him. He was near the edge.

Glancing at Beth was a mistake. She moved like a willow in the wind, her body slender and poised, dancing in harmony with the beat in his blood.

The song ended. Another began. Quieter. A love song.

Keegan took a deep, calming breath and brought Beth into his arms. The warm rise of heat from her body brought the sweet odor of her perfume and shampoo to his nostrils.

There was a freshness about her—a natural, womanly scent that came from her, not her cosmetics. He'd loved to press his nose against her at various places and draw her essence deep into him, all the way to his soul....

He pulled back, startling her. She stumbled. He caught and steadied her, then kept a cool three inches between them. It would be too easy to get trapped by passion again.

At the ridge last month, he'd found it hell to sleep, knowing she was only a hundred yards away. Next thing he knew, he would agree to let her have access to the water she so desperately needed.

He hardened his heart. No way would he fall for her again. It had nearly killed him the last time....

Laughter brought his attention to the couple beside him. Kerrigan had been miserable last spring, fighting his need for Rachel, unable to stay away from her. Things had worked out for the two of them.

A strange sensation fluttered in Keegan's chest, as if something fragile and full of hope sought to emerge into the open.

He smiled cynically. Yeah, *hope*, he mocked. Just what did he hope for? A woman who'd love him and stay with him no matter how hard life got?

In his experience most women didn't hold up when things got tough. His mother hadn't.

After her death no one had wanted the McPherson twins until they'd made their fortunes on the rodeo circuit. Then there had been plenty of women. None of whom he'd wanted.

Until Beth.

She'd been the unkindest blow dealt him by life. She'd been his dream come true, so wildly passionate and responsive, he had thought he'd found the other half of his soul.

Yeah, right.

He'd been a fool. Like his grandfather, she'd wanted what she could get out of him. Hell, he'd been fooled twice. Once in thinking if he worked really hard and did everything just right, his grandfather would love him; the second time in thinking Beth had felt the same about him as he had about her.

When she'd asked him to give her father access to the creek, he'd realized he'd been taken for a ride . . . again.

There wouldn't be a third time.

"You're hurting my hand."

He loosened his death grip on Beth's fingers. "Sorry."

"Were you thinking about us?" she asked softly.

The question surprised him. He had to give her credit for courage. She wasn't afraid to look a tiger in the eye. "Yes."

She smiled, and again he had an impression of sadness in her. He hardened himself against her charms.

"I could tell," she explained. "You always look so fierce."

"Thinking of you isn't the only thing that makes me mad," he informed her, holding a cool edge to his voice.

"It's the most obvious, though. Each time you glance at me, you scowl."

"I'll try not to be so easy to read in the future."

A slight tremor caressed her lips. He stared at the tempting flesh. All he had to do was lean forward and drop his head a bit, and their mouths would touch.

He could drink at the well of her sweetness forever and never tire of her taste. It was a realization that brought an immediate tightening of his muscles...everywhere. He realized he was scowling again and forced the frown from his face.

When the music ended, the other couples stayed on the floor. Beth turned from him and headed for the table. He put his hand on her back, letting his fingers splay out against the soft material of her sweater just where it ended on her hips.

Ignoring the pang of desire that shot through him, he kept his light touch on her, determined not to let her evade him.

"Stop it," she said, taking her seat.

"Stop what?" he asked innocently.

"You're trying to seduce me."

He laughed, then leaned toward her. "Honey, when I decide to seduce you, you'll go down like a lightning-struck steer."

Beth wanted to deny his statement. She wanted to erase the knowing look in his eyes. Knowledge that she had given him, she admitted. He knew every inch of her...where to touch her...how to caress her.

"Do you feel that you have to prove your manhood?" she demanded. "Is that what this is all about?"

Fire smoldered in his eyes. "I think I proved that quite effectively a few times in the past."

"Is this Plan A?"

She watched him carefully. Puzzlement was the only expression she could read on his face.

"Plan A?" he inquired.

"You admitted you were trying to scare me off that day in the pool," she reminded him, ignoring the pain that squeezed her heart. "It won't work. I'm not scared of you."

He leaned close. "You heat up in my arms, but you run like a chipmunk with a coyote after her when I let you go."

She stared into his hard gaze, wondering what his plans were. He wanted her off her ranch and out of his life. "You won't run me off."

In the silence following this declaration, a couple, a cowboy and a young girl, passed their table on the way to the dance floor. The cowboy said hello. Keegan smiled and nodded, then he returned to his study of Beth.

"I won't have to," he said. "The snow was below average again last winter. By the end of the month, you'll have no water. You'll have to sell."

"But not to you."

He stood when she did. "You sell to anyone but me, and I'll have your hide pinned to my barn door."

Beth removed the truck keys from her purse. She realized she was terribly tired. "I'll never sell," she said in a low, vehement cadence, spacing each word. "The Triple R is my land, my home, my heritage. I have a right to be there, and I'll never give it up. Nothing you can do will make me!"

Chapter Six

Beth pushed the chair aside and headed for the door. She'd taken one step when a vise grip captured her arm and spun her around. Keegan leaned close to her. "We'll see about that."

"You're right," she said in the same low, threatening snarl. "We'll see who stays and who goes. It won't be me." She twisted against his hold, but he held her wrist with little effort. "Let me go, Keegan."

"Maybe I like holding you." He grinned wolfishly, his eyes daring her to fight him. He'd never used his strength against her this way, but she wasn't scared of him.

"I'll kick you," she warned.

Keegan glanced at her soft red shoes and chuckled.

"You heard the lady, McPherson."

Beth looked around at her foreman with an annoyed frown. Just what she needed—a champion to complicate matters.

Keegan looked at Cawe. A slow, insouciant grin spread over his face. "Butt out, Cawe. This is a private conversation."

"I'm joining in." Cawe hooked his thumbs in his belt and leaned back on his heels in a challenging stance. "Release her or else..." He let the thought trail off suggestively.

"It's all right," Beth put in, trying to forestall trouble. "The discussion is finished. And I'm going home." She tugged at her wrist and gave Keegan a warning glance, which he ignored.

His eyes flicked from her to the foreman. "Or else what?" Keegan inquired in a soft voice.

Beth groaned tiredly. Honestly, *men.* She saw the fury in Keegan's eyes and felt it in the tensing of his muscles. "Keegan, don't. Please."

He switched his gaze to her. His smile changed, she thought, becoming gentler.

"No use talking nice to trash like him and his brother," Cawe told her with an arrogant tilt to his head. "There's only one thing he understands."

"Dammit, shut up," she said in exasperation.

Keegan laughed. "Such ladylike language."

Cawe stepped forward. "Let the lady go."

"Some hero for a lady in distress." The cowboy who'd spoken turned from the bar, a beer in his hand, and leaned an elbow on the oak edging. He gave Cawe a thorough perusal. "A man who can't tell his own brand from the Sky Eagle mark."

One of Cawe's men grabbed the cowboy by the shirt front. "You trying to say something about the way we do our business?"

"Yeah, it stinks," the cowboy remarked casually. "Now kindly take your hand off my new shirt. You're wrinkling the material."

Beth groaned as the tension escalated faster than an erupting volcano. Keegan muttered an expletive under his breath.

"Well, I sure wouldn't want to do that," Cawe's man said with a nasty grin. He released the shirt and pretended to smooth it out. "Heck, it's still messed up. I know, I'll just mess up your face so it'll match." He doubled his fist and threw a punch.

The cowboy ducked, blocked the blow, set his beer bottle down and shoved the Triple R man backward over a table. Cawe whirled around and socked the cowboy, sending him crashing down the bar, knocking two other men down like bowling pins.

The next thing Beth knew, the whole place was engaged in a free-for-all as two Sky Eagle men took on five Triple R men, and other people tried to flee or find a safe place along the sidelines to watch the scuffle and cheer on the winners.

She found herself pressed between the table and a tall, lean male body. Across the way, she saw the other McPherson twin and Tom Hunter push Rachel and Susannah against the wall by the back exit and shield them with their bodies. She tried to peer around Keegan to see what was going on.

He grabbed her by the waist and propelled her over to the other two women. "Stay here!" he ordered. "Watch the women," he said to Tom.

Then Keegan and his twin headed for the thickest part of the fighting, where two of Cawe's men held one cowboy while Cawe beat him senseless. Beth was shocked at this unfair conduct from the Triple R men. She started forward.

"Better stay back," Tom said, putting a hand on her arm.

She shook him off and waded into the melee. "Cawe, stop that right now!" she yelled over the noise of thrashing bodies and crashing furniture.

The rest of the cowboys and loggers had chosen sides and joined in the tussle. "For heaven's sake," she muttered. Beth shoved one staggering cowpoke out of her path.

He drew back a fist. "Sorry," he muttered around a split lip rapidly swelling to double in size.

"It's okay. Go home now. You're done for the night."

"Thank you, ma'am," he said in a daze and looked for the door.

She stepped around him in time to see Keegan tap Cawe on the shoulder. When the foreman jerked around, Keegan gave a little bow like the opening move in a karate match.

His twin wasn't so gentlemanly. He punched one of her men in the jaw and gave the other a kick in the knee. They released the man they'd been holding for Cawe. Kerrigan McPherson calmly proceeded to lay the punched man out cold before turning to the one holding his knee. Fear lit the man's eyes, and he refused to get up at Kerrigan's invitation.

Beth grimaced in disgust. Not only were her men bullies, they were cowards as well.

She pushed aside two wrestling bodies and plowed ahead. She saw the freed Sky Eagle cowboy shake his head to clear it, then grin at his boss and take on one of the two opponents, who was squared off with the remaining Sky Eagle ranch hand. At least the battle was even now.

She reached the cleared area in front of the bar just as Cawe delivered a left jab to Keegan. Keegan ducked, but not quite fast enough. The blow caught him in the eye.

Cawe followed up his advantage with a full-body right chop. Keegan dodged, then landed a slicing cuff to Cawe's face.

Beth crowded between them. "Stop it—"

She saw the fist...too late. Cawe's wild swing caught her smack on the upper curve of her cheek, knocking her head sideways. Starbursts and pinwheels exploded in front of her eyes.

Her legs buckled. They were no longer a part of her body, it seemed. Darkness hit her like a two-ton curtain. She went down for the count.

Keegan's irritation with Rolly Cawe, his old school rival, changed in a flash to white-hot fury. He rained a series of hammer blows to the man, hitting in the stomach, the face, anywhere. When Cawe sank to his knees, a surprised expression on his face, Keegan finished him off with a knee to his chin, his thoughts on only one thing—checking on the woman at his feet.

He knelt and lifted Beth's slight form into his arms. "Beth," he said, not recognizing his own voice, it was so strained.

His hand trembled as he pushed the unruly curls from her face. Her eyelids flickered, but failed to open.

"Beth," he said, a plea. He swallowed hard as he looked at the angry red mark that had already discolored her complexion. The tender flesh around her eye was puffing up like a blowfish.

"Is she hurt very bad?"

Keegan looked up into Rachel's worried frown. "I..." He had to take a deep breath. "I don't think so. She's dazed, is all. And she'll have a shiner to be proud of come tomorrow."

"Hmm, her eye should have ice on it for the next forty-eight hours. Let's get her home so we can take care of her," Rachel suggested. She glanced around with a rueful grimace. "And the rest of this outfit."

Keegan hefted Beth into his arms and started out. The sheriff walked in the door and blocked it with his body. The man was six and a half feet tall and weighed in at two hundred and fifty pounds. Not many cowboys or loggers argued with him.

"Not so fast," he drawled. He grinned, showing a gap in his bottom row of teeth. "Just how did this ruckus start?"

Keegan groaned silently. He'd knocked that tooth out when he and the sheriff were boys in high school. At that time, the sheriff had been a good friend to Rolly Cawe.

One of the Triple R boys limped over, favoring his right knee. "One of his men called us rustlers," he accused.

The sheriff nodded thoughtfully. "Them's fightin' words."

Keegan looked down when Beth stirred in his arms. She looped her arms around his neck and snuggled closer. With an obvious frown of pain, she opened her eyes.

"Everything is blurry," she complained.

"Your eye is swelling closed," he advised in a quiet tone meant to reassure her. "You took a hard blow."

"You should see your face, big brother," his twin advised with a chuckle, wiping blood from his mouth with a handkerchief.

Keegan shrugged his own aches aside. Fury still ate away at him. Beth had been hurt. He wanted to mop the floor with Cawe and his men.

"Who hit the little lady?" the sheriff wanted to know.

Susannah and Sita answered in unison. "He did." They glared at Rolly Cawe, who was totally taken aback at this attack.

"Rolly and his men started the whole thing," Susannah declared. She looked at the Triple R men as if spying a bunch of worms in her salad. "They always start trouble."

"All right. Everyone line up nice and quietlike in front of the bar here and let's get this straightened out."

"Beth needs attention," Keegan said tersely. "Cawe laid on the first blow to one of my men."

Susannah broke in. "Five of them ganged up on two of the McPherson men. It was an unfair fight from the beginning."

"Yeah," someone in the crowd agreed. "Until the twins stepped in and evened things up a bit."

Everyone laughed. The high school football coach had once said two McPhersons were worth four of any other players he'd ever seen.

Cawe and one of his men lunged for the man who'd made the quip. The sheriff grabbed them by the collar. "You boys are still riled up. A night in the cooler should chill you out." He signaled to his deputy. "Let's take 'em in."

"On what charge?"

"Disturbing the peace."

"What about them?" Cawe demanded, nodding at the twins and their two men. Keegan gave him a snarl of a smile, inviting him to try another dirty trick.

"You taking your boys home?" the sheriff asked Keegan.

He nodded.

"Well, I guess that settles it. You folks just go back to having fun. You boys come along." He herded the five roughnecks out in front of him, still holding Cawe's collar. He looked back at Beth. "You can get your men out in the morning. I'll just keep them overnight to let them cool off. You can check with the judge on the fine."

"Thank you." Beth would have smiled, but her face hurt. She could only manage a one-sided grin.

He nodded and left.

"Come on," Rachel said. "Let's get you guys home and put some ice on those bruises, else you'll look like—"

"You can put me down," Beth told Keegan in a low voice as Rachel clucked over her husband and his men.

Keegan glared at her, the anger still boiling in the icy depths of his gray eyes. "You're going home. Don't argue."

"I'm not arguing," she said in reasonable tones. She put a hand to her face, checking the swelling. "I have my truck."

He went to his truck, jerked open the door and set her on the seat. "You're in no shape to drive."

She had to agree. She could barely force her eyelid open. Her head echoed with pain as if a hammer were hitting an anvil inside it. She felt dizzy and nauseated.

Calling one of his men over, Keegan instructed the man to drive her pickup to her ranch. "One of her men can drive you to our place."

Beth gave up the keys without comment. She thought there might be a better arrangement, but she couldn't figure out what it was at the moment. Instead, she leaned her head on the seat back and sighed wearily. She let her eyes close.

When Keegan climbed in the driver's side, she shivered as the night air hit her. "My coat," she muttered.

He reached behind the seat. In a second she was engulfed in a warm blanket. He tucked the ends around her shoulders and made sure her legs were covered.

"Thanks," she whispered.

"Don't mention it."

She opened her good eye when she felt his breath on her face. He paused close to her, his breath caressing her lips. They watched each other for a long moment, neither speaking.

With a low snort he turned and started the engine. They drove off in a procession—Kerrigan and his wife, the cowboy in her truck, then Keegan and herself. The trip was a silent one. After a few minutes she fell asleep.

Beth had no idea where she was when she woke. She glanced around wildly when she was hefted into two powerful arms and carried through the dark. Panic hit her.

"I'm blind," she said in a hoarse whisper. She put a hand to her right eye and discovered a strange, painful lump.

"No, you're not." Keegan's rough tone reassured her. He always told the truth, no matter how painful.

Light flooded the garage, and she really was blinded. She pressed her face into his shoulder and held on while he carried her through an open door. "Where are we?"

"My place."

She stiffened in his arms. "I want to go home."

"There's no one to take care of you."

"Skully—"

"He's asleep. No need to wake him."

Inside the kitchen Keegan set her on her feet. Beth leaned against the cool white wall. With her one good eye, she looked around. Everything seemed to have a faint halo surrounding it. She blinked and looked again.

Rachel loomed in front of her vision. "Oh, you poor thing," she said. "Take her to one of the guest rooms, Keegan. Grab her. I think she has a concussion. I'll get the ice."

An arm encircled her waist. The scent of Keegan's after-shave lotion filled her senses. She pulled away, but had to lean against the wall to keep her balance. She felt terribly vulnerable all at once and very near tears.

Never show weakness in front of the enemy.

"Can you walk, or do you need me to carry you?" Keegan demanded. His impatience cut at her control.

"I can walk." She lifted her head and started forward.

"This way." He clasped an arm around her waist and guided her from the kitchen.

They went up some stairs that opened onto a hall. Two doors opened to the left, three to the right. He led her into the last room on the right and flicked a switch. Several lamps came on, bathing the room in brightness. It hurt her eyes.

"There's no one in the next room, so you'll have the bath to yourself," he informed her.

"Thank you," she said, squinting at the room done in pastel colors of spring. She still wasn't sure why she was there.

He sighed loudly. "Get undressed. I'll borrow a night-gown from Rachel."

"Absolutely not."

"You don't want a gown?"

"I will not get undressed. I . . . I want to go home." She sounded as querulous as a tired child.

Rachel bustled in. She flicked on the bedside lamp and turned out the others. "Of course she doesn't want to get undressed in front of you. You're not a doctor." She smiled at Beth. "I'll take care of our guest, Keegan."

Keegan cursed silently. With Rachel taking over and giving him a scolding, he could hardly insist on remaining. He stalked out. The door closed firmly behind him. Kerrigan came out of his bedroom with a nightgown in his hand.

"Rachel said to get a warm nightgown. What do you think?" He held up a flannel one dotted with little yellow flowers.

"It'll do." Keegan grabbed it. "I'll take it in." It was one thing for another woman to take over. It was something else for another man to barge into a bedroom with Beth in there possibly undressed. He wouldn't allow even his twin that privilege.

Twirling on the ball of his foot, he marched to the door, knocked, then went in. Just as he thought—Beth was half-naked.

A pang—pain, anger, he didn't know—plowed through him when she paused in unfastening her slacks and looked up. Her injury was a violent red that framed her eye like a target. By morning, the skin would be black. The eye itself was completely closed.

"Get out of here," she said to him, holding her sweater up to her front.

Not that there was anything to see. Her bra, a plain, modest white one, covered her better than most bathing suits he'd seen on the tourists over at the dude ranch.

"I brought you something to sleep in."

Rachel came out of the bathroom with a damp wash-cloth. "Thanks. You could have left it on the door."

Keegan felt frustrated with his sister-in-law. "Where the hell is that ice pack you were so all-fired anxious to get on her eye?"

"In the kitchen. I was just going to fix it. I'll do one for you, too." She handed Beth the damp cloth and headed for the door, giving him a warning frown as she passed.

Beth took the gown and went into the bathroom. When she came out a couple of minutes later, she was covered from neck to floor, not even a toe showing, in the long nightgown. She laid her clothes in a neat pile on a chair and crossed to the bed, which was turned down and ready for her.

Keegan strode past her and lifted the covers. Beth settled herself wearily against the pillows. "This is ridiculous, spending the night here when I have a perfectly good bed of my own a quarter mile away."

"There's no one in your house to watch you," he reminded her.

"I'm fine," she insisted. "A black eye is hardly a disaster."

The door opened. "Keegan is right," Rachel said, coming in with an ice pack in each hand. "You shouldn't be alone tonight. You might have a concussion." She smiled brightly. "Besides, I love having you." She handed Beth and Keegan each a cold pack. "Well, I'm off to see about *my* stubborn McPherson twin." She went to the door and paused. "Don't keep her up too late." Then she left.

"I don't feel like fighting anymore tonight," Beth said to her captor in the silence that followed. Captor? She did feel rather like a Rhine maiden, held for ransom by the conquering barbarian.

"The ice doesn't do much good if it isn't on the injury," was his reply, putting the pack to his wounded cheek. "And we're not fighting. I wanted to ask you something."

She propped the sloshing ice pack on her eye. "What?"

"Did you mean it earlier about staying?"

Her mind wouldn't grapple with the question.

"At the saloon," he reminded her. "Just before Cawe butted in. You said you'd never give up your land. Were you serious, or were you just trying to get at me?"

She stared at him, trying to decipher his mood. Anger? Definitely. Other emotions were held on the tight leash of his control, but she couldn't read them.

"I don't know," she finally said. "I don't want to think about it now."

He stood, a tall, powerful male animal at ease in his kingdom, sure of his place in the world he had created. She swallowed against the pain of loss and emptiness she felt inside.

"I'll fight you if you try to sell out without letting me know first," he warned her.

"I don't owe you a thing," she stated flatly.

"The courtesy of one neighbor toward another."

Her vision was blurring again. She could no longer hold her good eye open, nor force her mind to stay alert for his barbs. "The Code of the West?" She shook her head, then grimaced at the pain this caused. "Don't forget. I'm your enemy. How can you trust me to do the honorable thing?"

Keegan watched her drift into sleep. She looked tiny and pale against the sheets, a small, beautiful woman who'd briefly turned his nights as bright as day. He leaned down and adjusted the ice pack to cover her injury completely. His hands trembled when he grazed her cheek.

"Enemy?" he murmured, hardening himself against her allure. "Yes, and my nemesis, but I still want you more than any woman I've ever known."

Beth woke with a start. She stared up at Rachel McPherson.

"It's all right," Rachel assured her with a smile. "I was just changing your ice pack. We need to keep it cold to prevent any additional swelling."

Beth probed under the rubberized material. Her face felt so strange. Painful, too. She dropped her hand.

"I talked to the doctor this morning. He said if it wasn't better by tomorrow, he'd stop by and look at it. He's going fishing up the Rogue."

"Thank you," Beth said stiffly. She wasn't sure how friendly she wanted to be with Keegan's family. After all, if she was his enemy, it stood to reason that she was theirs, too.

"Now how about breakfast. Will you come to the kitchen, or shall I bring you a tray?"

"Oh, no, I can get up." Beth swung her legs out of bed. "In fact, you needn't bother with food. I'll just run over to my place—"

"No, you won't." Rachel smiled at Beth's surprise. "I've already prepared the meal, and I'm dying to eat with a woman for a change. Do you realize I've been surrounded by men for months out here on this ranch?" She laughed good-naturedly. "Let me find you a robe."

"I'll get dressed," Beth said quickly.

"All right. Come on to the kitchen when you're ready." She left the room.

Beth took a three-minute shower, then dried off and dressed in the clothes she'd worn the previous day. Fetching the comb from her purse, she gasped when she faced herself in the mirror.

Leaning closer, she studied the purple black skin. She could open the lid only a slit. Her heart was apt to end in a similar, bruised condition in any battle with Keegan. Sighing, she raked through her hair, put the comb in her purse and ventured into the hallway. The house was so quiet, she felt she should tiptoe.

"You look like someone making a quick getaway," Keegan said behind her.

Every nerve in her body jumped. She whirled around.

He grabbed her arm when she moaned and pressed a hand to her temple. "Easy," he said.

"Is that your room?" she asked, staring at the open door.

"Yes." He gave her a cool perusal. "You needn't worry. I haven't attacked a guest in years."

"Very funny," she muttered.

She noticed the bruise under his eye. It was hardly visible compared to hers. She headed toward the short flight of stairs leading to the lower level. She could remember climbing those last night. The kitchen should be to her left, if she was right.

Keegan strolled along beside her without a word. When they entered the big, roomy kitchen, she saw the table was set for four. "Hi. Ring for Kerrigan, will you?" Rachel requested of Keegan. She smiled at Beth. "I'm running a bit behind. As usual."

A noise brought Beth's attention to a high chair tucked in a pantry alcove. A baby chewed on a teething ring and played happily with a squeaky toy.

"The heir," she said softly, a catch in her heart.

"Yep," Keegan said. "Kelly Barret McPherson."

The child looked up. When he saw Keegan, he grinned and made sounds that Beth interpreted as ones of pleasure.

"Hey, dude," his uncle said, going over and squatting in front of the high chair. He held out a hand as if to shake.

The baby grabbed one callused finger and brought it to his mouth. He held out a gift to his uncle.

"No, thanks, I don't think I want to exchange my finger for your teether." With a laugh, he wiggled his finger free and stood up. For a second he looked at Beth; then he went to the door.

A triangle was suspended from a rafter. Picking up a metal rod attached to a string, he swung it around the inside of the triangle, making a loud musical sound. An answering yell was heard from the stable.

"He'll be in directly," Keegan said, closing the door.

Beth swallowed nervously. A family meal. "Can I help you with anything?" she asked her hostess.

Rachel scooped up a pancake and slid it on a plate. "All done. Take this stack to the table. We'll leave the others in the oven to stay warm." She picked up a platter of bacon and a pitcher of orange juice and carried them to the table.

Beth noticed that Keegan poured the coffee into blue mugs without being asked. He looked very...domesticated.

Yeah, like keeping a wolf for a pet, she scoffed.

"Sit across from me so we can talk," Rachel invited, taking a chair. "Your shiner is impressive."

Beth grimaced, then smiled. Rachel was so open and friendly, it was impossible not to like her. "Thanks. I think."

The two women laughed.

"The ice packs must have helped. You can open your eye this morning. I didn't think you would be able to."

"Oh, I wanted to thank you for that," Beth said, remembering waking once just as the door was closing and finding the ice bag on her eye, filled with fresh ice. It had been replaced again sometime in the wee hours of the morning. "You shouldn't have gotten up in the night, though."

Her hostess looked at her, then Keegan, then back again. "I didn't think of it," she confessed. She arched an eyebrow. "It must have been an elf." She gave a pointed look at her brother-in-law.

Keegan ignored them both.

Beth couldn't bring herself to ask if he'd taken care of her during the night. She didn't want to think about it. It seemed too intimate...too caring.

She put the platter of pancakes on the table and took the chair Rachel indicated. Keegan sat on her left. When his brother came in a second later, he washed his hands at the sink and took the vacant chair. To Beth's surprise, Keegan said a blessing before they ate.

"We like to observe the tradition on Sundays," Rachel explained. "It seems appropriate."

"Yes," Beth agreed. Family and tradition. She'd always believed in them.

"Speaking of tradition, we missed the annual birthday bash in April. We're going to have a Harvest Moon party next month, instead."

"Oh?" Her husband raised one dark eyebrow.

"Yes," she said firmly. She pursed her lips primly, but a smile kept turning the corners up.

"Hire Sita to cater it," he ordered. "I don't want you to overdo it. The eagles will be leaving soon, and you'll be up there taking notes from dawn to dark."

"Rachel is studying a pair of eagles who nest in the area each year. She plans to write a book on the return of wild-life to the national forest now that clear-cut logging has been banned," Keegan explained.

"Thanks to the Fightin' McPhersons," Rachel interposed.

Beth swung her gaze back to Keegan when Rachel didn't explain.

"My brother and I stirred up a campaign to stop it." He shrugged his shoulders as if it had been no great thing.

"They flew a bunch of experts to Washington to speak at the congressional hearing on the subject. Our state senator arranged a dinner with the key congressmen that night. Several people told me the twins were more effective over cocktails than the experts had been in the formal meeting." Rachel grinned. "They must have been. The bill passed."

"That's wonderful," Beth exclaimed.

A tinge of red crept into Keegan's ears. She realized he was embarrassed at the praise. Kerrigan was more at ease, though. He was used to his wife's loving attention.

For a second, Beth was unable to swallow the delicious bite of pancake in her mouth. Tears closed her throat as she saw images of her and Keegan sharing a home and a child with the obvious love that existed between his brother and his wife.

She managed to eat the meal without making a total fool of herself. When the others finished, Kerrigan stood and went to his son, scooping him out of the high chair and giving him a kiss on the neck before bringing the child to his mother.

"Here," he said to his wife, "top off his tank. I'll take him with me for a couple of hours this morning."

"Oh, that would be a help. I need to make out the payroll." Rachel turned to Beth. "I'm going to feed him. Will it embarrass you?"

Confused, Beth shook her head. She saw Rachel's hand go to her blouse and unbutton the pocket, which peeled down to expose a nursing bra. Rachel took the baby in her lap and pulled him close.

Beth lifted her coffee cup and took a drink to cover the pang of envy that went through her. A strange ache sliced through her breasts, and each of them contracted with a startling force. She caught her breath, regained control and let it out slowly.

Glancing up, she met Keegan's amused stare. A blush rose to her face. His smile became mocking, as if he saw her distress and gloated over it. She turned away and looked out the window.

"What a magnificent stallion," she said, seeing one of the men lead the animal to a pasture and set him free.

"Keegan, why don't you show Beth our blooded stock?" Rachel suggested while her son nursed hungrily.

"Oh, that's all right—"

"I'd be glad to," he cut off her protest. He rose smoothly and waited for her.

She went outside with him. They walked across the graveled area between the driveway and the fence. There, they leaned on the rail and watched the stallion. Beth realized there was another horse in the pasture. When the stallion tried to mount it, she realized the second animal was a mare.

"We intend to breed champion show ponies out of these two," Keegan said.

"I see." She plucked at a splinter on the rail. "Were you the one who replenished the ice?"

For a minute, she didn't think he was going to answer. "Yes," he finally said.

"Thank you."

"You're welcome." His tone was harsh.

There seemed nothing else to say. She turned her back on the pasture. "I'm going home now. I have work to do."

"You should take it easy with that eye for a few days," he advised without any softening in his manner.

"I will. Thank you," she added belatedly.

He muttered an expletive. "Wait here. I'll get the truck."

"I'll walk. It isn't far."

"It's no trouble," he ground out.

"I have to get my purse...and tell Rachel goodbye."

He nodded. She returned to the house while he went toward the garage. Rachel was cleaning up the dishes. Kerrigan and his son had disappeared.

"Keegan is going to take me home now," Beth said. "I wanted to thank you for your hospitality and kindness last night."

"It was nothing." Rachel waved further thanks aside. "I hope you'll do me a big favor."

"Of course." Beth waited anxiously to learn what it was.

"I need help with the guest list for the party. I want it to be special. It will be our first big affair since we married."

"I haven't lived here for years," Beth reminded her.

"But you were born here, and you've been back nearly every year. You still know Susannah and the people you went to school with. Will you help?"

Put like that, how could she refuse? "Yes. Let me know when you want to work on it. Here's Keegan. I have to get my purse."

She quickly retrieved her purse from the bedroom. Coming down the hall, she heard Kerrigan talking with his son and the baby answering in coos and gurgles. Glancing in the door, she saw the father changing the baby's diaper. From the back he looked like Keegan. And so did the child.

Quietly slipping down the steps, she went through the kitchen, expressed her gratitude once more and ran out to the truck.

Keegan drove to her house in silence.

"Thank you," she said when they arrived. Her truck was parked near the back door. The coolers were gone. Skully had already put the groceries away.

"Stay put," Keegan said.

He got out and came around to open the door for her. It was a courtesy she hadn't expected. It strummed a chord deep inside, sending a melodious note through her blood.

"Well, thank you again," she murmured, wanting to get away from him.

He heaved a heavy sigh. "Look," he said, "Rachel likes you. It would be nice for her to have another women to talk to once in a while. So..." He paused, then went on. "So let's call a truce for as long as you're in the neighborhood.''

He obviously didn't think she would last long. The thought stuck in her head. Ralstons had been the first settlers in this area. The *first*.

"I'm staying, Keegan."

His eyes narrowed. "You said that yesterday, but you didn't seem too sure about it later. How long do you think you can last out here without help?"

She raised her chin. "As long as you."

A ripple of emotion passed over his face. He sucked in an audible breath. "Don't bet on it," he advised.

Chapter Seven

Beth selected a hoe from the shed, picked up a pair of work gloves and headed across the meadow from the house. Supper was finished and the kitchen cleaned up. All the chores she'd assigned herself for that day were done. There was an hour of daylight left, so she had time for one more.

At the family cemetery, she chopped out the grass around the roses and clipped the plants back. Forty-five minutes later she straightened and glanced around, satisfied with her efforts.

Most of the graves had simple granite headstones. Her mother's had a marble cover as well. As a child it had been one of her favorite places to play with her dolls, or to rest and dream of her own family. She laid her hoe and gloves aside and sat down under the cottonwood tree, which seemed like an old friend.

Wrapping her arms around her knees, she gazed at the ranch buildings. For the past week, Skully and Ted, along with Jeff when he got home from school, had been working on the house. The repairs were finished, and the windows had been recaulked against the coming winter winds. Painting was next.

From her vantage point she could see beyond the cottonwoods and alders lining the creek to the Sky Eagle ranch. Cows grazed on alfalfa stubble next to the road. Last week two men had cut and baled the alfalfa for winter hay. It was now stacked and protected under giant plastic covers.

The Triple R had few resources to see them through the cold season ahead. The storm last month had afforded them some relief from the drought, thank goodness, but the fields had produced very little hay.

She hugged her knees tighter as little impulses of nervous energy ran under her skin. She had a hard year in front of her. The possibility of making wrong decisions loomed like a specter over her shoulder each time she went over the ranch ledgers.

To add to her troubles, she and her foreman had had words over the fight at the saloon. She'd warned him not to interfere in her quarrel with Keegan and to keep their men away from the Sky Eagle ranch hands. She didn't need to pay any more fines to bail them out of jail. Sighing, she put her hand to her eye. The bruises were almost gone.

Glancing up, she saw Rachel come out of the woods and slip between the strands of barbed wire that divided the properties.

''Hello,'' Beth called, standing and waving. She hurried to the house.

''Have I come at a bad time?'' Rachel asked, stopping at the porch steps.

''Not at all. I was just . . . daydreaming.''

"I wanted to go over the guest list with you in case I've left anyone out," Rachel said. "The party will be at the beginning of next month, the first Saturday. Is that convenient for you?"

"Uh, yes," Beth said. She led the way into the kitchen, which was now bright and clean the way it used to be when her mother was alive. "Would you like some coffee or tea?"

"Coffee will be fine."

Beth washed her hands, then poured two cups of coffee and set out a plate of cinnamon rolls she'd made that morning. She and Rachel sat at the dark pine table.

"This house is lovely," Rachel exclaimed. "Victorian, without all the gingerbread stuff. It's twice as big as ours, I think. How many rooms does it have?"

"Twenty, if you count the stillroom and out kitchen."

"A stillroom? May I see it?"

Beth led the way to several small rooms off the kitchen. "The butler's pantry," she explained as they passed from one to the other. She opened a cabinet and displayed rows of china, crystal and silver dishes.

"Lovely." Rachel pointed to a silver anniversary platter. "Were your parents married a long time before you were born?"

"Yes. Over fifteen years. The doctors thought my mother would never have children."

"So you were a surprise baby," Rachel concluded. "They were lucky. A child...umm...sort of completes a couple's life. Not that I wouldn't be perfectly happy with Kerrigan without the baby, but...you know what I mean."

Beth nodded, not trusting her voice. Opening a door, she stepped aside so her guest could enter the room. "The stillroom," she announced.

Sunlight poured into the room from windows on two sides and arching over part of the ceiling. Beth had brought in herbs from the garden and the countryside every chance she had and had hung them to dry from a latticework of wooden slats overhead.

A row of mortars and a pewter bowl of pestles indicated the medicinal use the room had once served. Glass-stoppered bottles were labeled with home remedies—yarrow, foxglove, tansy, ginseng—and the ailments they helped cure.

"It's like looking at history. Can't you imagine your grandmother collecting and drying these, then grinding them in one of these?" Rachel touched one of the mortars.

Beth was delighted to share her heritage with someone who appreciated it. "Tradition lasts a long time out here. My mother always put up her own herbs and sachets."

"And you're doing the same." Rachel sniffed a bouquet of blossoms over her head. "Lavender?"

"Yes. It comes up each year in one of the flower beds. I'll give you a sachet when it's ready."

"Oh, thank you. What's this one?"

Beth explained the plants and their uses. She led the way back to the kitchen and went over the guest list for the party with Rachel. An hour passed. A man with a child on his shoulders came out of the woods and across the stable yard.

"Here's your husband," she said, rising.

Rachel looked up from her lists, which included the menu and a schedule for preparing the food. "No, that's Keegan."

Beth paused, then went to the door. "Come in," she invited as Keegan and his nephew paused on the natural stones that formed the stoop. "Would you like some coffee? There's plenty."

Following him inside, Beth realized she was still in her work jeans and shirt. Her hair had a tendency to hang in her eyes and straggle down her neck. She hadn't had a haircut and shaping in weeks. Nor a manicure. And she needed a bath.

"That would be nice," he said.

Like his sister-in-law, Keegan had bathed and changed to slacks after the working day was over. His white knit shirt outlined his lean torso. When he lifted the child down, the muscles flexed in his arms and back, giving only a hint of his great strength that had once wrestled steers to the ground in his rodeoing days.

The baby held out its arms to its mother and gave a wobbly-chinned cry. Rachel cuddled her son against her.

"Hey, what's wrong? Did you think I'd gone off and left you forever?" She gave Keegan an apologetic smile. "Beth and I got to talking. I forgot all about the time."

"I figured as much," Keegan said easily, settling in a chair at the table. "Looks like homemade cinnamon rolls."

"Help yourself," Beth invited. She set his coffee mug on the table and got a plate out of the cabinet.

"Don't bother," he advised, taking a roll and biting into it. He chewed slowly, swallowed, then sighed. "I haven't had anything this good since your mother used to send over treats to me and Kerrigan when we were kids."

"It's her recipe," Beth said.

Rachel bounced the baby on her knee. "I suppose I'd better get home and get this monster to bed." She stood. "It was wonderful having a woman to talk to. Come over for lunch with us tomorrow about one. We'll finish our plans."

Beth hesitated. It probably wasn't wise getting mixed up with the McPherson family. She liked Rachel tremendously, but...

She glanced at Keegan. He was watching her with an impassive expression. He'd wanted a truce between them because of his sister-in-law.

"All right," she agreed.

A smile kicked up one corner of his mouth, not much of one, but she took it as approval. She walked Rachel to the door. Both women paused and looked back.

"I'll be along soon," he said. "I want to finish this." He held up his second roll.

Rachel teased him about getting fat, told Beth goodbye and left them. Beth closed the door against the night chill and returned to the table. She refilled her coffee mug, then Keegan's, when he indicated he'd like more.

"Got any milk?" he asked.

"Nonfat."

"I'll take a glass."

She poured it and returned to the table. She kept her gaze anywhere but on him, while he finished off the roll and milk.

"I'd forgotten anything that good existed," he said with a satisfied smile, when he sat back and lifted the coffee mug.

"Thank you."

He studied her for a minute. "I saw you up at the cemetery earlier," he said all at once.

The conversational gambit surprised her. She'd been expecting some diatribe on selling her ranch to him and had been preparing to resist his arguments.

"Do you miss your mother?" he asked.

Beth nodded slowly. Tears pressed against the backs of her eyelids. Returning to the ranch made the loneliness greater.

"She was the gentlest person I ever met," he continued. "And the most fun. She showed me and Kerrigan where to find marine fossils. I remember being amazed that this land was once a sea. I was even more awestruck that one person could know so much."

"She loved to read," Beth mused. "And she loved knowing about the land."

He set the mug on the table and leaned over it, staring into the swirls of steam rising from the coffee. "Kerrigan worries about Rachel being alone out here. He thinks she needs a friend, a woman friend. She likes you."

"I like her, too."

"Yeah, well that's good." He took a drink.

Beth watched his throat move as he swallowed. The column of his neck was firm and tanned. She'd liked to snuggle her face against him and sneak her tongue out for a taste of the salty tang of his skin after he'd been working all day. Before they tossed off their clothing and clambered into the hot pool.

"Don't try to get at us through her," he advised and stood.

When his words registered, Beth was so outraged, she wanted to throw her coffee in his face. Instead, she held herself rigid and forced the anger at bay. "You should warn her of the type of person I am," she suggested with a cynical smile. "Now, if you'll excuse me, I need to clean up."

A flare of desire hit his eyes before he pivoted and headed for the door. She knew what he was thinking—of the pool and their meetings there . . . the way they used to wash each other . . . their hands soapy and caressing . . . their words hushed in the twilight . . . the buildup of the yearning . . . the coming together . . .

And then the wonder of it . . . the wonder . . .

He gave a snort of disgust, with himself or her, she couldn't tell, then he walked out, slamming the door behind him. Beth stood still for several minutes. Until the flood of anger washed all the pain away. Trembling, she went to her room.

Keegan stood by the stall and watched the mare. "She's getting weaker," he said. "You want me to call the vet?"

Kerrigan nodded. "Yeah. I give up. I can't turn the foal." He withdrew and peeled off the plastic glove that covered his arm to his shoulder. "Damn," he said.

Keegan nodded in sympathy. He headed for the house. At the open kitchen door, he stopped when he heard a woman's soft laughter inside the house.

Beth.

His heart set up a rapid cacophony like tom-toms in an old jungle movie indicating the natives were restless. That was certainly true, he admitted with a sardonic grimace at the tightening of his body. Glancing at his watch, he realized it was after one o'clock. Sunday dinner was going to be late.

He opened the door and stepped inside. The sight that greeted him nearly brought him to his knees. Beth held the baby on her lap while Rachel took care of the meal.

"How is Queenie?" Rachel asked. "Is she ... is she ..."

"No," he said. "She's weak, but she hasn't given up. I'm calling the vet to see if he can get out here."

Beth, he noted, didn't say anything, but her green eyes flicked from him to his sister-in-law and back again. The baby dropped his teething ring and reached up to pat her on her peach-colored sweater.

Heat flared in him like the exhaust from a rocket; red-hot, creating a roar in his ears.

"Queenie—her real name is Rogue's Queen—is our prize breeding mare. Kerrigan calls her the Queen Mum. This is her first foal," Rachel explained to their guest. "Things aren't going well at the moment."

Beth waved a rattle and let the baby take it from her. "I'm sorry. I hope everything..." She stopped as she realized what she was saying. A faint red climbed her face.

"Comes out okay?" Keegan finished for her. "So do we." He spoke to Rachel. "Wills rode out and got Hank. They'll stay with the mare. Kerrigan will be along in a minute."

Rachel gave a disbelieving snort and ducked her head to peak into the oven. "I won't take the food off the stove until I see the whites of his eyes."

Keegan saw an understanding smile curl up the corners of Beth's mouth. He suddenly wanted to kiss her. He frowned at the impulse. The smile disappeared from her lips.

He strode into the office and picked up the phone. After talking to the vet, he went down the hall to his room. He stripped out of his jeans with a grunt of relief. His body was hard and aching, the pants too confining.

Last night his sleep had been riddled with erotic dreams of Beth and steaming pools of some magic elixir where they floated like lilies, their skins warm and golden in the light filtering through the trees. Exotic fruits hung within easy reach. They'd fed each other, then made love until all hungers were sated.

Muttering curses upon his dreams and his imagination, he headed for the shower. But there, rubbing soap briskly over his skin, he was drawn back into the mixed dreams.

In one, he and Beth had been mounted on magnificent horses. They were rounding up a breed of cattle never seen on earth. The cattle had sported horns of solid gold, and their hides had been the color of pearls. He and Beth had laughed and talked, enjoying their work and the anticipation of bedding down for the evening.

"Hell," he said as a surge of hot need clenched at his insides. The one thing he *didn't* need was to get mixed up with Beth Ralston again. He'd warn Kerrigan about encouraging the women to socialize. The Ralstons were devious. They would do anything to save their going-down-the-tubes ranch. He'd learned that lesson three years ago.

Feeling better at having made this decision, he forced the image of Beth holding the baby out of his mind. When he returned to the kitchen, he was in complete control.

Until he saw her.

She was spooning food into Kelly's open mouth. Her lack of experience, combined with the child's eager hunger, resulted in more food landing on the bib than in the baby. A towel covered her peach outfit, attached with clothespins at her shoulders.

"Rachel, help," she called out, laughing and ducking a splutter. The baby grinned and patted his sticky hands together, thoroughly enjoying the attention of the pretty stranger.

Keegan experienced another tightening of his body, not all of it desire, he acknowledged. A stabbing pain in his chest warned him of his vulnerability around her. He wanted her. God, he wanted her—with a need that was more than physical. . . .

Beth looked up and saw Keegan standing in the archway between the family room and kitchen. There was a grimness in him that was plain to the naked eye. He didn't like seeing her in his home.

Grief rose, dark and despairing, inside her.

She was an outsider here. Keegan didn't want her to stay. No one else really cared whether she did or not. It wouldn't make a bit of difference in the scheme of things if Ralstons were to disappear like the dinosaurs.

The screen door opened, and Kerrigan came inside, stirring the warm air of the kitchen. He went at once to his wife and dropped a kiss on her neck.

Beth looked away, staring out the open door rather than at the loving couple. The September day was perfect—sunny, the air crisp and invigorating, the sky an overturned bowl of blue. It was a perfect Sunday for visiting friends and sharing the joy of living. It was all an illusion.

She gave the baby another bite. It half dribbled down his chin.

"Here, this is how you do it," a masculine voice said near her ear. Keegan bent over and took the spoon from her. He scooped the food back into his nephew's mouth, then deftly slid the spoon out with an upward motion, leaving the food inside.

"Thank you," she said stiffly, taking the spoon back when he held it out to her.

"Are you going to shower or wash up?" Rachel asked her husband.

"Do I have five minutes for a shower?"

"Umm-hmm." She peeked into the oven again. "I'll start pouring everything up. It'll be ready when you are." She gave him a smile and a push on the shoulder when he bent to kiss her again. "To the shower," she reminded him with a soft laugh.

Beth glanced at Keegan, wondering if the couple's love play, light as it was, bothered him. He was still watching her feed the baby, his expression unreadable.

"You're making me nervous," she murmured. Her laughter sounded tremulous to her ears. "And I'm having a hard enough time doing this."

"I'll finish his feeding," he volunteered. "You can help Rachel, if you like."

He took the spoon from her again and waited until she stood, before taking her chair. "Come on, dude, you gotta finish this delicious—" he looked at the label "—chicken and dumplings."

"What shall I do?" Beth asked Rachel.

"Set the table in the dining room. We'll eat in there today. Use the china with the rose pattern. Silver is in the top drawer."

Going into the dining room, Beth quickly set the table as directed. Cloth napkins were already laid out. She folded them in a swan design and set them on each plate.

Rachel came in and set platters on a sideboard within reach. "Use these water glasses. I've already chilled a pitcher of water. If you'll get it and pour the water, I'll bring in the rest of the stuff. How delightful," she said, indicating the napkins.

Keegan came in, Kelly in his arms. "Give him a kiss. He's ready for sleep time."

The baby held his face up to be kissed. Rachel gave him a loud smack, which caused a gurgle of laughter. As Keegan turned to leave, Kelly held his arms out to Beth.

"He wants to give you some sugar," Keegan explained. He stepped close to her. Kelly turned his cheek, a giggle already bubbling up.

Beth leaned over and kissed the baby on the neck. He clasped his arms around her and held on. She looked up at Keegan, not sure what to do.

"He wants you to take him." He handed the child over.

Beth locked one arm under the baby's padded rear and laid a hand on his back. She started toward the baby's room.

"Go with her and show her what to do, will you?" Rachel requested of Keegan.

"Sure." He ambled along beside Beth. In the bedroom, he pointed at the changing table. "Better change him first."

She laid the child down. He gave her a drooling grin and stuck his finger in his mouth. "What...what do I do?"

"Haven't you ever changed a baby?" Keegan asked.

"No."

"Come on," he scoffed. "Never?"

"Living so far out of town, I never baby-sat when I was growing up. In San Francisco, none of my married friends have children this young."

He reached over and touched her cheek, drawing his finger along her jaw, then over her lips, making them tingle. "Poor, lonely little girl," he murmured, half mocking, half something else that she couldn't decipher. "Would you like a baby?"

She pushed his hand away. "Maybe." *With the right man, under the right circumstances.* "Are you offering?"

"No. Have you tried your stockbroker? Maybe you'll lure him into marriage."

"He's already asked."

She didn't miss the pause before Keegan lifted a fresh diaper from a neatly folded stack. He stepped close to her. She moved over, giving him room. "Stay here. There's a first time for everything. You may as well learn to do this now."

He directed her in changing the diaper. Heat seeped into her face as he told her how to clean the baby's bottom and arrange the tiny private parts.

"One would think you'd never seen a male before," Keegan remarked. His voice was husky.

Beth was aware of his body heat as he stood beside her, one large tanned hand on the wiggling child's tummy to keep him from tipping off the table while she struggled with the unfamiliar task.

"He looks so tiny and . . . and vulnerable."

"We all start out that way."

Her insides churned as raw emotion took hold of her. If she could have found a graceful way to leave, she would have. But she couldn't hurt Rachel's feelings.

"Even you?" she quipped, striving for a sardonic tone to match his. "I thought you were born tough and cynical."

"Nah," he drawled, lifting the baby when she finally finished. "I thought life was a lark until I turned seven."

"The year your father died. You must have missed him very much. I remember your saying he loved to laugh and joke."

"Yeah." He gave her an odd smile. "I used to wonder what it would have been like if my father had married your mother."

Beth could only stare at him, astounded.

He took his nephew to the crib and put the child down. The baby smiled sleepily up at his uncle, then closed his eyes. Keegan turned toward the door, then waited until she went out first before closing it behind them.

"I thought they would have been perfect. His strength, her gentleness. His laughter, her smiles. He was noisy. She was quiet. A perfect combination. Or so it seemed to me."

They stood there in the quiet hallway, the cool September breeze stirring the air as it swirled through the house. Beth could hear Rachel and Kerrigan talking in the kitchen. She released the breath she'd been unconsciously holding.

Rachel appeared in the archway. "Ready?"

"Ready," Keegan replied. He placed his hand on Beth's back and guided her to the dining room. There, he seated her on one side of the table and took the chair opposite when Rachel was seated. Kerrigan said the blessing this time.

"This house is lovely," Beth commented to her hostess. "I love the colors and the way you've used various mixtures of blue and sandstone throughout to tie the rooms together."

"Thanks," Rachel said, "but you have the wrong person."

"Keegan supervised the building of the house. He also did a lot of the work," Kerrigan said. "It was good therapy after he retired from the rodeo circuit."

"A forced retirement," Keegan said dryly. "After tangling with that bull, I couldn't sit astride a saddle for months."

Memories rushed into Beth's mind. The house had been under construction during that wild autumn affair three years ago. At night, she'd massaged his leg when it ached. She'd kissed the angry red welts, slowly moving her lips along his thigh—higher and higher...

"However, I could still swing a hammer and drive a nail."

"On a ranch, there are always a ton of things to be done," Rachel said with a sigh.

"Yeah," Keegan agreed. "A man could work day and night if he had the energy."

Beth kept her eyes focused on her plate, not wanting to see the mocking look he was probably giving her.

"Oh, speaking of ranch work. Hank came up to the house while you two were putting the monster to bed," Rachel informed them with a big smile. "We have a new filly to continue the breeding line from Queenie. He called the vet and told him not to come out."

The two brothers made identical sounds of satisfaction.

The conversation revolved around ranch life and some new government restriction on land use for the rest of the meal. Then they firmed up the plans for the party. All of them helped clear the table and clean up the kitchen. Done, they eagerly rushed out to see the new foal.

In the stable, the four of them leaned over the stall door and peered into the gloom. The mare pushed her nose against Rachel's hand. The newborn nestled in the clean straw, sleeping contentedly after feeding for the first time.

Again, raw emotion shoved its way into Beth's consciousness. This time she recognized some of her feelings. Envy. Anger. Yes, and longing, too. The longing was the worst.

She stepped aside, ostensibly to let Rachel see better; in reality, to get away from Keegan's warm presence at her back.

He followed her when she walked on down the row of stalls to look at the other horses. "What is it?" he asked, a frown nicking a line between his dark brows.

"Nothing." She managed a tight smile.

"Don't give me that. What's bothering you?" He opened the door, and they walked into the sunlight, then stopped by the fence to watch the yearlings romp through the pasture.

We could have had this, she wanted to say. We could have been a family, had children, loved and dreamed and grown old together. If you'd loved me enough to trust me.

"Are you jealous of Rachel and Kerrigan?" he asked.

She stared at him, taken totally aback by his insight.

He smiled in his sardonic way. "Don't you think I've ever looked at them with envy eating me alive?"

Chapter Eight

Beth tossed the shawl around her shoulders. The black velvet was lined with teal green silk that matched the dress. She held the dress up under her chin, stepped into the kitchen and smiled.

"Ta-dum," she sang out.

Skully paused in washing the supper dishes. Ted put a plate away and turned around. Jeff, at the table doing his homework, closed his math book. They smiled in unison.

"What do you think?" She stood still for their inspection.

"Like, *wow!*" Jeff said.

"Pretty as a picture," Ted added.

Skully cleared his throat. "Your ma would have been proud."

A momentary quiet descended. Beth saw memories flick through the two old men's eyes. They'd loved her mother, she realized.

"Well, I'm off. Rachel needs help until Sita gets there." Clutching the bag containing her evening shoes and cosmetics, Beth dashed out the door to the truck, which Jeff had washed and shined that afternoon.

The October air swept through her cotton shirt, adding a real chill to the goose bumps that chased along her spine. She was as nervous and excited as she'd been at her first dance.

She drove to the county road and immediately turned onto the McPherson drive next to her own. She saw the gravel had been newly graded and smoothed. Old railroad lanterns in amber, red and green cast interesting patterns of light along the sidewalk when she got to the house.

The wide bank of windows along the porch spilled a welcoming light through the polished glass. She parked and hurried inside, choosing to enter through the kitchen rather than the front door.

Rachel greeted her with a distracted smile. She held the baby to her breast. "Oh, I'm so glad you're here. Sita's tied up at the diner, and I'm terribly behind."

"What can I do to help?"

"Take your things to the bedroom you used the other time, then we'll get started."

Beth did as directed and hurried back.

"There's an apron." Rachel pointed it out and lifted her son to pat his back. "Watch the quiches in the oven, will you? I'm afraid I'll let them burn."

Beth peeked into the oven. Four quiches were baking to a golden brown. "Umm, they smell delicious."

"I hope I remembered to put everything in. Kelly was crying the whole time. It made me so nervous."

Footsteps sounded on the porch. Beth's heart speeded up, then slowed in disappointment when Kerrigan bounded in.

"Sorry I'm late, sweetheart. I'll take a fast shower. Here, give me the monster. I'll bathe him, too, if he's through eating." He stopped long enough to kiss his wife and scoop up his son.

"Thanks, darling. See if you can get him down for the night. Beth and I have a zillion things to do." After he left, Rachel turned to Beth. "If you'll fix a fruit and cheese platter, I'll do the meat. Then we'll set out the various chips and dips, and we'll be finished. Thank goodness Kerrigan insisted I keep it simple. Last year, Sita prepared all kinds of Mexican dishes."

"I could have done those if I'd known you wanted them. My grandmother was from Mexico. She was a wonderful cook. So was my mother. I have all their recipes."

"Would you share some of them?" Rachel asked eagerly. She selected two huge platters, gave one to Beth and set out the fruit that was to be arranged on it. She began working on a meat platter.

As usual, Beth enjoyed Rachel's company immensely. They didn't once run out of conversation while they worked.

When she heard footsteps on the porch, Beth tensed. This time it was Keegan who came in on a swirl of cold air. She glanced at him once, then concentrated on her task.

But his image lingered in her mind. Broad shoulders encased in a red shirt and a faded denim jacket. Long, muscular legs outlined in equally faded jeans. Plain leather boots.

"Frost tonight for sure," he said, closing the door.

"I'm glad we're having the party inside rather than in the hay barn." Rachel rolled a slice of ham and placed it on top of the pyramid. She placed a row of radishes between the ham and the turkey slices, put down a lettuce leaf and started rolling and stacking the roast beef.

"We had no choice. The barn's full at this time of year," he reminded her. "Something smells delicious. I'm starved."

"Better hurry and get dressed," Rachel advised. "Our guests are due to start arriving in fifteen minutes. Beth, you need to change clothes, too. Do you want to go now?"

Beth felt the flick of Keegan's eyes over her jeans and shirt. "Why don't you go on while I finish the fruit?" she suggested.

"Hmm, okay. I think everything is under control. I'll be back in a sec." She put the last of the roast beef on the platter, added some more radishes, then hurried out.

Keegan ambled over to Beth. He filched a pineapple cube and ate it. "Would Rachel notice if I stole a piece of meat?"

"I'll fix it," she said. "Take what you want."

"Anything I want?" he asked.

She grew flustered at his intense perusal. "Do you want a piece of beef, ham or turkey?"

"One of each. How about a couple of slices of that sourdough bread, too?"

She fixed him a sandwich, spread it with brown mustard the way he liked it and handed it to him. She shifted the meat stacks to hide the missing slices, then went back to cutting oranges into slivers that could be eaten easily. She added grapes and cheese cubes.

"There, that's ready," she said, satisfied with her work. She bent and peeked into the oven. The quiches were rising and turning a luscious golden brown. She opened several kinds of chips and put them into bowls, then searched the refrigerator for the dips and set them out.

The entire time, she was acutely aware of Keegan leaning against the counter, watching her every move while he ate. She had to walk around him to finish the chores, but he made no offer to get out of the way.

"Excuse me," she said, giving him a pointed glance.

He stepped aside just enough to let her reach into the drawer and grab a big spoon. She scooped out the salsa and dips into a condiment carousel and placed it next to the chips. She was finished with all she knew to do.

Keegan polished off the sandwich. "That was good. I could eat about three more like it."

"Don't you dare mess that platter up," she warned.

He rolled his eyes. "Women," he murmured, a grin kicking up the edges of his mouth. "It's going to get messed up when everyone starts digging in."

"Yes, but then it will be the guests, not the host, who's doing it. Everything must look nice when they arrive."

"Appearances," he scoffed. He eyed the stack of fruit, then deftly grabbed a cheese cube. He nibbled on it, his face taking on a moody cast as he studied her.

She removed the apron and wished Rachel would return so she could leave. He was making her nervous. The way he stood there, his lean, powerful body inclined against the counter edge, the way he watched her. His light gray eyes, moving from her eyes to her mouth and back, made her uneasy.

The quiet became stifling. She glanced around, looking for some task to occupy her trembling hands. She had managed to avoid Keegan during the past two weeks, although she had seen Rachel almost every day.

"I'd better get my shower," he said at last.

She nodded.

"You could join me," he suggested very softly.

Her head whipped around as if attached to a string. He didn't smile. Neither did he hide the passion that flared in his eyes.

The trembling dipped deep inside her. "I've had my bath, thanks." She met his gaze with determined calm.

"Too bad I wasn't there."

Before she could get her shocked mind to working, he was gone, bounding down the hall with his long stride, then up the steps and out of sight. She leaned into the corner of the counter, too shaken to move for a minute.

He was teasing her, she decided. Tormenting her was the truth of it, she admitted. Although she knew it was foolish, some part of her reacted to his presence without regard to common sense.

After this party she'd back off from Rachel's companionable friendliness. That would be best.

"Okay, your turn," Rachel said, dashing into the kitchen. She wore black velvet slacks and a gold sequin top that looked stunning with her blond hair and golden eyes. "I'll do the hot crab dip."

"Right. I'll just be a minute."

Beth went to the room assigned to her. It only took her a minute to slip out of her jeans and shirt. She found she could zip the silk dress, but she couldn't fasten the hook and eye at the top of the zipper. She would ask her hostess to do it.

After pulling on her panty hose, she quickly combed her hair into place. The loose curls brushed her shoulders now. She still hadn't gotten to a stylist to have it trimmed.

There weren't enough hours in the day for all the work that needed doing, much less for luxury items such as haircuts.

A knock at the door startled her. She froze in place for a second. "Yes?" she finally called.

"Can you give me a hand for a sec?" Keegan called out, plainly irritated about something.

"I suppose." She went to the door and opened it.

He stepped inside and held out his hand.

She automatically put hers out. He dropped two onyx studs onto her palm, then held the cuff of his shirt toward her.

"I can't fix these blasted French cuffs," he complained.

"Oh." She quickly bent to the task, hoping he wouldn't notice the slight tremor his nearness caused in her fingers.

Down the hall they heard his brother come out of his room and run down the steps. Then all was quiet. Other than the sleeping baby, they were alone in the bedroom wing of the house.

The familiar scent of his after-shave lotion wafted around her head. She felt dizzy as memories and longing swelled within her chest. Once she'd been able to respond so freely and naturally to the attraction she felt for this man.

"There," she said.

He turned and held out the other arm. She slipped the stud through the buttonholes and fastened it.

"Thanks. Anything I can do for you?"

He gazed down at her, his eyes taking in the low scoop of the dress between her breasts. A smile curled the corners of his mouth when he stopped at her stocking-clad feet.

"You could fasten the hook on my dress." She realized what she'd said. "Or I can have Rachel do it," she quickly added.

"I don't mind. Turn around."

His fingers clasped her dress as he pulled the hook and eye together. He brushed against her skin as he fastened them. Little tingles like lightning streaked over her back.

"Thank you." She cleared her throat of the huskiness caused by his presence. When she looked up, she was caught by their images in the mirror across the room.

The teal green of her dress contrasted vividly against his white dress shirt and black pants. His tie picked up the black of his hair and the gray of his eyes. He looked wonderfully handsome.

A thrill went through her at the hunger in his eyes as he, too, observed them. Although she wore no makeup yet, her cheeks were flushed. Her lips were pink, as if she'd been kissed.

He laid his hands on her bare shoulders, his fingers near the tops of her breasts. With gentle motions he traced circles on her skin. "You always had the softest skin," he murmured. "I loved to touch you. Do you remember?"

"I . . . yes," she whispered. But she didn't want to.

"It was so good . . . so damned good."

With an oath, he whirled and walked out. She sat down, her legs too weak to support her weight. After a moment she calmed down, put on her makeup and slipped into her shoes. In the future she definitely would stay away from here.

The need was too great between them. It was getting harder to resist, a fact both of them recognized. Reluctantly she left the bedroom and returned to the kitchen. After she checked on the quiches, she turned to Rachel for her next project.

"What's next?" a masculine voice inquired.

Beth glanced over her shoulder. Keegan stood in the doorway to the dining room. His gaze roamed over her.

"Umm, take the chips and dips in," Rachel ordered. "I'll have the cream whipped for the fruit in a minute. Sita is here. She's doing the centerpieces for the table," she said to Beth.

Beth motioned to the oven. "The quiches look done to me," she said. "How long have they been in the oven?"

"I'm not sure. I forgot to set the timer." Rachel shook her head in exasperation, then grinned. "I'm more nervous about this party than I ever was helping my mother with one at the embassy."

"This is your own party," Beth said in sympathy. "And these are your neighbors. Don't worry. Sita is good at this."

"Yes, thank goodness. With her here, we're back on schedule. Kelly was grouchy today. He's cutting teeth, I think."

"I should have come over earlier."

Keegan walked back into the kitchen. "You were busy with your cattle most of the day. Looks like you sold off a lot of calves plus several cows."

"Yes. Father was trying to get into the prime, heavy beef market, but I decided to go back to a cow and calf operation."

"A wise decision."

Although his tone was noncommittal, Beth felt he was mocking her efforts to put things right on the Triple R. "Yes," she said coolly. "I thought so."

"Please, no ranch talk tonight," Rachel interjected. She held out a bowl of whipped cream. "Where's Kerrigan?"

"With the baby."

Rachel frowned. "I hope Kelly doesn't act up tonight. He hasn't been sleeping well this week," she explained to Beth. "I'd better see how he's doing." She hurried from the kitchen.

Beth decided the quiches were done enough. She turned the oven off and left them inside to finish cooking.

"Those don't look firm in the middle." Keegan crossed the kitchen and peered over her shoulder.

"I know. They'll finish setting up if we leave them in the oven until we're ready to serve them."

"Hmm," he drawled. He crossed his arms over his chest as if closing her out of his space. "You seem to know your way around the kitchen."

"Surprised?" She couldn't stop the little triumphant grin that tugged at the corners of her mouth.

His gaze flicked to her lips, then away. He shrugged. "I suppose you were bound to learn something from your mother."

"I did. I learned—"

Beth suddenly remembered how grim her father had become after her mother died. As if the light had gone out of his life. With a start she realized her parents had loved each other with a deep, abiding love and that her father had never recovered from the loss of that love.

Like a door opening, she realized how it must have hurt him when she tried to cheer him up by fixing one of his favorite dishes her mother had once prepared. If only they could have talked, she thought. Instead, they'd lived in the same house, a lonely man and a lonely child, too alike to reach out to the other.

Perhaps it was a Ralston trait—to love once and only once, then to grieve in solitude.

"You learned what?" Keegan prompted.

She forced a bright smile to her face. "All the things a lady needs to know. We'd better get the rest of this food out. Here come your first guests." She picked up the plate of attractively arranged meat and walked past him.

The party rapidly got into full swing after that. Couples continued to arrive for the next hour. Keegan and his brother were good hosts, she noted, greeting each person with a personal tidbit before directing them to the food.

The neighbors unabashedly asked Beth about her intentions for her land. "Heard one of those Japanese conglomerates is interested in your spread," a nearby rancher mentioned at one point.

"Yes," she admitted. "But I'm not interested in them."

"That's good news."

She saw several relieved smiles. The local people didn't like the idea of change. But it was coming. She could see it in the increasing tourist trade, in the bed-and-breakfast places, in the ski resorts and dude ranches that were springing up in the area.

Taking a glass of wine and a plate of food, she withdrew to the formal living room and found a quiet place to sit. She listened to the talk around her while she ate.

"The quiche is delicious," a deep voice murmured.

She glanced up at Keegan. He took a seat on the sofa next to her. Her heart set up a fluttery beat. She ignored it.

"That's an apology," he growled, low-voiced.

"For what?"

"For mentioning your mother."

Beth met his eyes. She saw he was sincere. "That's all right. It doesn't bother me to talk about her. She was wonderful, and I miss her, but life goes on. She taught me that."

There didn't seem to be anything more to say. The party surrounded them, laughter and conversation flowing past them as if they were in a bubble.

"So there you are!" Susannah rushed over, her husband in tow, and gave Beth a hug. "I haven't seen you in a month. Don't you ever come to town?"

Beth smiled at her friend and said hello to Tom while the two men shook hands. The interruption relieved the tension between her and Keegan. "I've been pretty busy," she explained.

Susannah rolled her eyes. "Ranchers. This is a party. Come on. Let's dance." She urged Tom to a cleared space at the end of the large living room.

Someone turned the music a bit louder. Again she and Keegan sat in taut silence and watched as other couples seized the chance to be in each other's arms. Sita came in and checked over a table filled with nuts and candy. She paused to watch the dancing.

Rachel entered. A pleased smile lit her face when she saw everyone having fun.

Hank, one of the McPhersons' cowboys, dressed in fancy boots, blue slacks and a white shirt with a tie, stood silently in a corner.

Beth saw Rachel take Sita's arm and lead her to the cowboy. She must have said something amusing for Sita laughed and gave the man a teasing smile. He grinned and took her hand. They went to the dance floor and joined the others.

"Oh-oh," Beth muttered when Rachel saw her and Keegan. She knew what was coming when she spied the look of determination on her hostess's face.

Keegan gave her a sharp glance, then looked up when Rachel stopped beside them. He stood. "Here, have a seat. You probably need a rest."

"I do." She sat down gratefully in his place. "You two can dance while I prop my feet up. Go on."

Beth had no choice but to rise. Rachel promptly swung her legs up on the sofa, her feet dangling over the side. She leaned her head back and gave them a mischievous smile.

"Don't let me keep you," she said.

Keegan scowled at his sister-in-law. The one thing he didn't need was Beth in his arms. He didn't know why he'd sat beside her, except he'd noticed her sitting alone, watching the activity around her like a kid who'd been left out.

"I should go freshen up," she said.

Her reluctance to dance with him grated on his nerves. He took her hand and guided her to a space next to the other couples. "You can do that later."

Her lips tightened, but she didn't protest further. He held her lightly, keeping distance between them. Tom and Susannah drifted by, locked in a tight embrace, their eyes closed.

Keegan looked at Beth. She stared over his shoulder, her face without a trace of emotion. Anger raked through him. He wanted to pull her against him and caress her until that wall of reserve came crashing down and she melted in his arms.

He restrained the impulse.

Gradually other sensations built in him. The scent of her perfume, faintly exotic, wafted around them. He pulled it into his lungs, hunger for the heated fragrance of her slender body sweeping over him.

The warmth of her skin made his palm tingle where he touched her waist. He moved his fingers lightly over the silk, aware of how thin the material was that separated them.

A scene came to him. Moonlight. Her in his arms, humming a love song while they danced on the sand. Steam off the hot spring eddying around them. Their clothing heaped on a boulder.

Before he knew what he was doing, he'd pulled her solidly into his arms so that she was crushed against his chest. He heard her surprised gasp and felt her stumble as she stiffened. He eased his hold. She pulled away.

"I...I need to go..." She was gone in a blink.

Keegan let his arms drop. He rammed his hands into his pockets and leaned against the doorjamb, fighting a battle with the need that rose in him.

Damn, hadn't he learned anything three years ago? He couldn't allow himself to be weak for a woman again.

Rachel came over to him. Her eyes were full of concern. "I think there's something between you two," she said, tilting her head thoughtfully as she studied him.

"Think again." The words came out harshly, when he'd meant to give them a sardonic twist.

She laid a gentle hand on his arm. "Love is a gift. Don't throw it away. Remember how much time Kerrigan and I lost because we were both stubborn and stupid."

A man had no peace even in his own house. He shrugged off her touch. "Dammit, keep your nose out of my love life. When I want help, I'll ask for it."

A hand settled on his shoulder. "Watch it, brother," Kerrigan warned. "Rachel is worried about your happiness. She seems to think you're suffering from a broken heart."

Keegan felt surrounded. He went on the defensive. "Don't worry about my heart. Just make sure our sweet neighbor doesn't con you with her lies." He pushed past them and headed for the door.

Outside, he pulled the cold air deep into his lungs, hoping it would cool his blood. Not a chance, he thought, mocking the effort and exhaling in a sigh. Not with Beth in his house, tempting him in that silky outfit the color of her eyes.

The way it dipped low beneath her breasts made him ache to explore the satin-smooth skin underneath the silk. Damn her! Just being in the same room with her upset his equilibrium. Now he'd been hateful to Rachel—which he was sorry for—and made his brother mad—which didn't particularly bother him—all over a woman who wasn't worth a second thought.

The startled clucks of some chickens near the creek brought his head around. He heard a sound like the flap of a scatter rug being vigorously shaken out and recognized the dark shape of an owl as it rose on the wind.

He looked at the cars lining the drive and the area between the house and the stable. All the tradesmen from town as well as the local ranchers had shown up for the party. Probably wanted to see how the McPherson kids were doing.

They were doing damned well, he'd be glad to tell them, if they asked.

He waited for the sense of satisfaction that usually followed that realization. None came.

He hadn't been pleased with his life since that episode with Beth three years ago, he realized.

It was all her fault—his restlessness, the angry words with his brother, all of it. Why the hell did she have to come back to these parts?

Down the porch, the door opened and closed quietly. He recognized the dark, curling hair that had grown long enough to reach the white shoulders left bare by the silky dress. She seemed to glow in the moonlight.

"Leaving so soon?" he asked.

Beth whirled around. Keegan appeared like a specter beside her. She pressed a hand to her heart. "Oh, you scared me."

"Guilty conscience," he concluded.

"Why would I have a guilty conscience?"

"You're driving a wedge between me and my family. You have Rachel fooled into thinking you're some kind of paragon. But I know better."

As her eyes became accustomed to the pale wash of light from the moon, she could discern the bitter twist of his mouth. "I'm sorry I hurt you," she said stiffly. "It's something you're going to have to come to terms with, though. No one else can help you."

He stiffened, then laughed. "I got over you a long time ago, honey. It's only my body that remembers. I admit, when you're around, I still want you."

"A liar and a con artist like me?"

There was a second of stark silence between them.

"So you heard."

"Anyone standing in the hall could have." She didn't look at him, but gazed off into the distance at the moon-struck landscape. The anger still raged in her. She refused to recognize the pain.

"Is that where you were?"

"Yes."

"Was anyone else there?"

She swallowed hard. "No." She'd paused in the hallway to let her breath steady and her heartbeat return to normal after fleeing from the living room and the invitation in his arms.

"Good." He sounded relieved and suddenly tired.

Curious, she stared at him in the soft light of the antique lanterns. He turned his head as if drawn to her gaze against his will. His lips parted, and she watched his chest lift in a deep breath. Then their eyes met.

A chill spread down her arms. She pulled her shawl tighter around her, her eyes captured by his.

"Why?" she asked. "Don't tell me it would bother you for people to know what you think of me."

"Our quarrel is between us, no one else," he said, his voice going deeper, the edge harder. "What I said inside...it was said in anger. You women can back a man right up to the wall."

"It's a tough world." She headed toward her truck. She wasn't going to engage in a battle of the sexes with him. There were too many other things on her mind. Important things. Like losing her home.

He swung into step beside her. With unconscious courtesy, he opened the truck door. When she was inside, he stood there for a minute, blocking her from closing it.

"I don't know how much longer I can keep my hands off you," he warned her in a low voice. "Maybe it would be better if you backed off from being so thick with Rachel."

Beth trembled at his confession. "It's too late. Rachel and I are friends. Why should we avoid each other because of you?"

"She doesn't know you like I do," he said harshly.

Beth pulled on the door. He stepped aside.

"You don't know me at all," she said and closed the door.

The house was dark when she arrived. She realized she'd left her shirt, jeans and sneakers at Keegan's house. After changing to pajamas and washing up, she went to bed and lay there in the dark—tense and hurt and aching for something that could never be.

Nothing had changed between them. Nothing.

After a while, she fell into a restless sleep.

Who-o-o who who-o.

She sat up in bed with a start.

Who-o-o who who-o.

The dream fled. Happiness flooded her. Mindlessly she flung out of bed, jammed her feet into slippers and tugged her robe on as she raced out the door and down the steps.

She was halfway across the yard when a great flapping came from the woods. An owl erupted from the trees, a dark, menacing shadow that skimmed over her head before disappearing behind the barn. She stopped dead still.

The cold air surrounded her. She wrapped her arms tightly across her chest as she realized what she'd done.

The hoot of the spotted owl had been Keegan's signal to her. She'd reacted without a thought, rushing to their meeting place as instinctively as a bird returning to its mating ground.

Trembling uncontrollably, she stared at the thick shadows of the trees. She could almost feel his presence. It seemed to reach out to her. . . to beckon her. . . .

Despair rushed over her like a raging wind born of desperation and longing. Moving stiffly, she retraced her steps to the house.

On the porch she stopped, drawn against her will to the woods that separated her land from his. She gripped the railing as the full realization of her wild response rushed over her.

She'd loved him three years ago. She loved him still.

Chapter Nine

Beth pressed a hand to her aching chest. Her heart pounded erratically against her ribs, making her aware of needs too long denied. The vast emptiness of her life stretched before her.

She was lonely, she realized. Lonely in ways that friendship couldn't assuage. She needed warmth, companionship, fulfillment.

The longing grew, and with it the knowledge that she might not ever find happiness. The thought brought the sting of tears to her eyes. She wouldn't give in to them. When had tears ever solved any problem?

Grimly she calmed the tempest of emotion. Slowly, she became aware of the hush of the night. The half-moon shone with an eerie radiance, bright on the dormant grass but dark on the woods, as if they absorbed all light in their velvet blackness.

As she watched, a tall, lithe form separated itself from the trees. She bit back a gasp.

Keegan.

He stepped on a boulder and lightly jumped over the fence and onto her property. Hardly making a sound, he walked toward her. She blinked, not sure she wasn't dreaming. The night was unreal.

"You left these," he said, his voice deep, melodious, resonant—the way the wind sometimes sounded in the cottonwoods. He climbed the steps and laid her clothes in the swing.

For a moment she couldn't speak. Finally she forced a brief "Thanks" out of her paralyzed throat.

He nodded. Instead of leaving, he moved closer. Leaning his shoulder against the support post, he studied her. "You answered the signal."

She jerked around, startled...hopeful, she realized. "Was that you? I thought...but there was an owl." She stopped in confusion, not sure if he'd called or not.

His voice was harsh when he spoke. "It was the owl. I apparently disturbed it when I cut through the woods."

"Oh." Humiliation washed over her. Every nerve felt raw and open to inspection.

"But I wanted to signal," he admitted. He spoke in a low, strained tone.

"And hated yourself for it. And me." She spoke quietly, used to the pain of his distrust.

"No," he ground out savagely. "I don't...hate you." He doubled his fist and silently hit the railing with one blow. In a hoarse voice, he added, "I want you too much."

A wild flutter went through her. Could he... Did he still love her? She searched his face, desperate for the truth. She saw only desire. The hope died. There was only the need.

He reached out to her. His hands settled on her shoulders, his touch light yet compelling. She felt his breath on her forehead, and a tremor went through her. His hands tightened; then he drew his fingertips over her, slowly, teasing her with the promise of his passion. He trailed a path up her neck and into her hair until his long, slender fingers cupped her head.

She watched as his head came nearer, blocking out the moonlight; then his mouth touched hers.

Sensation darted off into the inner regions of her body. Like a completed circuit, electricity flowed between them, fusing them together. His tongue probed the prim line of her lips. She opened to his demand.

Pleasure, sweet as autumn wine, filled her. She inhaled the aroma of his after-shave lotion and was catapulted back to a more innocent, trusting time when the world had been theirs.

A shiver of apprehension reminded her that life didn't keep its word, that passion whispered forever and lasted only minutes.

She pulled back from his embrace. "Keegan, don't."

His gaze roamed her face, his eyes as darkly mysterious as the night. "I can't help myself. I see you and . . ."

He didn't need to explain. She knew. Each time they were together, the harder it was to part. She was aware of her heart beating, of time passing with each thump.

"I wish I could remember that you're my enemy," he said. He rubbed his fingers in circles on her scalp, then let them glide down her neck, onto her back. He encircled her with his arms.

"I'm not." She'd thought she would be able to keep her distance, that they might even become neighbors in the true sense, but now she knew how foolish that had been. There was too much fire between them for a casual friendship.

And too much distrust for love.

Unable to help herself, she reached up and touched his cheek. She traced a line to his firm chin, then ran her fingers over his mouth. He closed his eyes and said nothing.

She bit down hard on her lower lip to keep from crying out. He seemed vulnerable, all at once, like a man who had reached the limit of his control. It came to her that he needed the same things she did—the warmth, the tenderness, the caring.

Pain and longing swirled through her. "Please," she whispered. "Keegan, please."

He exhaled a deep breath and opened his eyes. "Please what?" he asked hoarsely. "What do you want from me?"

"You, only you." Couldn't he understand that? There was nothing between them but *this*. She wrapped her arms around his neck as a wild surge of hunger shook her.

She felt the instant contraction of his muscles against her aching breasts. Then his hands tightened. She was lifted off her feet. He carried her into her bedroom and kicked the door closed behind them. Then his hands were between them, opening his jacket. He threw it aside. He unbuttoned his shirt, but fumbled with the studs on his cuffs.

"Unfasten the damned things before I tear it off," he said.

With shaking fingers, she removed the onyx studs, slipped them free of his shirt and placed them in the pocket. He slung the shirt aside. Then he took her hands and guided them to his chest.

"Touch me," he said.

She heard the desperation in him and knew it matched her own. She ran her hands over his chest, loving the hardness of it, the crisp feel of the dark hair under her fingers, the corrugations of bone and muscle along his torso.

His mouth swept over hers, and she closed her eyes. Flames leapt at her from a fathomless pit someplace inside her. They licked at her soul. The kiss became hungrier. He demanded more of her.

She moaned when his hand pushed her robe open and touched her breast through the cotton knit of her pajamas. He stroked the tip until it was the size of a small, hard pebble. She felt his breath against her cheek, becoming hot and heavy with his need.

The kiss deepened yet again. She knew she should stop this madness and send him away, but desire consumed her, making it impossible for her to move beyond his embrace. When he released her mouth, she buried her nose against his throat and pressed closer, feeding the hunger that drove them both.

They stood there for a long minute, just holding on to each other. Then he pulled away enough to look at her . . . hesitating . . . as if he waited for a protest from her. She had none.

Then he was pushing the robe off her. He made quick work of her pajamas, lifting the top over her head and sliding the bottoms along her hips and legs, then leaving them in a pool around her feet. He lifted her out of them and her slippers and laid her on the bed.

She ached for the feel of him against her during the moments it took for him to strip out of his dress pants and the rest of his clothing. Then he propped a knee on the bed beside her. She reached up to meet his descending mouth. He slid down and covered her completely.

With a cry, she arched upward. Joy sparkled through her like bubbles of rare champagne. She was floating, effervescent, doubts transcended by the hunger of her love.

His lips were magic on her flesh, skimming along her throat down to her breasts. He kissed each of them and laved them with the hot moisture of his tongue. When he paused, breathing heavily, she cried out with need.

"Let me see you," he whispered.

She reached out without hesitation and flicked the bedside lamp one time. The frosted pink globe of the nightlight softened the shadows cast by the moon on the carpet.

He drew back, his gaze on her breasts, which lifted and fell with each husky breath. "You're so damned beautiful. I thought I must have imagined it, but..." He shook his head, his eyes never leaving her.

Beth flushed with pleasure at his praise. He'd always found her much more appealing as a woman than she'd ever thought she was. Through his eyes, she saw herself as voluptuous and desirable. She ran her hands over his chest, loving the wonderfully masculine feel of him against her palms.

"I've wanted you like this since the moment I saw you on that damned road, stranded and waiting for someone to come along."

"And that someone had to be you," she whispered.

"Yes, *me,*" he said, breathing against her neck as he nibbled and kissed from her ear to her shoulder.

He cupped her breast and inspected it with a heated gaze that seemed to send funny, aching darts right through her chest. She shifted impatiently against him, her eyes never leaving his face.

With a gentle touch, he skimmed along her stomach and ran his hands over her thighs. He paused at the triangle of dark curls. "Like silk," he murmured, "black silk on white satin."

She closed her eyes as he caressed her thighs again, then glided his fingers between them, touching her with an intimacy that made her cry out and draw her breath in sharply.

"Yes," he said. "Yes."

Wildness invaded her. A storm of passion broke over her. "So hot . . . and aching. It hurts . . . to want you so much."

He held his weight off her but let her feel the full embrace of his body on hers. She held her breath. He stroked up and down, the dark, wiry hair on his chest teasing her breasts unmercifully, then eased away. The breath rushed from her. She experienced pure ecstasy from everywhere they touched.

"I know," he soothed. "Let me go. Just for a moment."

She released her desperate hold on his shoulders and watched him retrieve a packet from his wallet. He held it out to her.

"Cover me," he requested, his wintry gray eyes no longer cold and wary.

With shaking hands, she opened the packet. When she touched him, he sucked in a harsh breath. She waited, drawing out the love play, knowing she was driving him to the edge. With a slight smile, she reveled in the knowledge of her power over him.

"Scamp," he muttered, an endearment she hadn't heard for three years. She gathered it hungrily to her, reviving old memories, adding new ones. Leaning down, she kissed the jagged line of the scar on his thigh. Lovingly she played erotic games with her mouth and hands.

For several minutes he endured her exploration; then he caught her hand. "Get on with it," he growled, playful, yet serious, too.

She finished the task. Inside she was melting, ready for him, but he wouldn't let her guide him to her.

"Watch," he said.

Completely under his spell, she let her gaze slide down to the point of contact between them. Again he moved against her, casting soft brush strokes of feeling over her, tantalizing her... no, both of them. She arched against him, unable to control the wildness that raced through her.

She looked up and saw him watching her, a half smile curling his lips. "Now," he whispered hoarsely, raggedly.

With a tiny push, he began to move into her. She bent her knees and thrust upward. They slid smoothly together. A slight discomfort surprised her. It must have flickered over her face.

"It's...it's been a long time," she told him, unable to be less than honest with him.

"How long?" He sounded strained, his voice raspy.

"Three years," she admitted.

"Not since..."

She closed her eyes and shook her head.

His breath touched her face as he leaned close to her, his mouth a whisper from hers. "I'll be gentle."

The tenderly spoken promise nearly made her cry. If he could believe her in this, why couldn't he believe her in all things?

With his kiss, she forgot the past and its problems. There was only this moment and the smooth glide of flesh on flesh, hot and sensuous and compelling, building need on need, hunger on hunger, until the crest was broached.

A cry of pleasure was torn from her as she writhed under him. He answered it with his own thrust to completion.

Then they lay in each other's arms, silent and replete.

Warmth. Companionship. Fulfillment.

Beth fell asleep, lost in a lovely dream. It seemed but a moment later that the phone rang. She opened her eyes, puzzled at who would be calling at night. The bright light of day greeted her from the window.

Keegan sat up at the second ring.

She picked up the phone and murmured, "Hello."

"Beth? Jack Norton. Sorry to bother you on a weekend, but I've been going over some old records your father gave me..."

Her attorney's words were clearly audible to Keegan, who was watching her with a narrow-eyed scrutiny.

"Uh, Jack," she interrupted, "could we discuss this later? I have a...guest with me at the moment."

"Sure. Why don't you come down to the office tomorrow and we'll go over the details."

"I will. Thanks." She said goodbye and hung up.

Keegan threw back the covers and headed for his clothing. He pulled them on savagely.

"Keegan—"

He turned on her, the ice back in his eyes. "I vowed never to become entangled in your web of passion again and look where I end up." He laughed, a sound of disgust with himself and anger with her.

"We could work this out," she began hesitantly.

"Are you going to drop the suit?" He rolled his shirtsleeves back on his arms and slung his jacket over his shoulder.

The question was like a bucket of cold water in the face. "Was that what last night was all about?" she asked quietly.

A tense silence hummed between them. "Maybe," he said. "Why shouldn't I use the same tactics on you to get what I want? You're as susceptible to me as I am to you."

His gaze challenged her to deny his statement.

"I know." She tucked the sheet under her arms, embarrassed by her nudity in the cold light of day.

When she said nothing further, he turned with a curse and headed out the door.

Tremors ran over her. The house settled into its customary emptiness. Twenty rooms, she thought illogically. And only one person to fill them. It seemed so unbearably sad.

"Get back there, you stubborn heifer," Keegan yelled. He swung the red mare in a tight circle and darted in front of the cow, running it back in with the herd. He stopped and wiped the sweat off his forehead.

He and three other men were rounding up the breeding herd in preparation for trucking them down to their Rogue Valley ranch for the winter. In April or May, according to how mild or severe the winter turned out, they would bring them back. Only a select bunch of steers would remain on the home pastures.

He'd spent most of October in the rough country bordering the Rogue River National Forest. This land was the backside of his grandfather's old ranch, and it was the devil to ride. The crinkled hills, valleys and occasional outcropping of lava rock could hide a whole herd of elephants, not to mention the mavericks that seemed to comprise the Sky Eagle stock.

"Okay, let's bed 'em down," he called.

They had about two hundred head of cattle milling around the highland pasture. Steep ridges acted as barriers on two sides. Thick woods, traversed by a logging road, led down to the home pastures on the third. They were vulnerable only on the northeast corner, which adjoined the Triple R ranch and the national forest.

"We gonna post a guard tonight?" a cowboy called out.

Keegan considered. The men had been putting in long days. While the pasture wasn't fenced, there were no predators in the vicinity, nor was there any indication of a storm that might spook the herd. The last of the mavericks were grazing peacefully, so all was in order.

"I don't see any need. We could all use a good night's sleep for once. Tomorrow will be hard enough."

They'd have to drive the herd down the logging road to the holding pens where the loading chutes were located, which would mean another twelve- to fourteen-hour day in the saddle.

He sent two men to make camp near the logging road. He and the other man pitched their tents in a copse of trees at the back of the herd. After turning his horse loose to roll in the dust, he hiked over to the ridge. A stream ran at the base of it.

Peeling off his clothes, he plunged into a deep, narrow pool. He swam until the kinks smoothed off his shoulders and legs, then washed with the sliver of soap he'd brought and dried off by wiping down his body with a bandanna. He let the rapidly cooling air finish the job, then dressed and headed for his bedroll.

It seemed he'd hardly gotten to sleep when he was awakened by a noise unlike any he'd heard on the range before. The next sound brought him upright as hooves pounded the dirt.

Stampede!

With a curse, he grabbed for his pants, yanked them and his boots on and dashed from the tent. The herd was moving fast now. Any chance he'd had of turning them was past.

"What the hell!" yelled Hank, coming out of his tent.

As the last of the cattle thundered by, Keegan saw three men bent low over their horses. In the moonlight, their faces looked grotesque. He realized they were wearing masks. The unidentified noise he'd heard earlier came from the Halloween whistles clenched between their teeth.

He and Hank watched twenty-four days of work disappear into the back country again.

"Kids," Hank spat in disgust. "A damned Halloween prank. You think it was Elmer's nephews?" He pulled his shirt on and reached into the tent for his jacket.

"I don't know." Rage held Keegan immobile for several seconds before he, too, felt the chill of early morning and turned back to his tent to finish dressing. "But we'll find out," he promised in a dead-level tone.

Hank gave his boss a wary glance. "Sure hope it wasn't those dumb kids," he muttered. "Fool thing to do."

Keegan glanced at the eastern skyline. "It's two hours before first light. At dawn, the other two can begin the roundup again. You and I will start tracking. Be sure your rifle is in working order," he said. He whistled for his horse.

Beth gave a sigh of satisfaction. The heavy rain that had fallen earlier in the month had been a lifesaver. She'd had to have water trucked in during September, but things were looking up now.

Skully met her at the newly repaired and painted stable. He took her horse. Ted and Jeff were feeding the remuda, she noted.

"How's it going?" Skully asked. He lifted the saddle off.

"Great. We got the last of the stock moved down today, so we're set for the winter. If we don't get any blizzards, we'll be in good shape next year."

If the spring calving goes okay. If the costs stay down and the price stays up. If we don't have fire or flood or disease or any other of a thousand things that can befall a cattle ranch.

"Supper's ready. Didn't the men come in with you?"

"Two of them helped me bring down the rest of the strays. They'll be along shortly. Cawe and the other two are

going to check those hidden ravines up by the forest
boundary one more time before coming in.''

Skully finished rubbing down the horse and put it in a
stall with a bucket of feed. He went to the house with Beth.

"I'm dying for a hot shower," she told him with a tired
smile. "I dreamed about it last night—oceans of hot water
to bathe in."

"Get one, then come eat. I've fixed beans and corn bread
with jalapeños."

"Skully, you doll!" She gave him a kiss on the cheek.

He bent a mock frown on her. "Those peppers will fry
your insides one of these days," he warned.

Beth laughed and headed for her room. In the steamy
shower her smile disappeared, replaced by a slight frown.
She wished she could find other cowhands to replace Cawe
and his men. They were incompetent. She'd found several
cases of pink eye, some festering sores and other problems
with the care of the animals. They were also slow and almost insolent in taking orders.

Plus, she had a firm dislike of her foreman.

With a grimace, she admitted that was the main reason
she wanted him gone. He was one of those men who made
a woman feel uncomfortable when he looked at her. Shaking her head, she scrubbed harder, then rinsed. Dressed in
her pajamas and robe, with fuzzy slippers warming her feet,
she headed for the kitchen.

After fixing a plate, she took it into the ranch office to
work on the books while she ate. The tax bill had come in.
She looked at it as if by staring, the numbers might change
to a more nominal amount. They didn't.

It would take the last of her personal money to get them
through the rest of the year. If she sold her condo and
flower shop, then she could make it through next year. If

the ranch had a good year... She sighed. She'd been over that ground.

A letter from her lawyer was under the tax bill. She read it while she finished her supper. The hearing over the land next to the creek was scheduled for November seventeenth.

She glanced at the calendar. Surprise lit her face. Tomorrow was the first of the new month. Today was Halloween. She knew someone she'd like to haunt.

Keegan came to mind. She'd missed him this past month. She missed his passionate glances that burned her right to the core. She missed the unexpected way he would sometimes smile at her. She even missed his dark scowls, which might make her angry but never intimidated her.

That was one thing she knew—he would never physically hurt her. Being on the receiving end of his verbal lashes was quite enough, she admitted wryly.

She finished eating and rested her head on the chair, moodily watching the deepening twilight. She tried not to remember that he'd come to her, that they'd made love and slept together; then he'd left her in anger. Didn't he realize there was a simple solution to their problem? If they married, the ranches would be merged. If only he trusted her...

She sighed and stretched wearily, knowing she was pushing herself to the limit. With winter coming, the work would ease off. The herd was down to a manageable size. She would have to buy hay, but she thought they'd make it okay. If there were no blizzards...if the calving went okay...if...

She closed the ledgers, took her plate to the kitchen and saw it was after nine. The men had eaten. The kitchen was clean. She went to bed.

Beth and Ted were discussing the treatment of a swollen ankle on her favorite horse when a truck came up the road.

Keegan stopped and got out, then headed for the house, his stride long and smooth...and angry. He looked as grim as death.

She straightened and dusted her hands off on her jeans. Her heart was suddenly loud in her ears, a typical reaction to fear. She raised her chin. Ralstons weren't afraid of anyone.

"Hello," she called, leaving the stable and going toward the house. Keegan turned and waited for her.

He'd replaced his summer cowboy hat of white straw with a gray felt Stetson. His faded denim jacket and jeans were no-nonsense working clothes, yet he looked as handsome as a prince. Just the sight of him wrenched her heart. She met him at the porch.

"Looks like trouble," she commented, meeting his dead-level gaze with more courage than she felt.

"In spades," he agreed. "Where's Cawe?"

"Treating some cows near here. What's the problem?" She stuck her hands in her back pockets and waited for the bad news.

"Night before last some pranksters spooked my cattle, causing a stampede." He gave her a glance that chilled to the bone. "Hank and I tracked them to your land."

She couldn't believe the implication. "Are you saying Triple R men stampeded your herd?"

"Yeah." He thrust his hands into his back pockets and settled back on his heels, his cold gaze on her reaction.

"You're wrong." A shimmer of doubt ran through her. Surely Cawe wouldn't... She remembered the hatred in her foreman's eyes at the saloon the night of the fight. But a stampede... That would be stupid, childish and dangerous. "Did you see them?"

"Not their faces. They wore Halloween masks."

"Then how—"

"Their tracks led over the ridge to your land. One of them rode a mare who leads with her left and has a nick in the front horseshoe on that side." He described the nick. "I want to examine the horses you've been using."

Ted came out of the stable. "I took fresh horses out last night," he said. "I have the others here."

"Let's check them," Beth suggested, keeping her tone as cool as Keegan's. "How many pranksters were there?"

"Three," Keegan said. He strode toward the stable with Ted.

She marched behind the two men. In the paddock behind the stable, three horses cropped at the new spurt of grass caused by the recent rains. Ted went to a brown mare and led her over.

The three of them bent to examine the front hoof when Ted lifted it. A flaw in the horseshoe matched Keegan's description. Beth felt her heart zoom down like a falling elevator.

"Who was riding this one?" she asked.

Ted gave a grimace of disgust. "Cawe."

"I'll go out to the pasture and bring him in," she said.

"I'll ride along." Keegan went to her truck.

She remembered there were two other men with the foreman and that Keegan was alone, except for her. "You'd better stay here," she said. "In case things get rough."

He gave her a scathing glance. "Do you think I'd let you face those polecats alone?" he demanded.

"No, of course not," she replied in the same vein. "The Code of the West says you have to act the hero even if you get killed doing it."

Tension sizzled between them. They stood at the back of the truck; she was on one side, he on the other, like kids hurling insults across a barrier. It would have been ridiculous if the situation hadn't been so serious.

"You'll be outnumbered three to one," she advised.

He climbed in the truck and slammed the door. She did the same and drove in silence to the pasture where Cawe and his men were running cattle through a chute in order to tag their ears. She and Keegan got out and walked over.

"Hey, boss lady," Cawe said in his usual unctuous manner. His gaze shifted to Keegan and back to her. His smile disappeared.

"We have a problem," she said. "McPherson says his cattle were spooked a couple of nights ago. He tracked the culprits to our land."

"Is that so? I didn't see anyone. Did you, boys?" He glanced behind him at the two other men.

They stopped the tagging operation. Beth noted the uneasy glances they exchanged. They didn't say anything.

"That's because you weren't looking in a mirror," Keegan said with a caustic grin.

Cawe's eyes narrowed. "What are you trying to say?"

Beth stepped forward, putting herself between the men. "We know you three did it. The question is, why?"

"You gonna take his word over your own men?" Cawe demanded, indignant and virtuous.

Keegan moved up beside her. She could sense the fury in him. "McPhersons don't lie," she said, tired of her foreman's bluster. "Besides, you left evidence."

At her statement Cawe's bravado disappeared. He looked around as if checking for an escape route.

"Pack your things and get out, Rolly. I'll have the payroll ready when you leave."

"If I go, my men go with me," he warned with a snarl.

"That was my thinking, too." She headed for the truck, giving Keegan a push in front of her. To her surprise, he went without a word. She turned back to the ranch hands.

"By the way, aren't you men a little old for Halloween tricks?"

If she'd needed further proof of their guilt, the sudden shifting of feet and the red tint of their ears provided it. She climbed into the pickup beside Keegan and headed for the house. On the way she was acutely aware of Keegan's eyes on her.

"What is it?" she finally asked.

"You," he said. "I don't think I'll ever figure you out."

She flashed him an angry look. "Did you think I'd keep them on after they pulled a stunt like that? I'll start rounding up your cattle for you—"

"I've got two men on it."

"As soon as Cawe is gone," she finished.

"Don't bother."

She stopped the truck beside his. "Ralstons always pay their debts," she informed him. "I owe you for what my men did."

"Who are you going to use?" he demanded. "Those two old men who should have retired years ago and a kid still in school?"

"I have two other men working for me," she informed him.

He gave a snort of disgust. They got out. He came around the truck. They stood there in the morning sunshine. On a distant hill, aspens added a splash of color to the deep green of the fir trees. She stared at the bright, shimmery gold and didn't let herself think of Keegan and how strong and handsome he was.

And how she had let him make love to her.

For days...and nights...she'd wrestled with the knowledge that she still loved him, still wanted him.

A wave of longing rushed through her. She wanted to press her face against his neck, right where the white of his

T-shirt formed a triangle between his tanned throat and deep blue shirt.

"I'll pay for your men's time," she said.

"Skip it." He stalked toward his truck.

She caught his arm. "I said I'll take care of it."

He looked at her hand on his arm, then into her eyes. "You'd better save your money. This place needs all the help it can get."

Her pride was stung at his cynical quip. She dropped her hand and stepped back from him. "How nice of you to worry about us."

"Dammit!" he bit out. "I..." He resettled his hat. "The less we have to do with each other, the better it'll be for both of us," he reminded her savagely.

"I agree," she said coolly. "So my men and I will take over. Are your cattle on my land or in the national forest?"

"National forest," he snapped. "The northwest sector across the ridge from my grandfather's old spread."

She nodded.

With a curse he leapt into his truck and drove off. She stood there in the small tempest of gravel dust that was stirred up by his leaving. She was terribly tired all at once. Going into the house, she made out checks for the three men who were leaving.

When the men arrived at the homestead, she wasn't particularly surprised to see that the other two were with them. She made out another two checks and entered the amounts in the payroll ledger.

She'd go get the McPherson cattle by herself.

Chapter Ten

Ted drove the truck, pulling the horse trailer. "You can't go off in the woods by yourself," he said for the tenth time. "You should have brought Jeff."

"He has school."

"He can miss a few days."

"No. The dogs will do fine."

He muttered about the Ralston trait of stubbornness.

At the end of the road, they unloaded the two saddle horses and the pack horse she would use while she rounded up the Sky Eagle cattle. Two blue heelers—Australian herding dogs purchased from a neighbor on Saturday—leapt out of the truck.

The dogs sniffed the air, eager to be off. The horses were ready to go, too. Beth swung into the saddle. The dogs looked at her for direction. She'd worked part of Saturday and all of Sunday with them. It was Monday. They were ready to go.

"I'll see you at the end of the week. Saturday."

"Keep your gun at hand and your eyes open," Ted advised.

Beth nodded. Ted and Skully were worried that Cawe and his men might return, but she didn't think they would. With the evidence against them, Keegan could have them arrested.

She rode off into the rough country, then paused to look back once as Ted returned to the ranch house. A ripple of loneliness ran over her. She knew this country well, but it had been a long time since she'd roamed around it on her own. It seemed as vast and empty as she felt.

The dogs sniffed the air once more, then bounded forward. They turned to see if she was following. "Lead on," she said.

Cutting through a deer trail, she rose over to the point where her land adjoined the national forest and the McPherson ranch. She studied the ground for a moment, noting tracks through the dust.

"Heel," she called to the dogs. They immediately came to her. She turned right onto Keegan's land. In a moment hearing men's voices, she rode out of the woods into a clearing. "Stay," she said. The dogs sat down, their noses quivering as they watched the herd for any strays.

Keegan and two of his ranch hands had a hundred or so beeves rounded up. She saw him speak to his men, then wheel his horse around and come to her in a gallop. He pulled up four feet away. His gaze encased her in ice. Hard, implacable male.

"How many are you missing?" she asked without bothering with the niceties.

"We're fifty-seven short of our count."

"I'll check the ravines in the forest next to my land," she volunteered. It was the roughest country, easy for mule-tempered cows to hide in. And die in, she added. If a blizzard came. If a cow got caught in a landslide or a flash flood. If...

"I see you brought help." Keegan nodded toward the heelers. "Elmer's?" He referred to a neighboring rancher who raised the pedigreed dogs.

"They were. I bought them."

"Think you can handle them?"

"Yes."

His eyes narrowed to wintry slits. He studied her as if testing her mettle. She set her mouth and gave him back his dead-level stare. "Wait here," he said suddenly.

When he rode off to talk to his men again, she searched for a good camping spot. She found one at the base of a steep drop-off. A tiny creek carved its own shallow ravine between the cliff and an outcropping of rock. There was a sheltered place in the trees close by. It would do.

Quickly she set up her tent and suspended her supplies from a tall tree. After hobbling the pack horse and her spare work horse, she left them to graze, then mounted up and started out.

"Heel," she said to the resting dogs. They immediately swung into place behind her.

Keegan caught up with her before she went over the ridge. "You don't listen worth a damn," he informed her.

"I'm here to do a job." She stared straight ahead. Ignoring him didn't stop her from being aware of his masculine presence. He was a man who looked good on a horse, lean and spare, at ease in the saddle. Equally at ease in bed.

He sighed loudly. "We'll do it together."

She whipped her head around. "I don't need help. I'll get your fifty-seven cows back." Briefly, she thought of failure. "Or I'll pay you for their loss."

That was as fair as a person could get.

"It's November," he reminded her.

Which was to say the weather was uncertain. He didn't have to tell her that. She remembered what the winters were like in the area. While she didn't expect snow, it could happen. More likely, if a storm came in, it would bring freezing rain or hail.

"I'm staying," she said.

"Fine," he said just as coolly. "I sent the men on down to the home pastures with the herd. They'll be back at the end of the week to get any that we round up."

A flare like a Roman candle went off inside her. She waited for the hot brilliance to pass before speaking. "Just keep out of my way."

"Don't worry. I intend to."

Once over the ridge and on federal land, he turned off to the right on a game trail while she went left. She headed up the first narrow valley between the crinkled hills and volcanic peaks.

With a sweep of her hand, she set the dogs to work. Together, they combed the ravine and found three cows munching contentedly on the grass growing next to a seep. The cows didn't want to leave, but the dogs quickly convinced them to move on.

By nightfall, she had a grand total of seven cows. She and the dogs herded the beasts into the large meadow over the ridge. She counted ten others already there. Forty more to go.

She set the dogs on guard and headed back to camp. Every muscle ached when she dropped to the ground. With a groan, she lifted the saddle off and laid it next to the tent.

She and the horse headed for the creek.

To her consternation, she spied a bedroll tucked under a tarp, which was supported over a limb and tied at the corners. A fire ring had been readied. A coffeepot sat on a rock.

Keegan was at the creek. Kneeling, he pumped water through a purifying filter into a plastic bottle.

"The water is usually warm enough to wash in, over in that pool," he advised. "It's warmed by the sun most of the day."

His gaze took in everything about her. She knew how she looked. Tired. Dusty. Irritated. No makeup. Straggly hair. Yeah, she knew. She was way too tired to care. He'd seen her like this before.

Moving her horse downstream of Keegan, she went back for her toiletry kit and clean clothes. He had the bottle filled by the time she returned. "Supper in twenty minutes," he said.

She nodded. If he thought he was going to upset her, he could think again. One night of lovemaking didn't mean a thing.

Her heart drummed wildly, contradicting her rational thought. She laid her clothing on a rock and washed in the water that was slightly less frigid than zero degrees. Dressed in fresh clothes, she quickly washed out her others and hung them over bushes to dry.

She checked the other horses before heading for the campfire that sparkled in the near dark like a homing beacon. There was only Keegan and the long night to face now.

He was bent over the low flames in the firepit, stirring a pot of beef stew. Her mouth watered at the aroma. She saw he had made a seat for her, using a flat rock for the base and her saddle for the backrest. She sank down with an audible sigh.

He glanced over at her. "You should be used to long days in the saddle. You've been doing half of the work on your place since you returned in August."

"Two and half months ago," she mused. "August thirteenth to November..." She couldn't remember the date.

"It's the third."

"November third. It seems longer. A lifetime."

"Time slows down when life gets rough," he said, without any inflection in his tone.

"The years with your grandfather must have seemed forever."

His expression became closed, effectively telling her his life was off limits. "Where's your plate?" he asked.

She fetched her plate and utensils. He evenly divided the meal into portions. "You're bigger than I am," she reminded him.

"You worked just as hard," he replied tersely.

They ate in silence. The moon came up over the ridge shortly after dark. Beth dozed off, staring into the fire. She woke as her head nodded to one side. Jerking upright, she glanced around in confusion. Keegan watched her across the fire pit. A great joy rose in her, and she smiled at him.

"You'd better go to bed," he advised.

"Yes. Are you coming, too?" she asked without thinking.

A sardonic smile slashed across his face. "Are you inviting me?" He gave her a thorough perusal, a challenge in his eyes.

Her mind finally caught up with her instincts. She thought about them and what the night would offer. The passion was there. Would that be enough?

Like the caress of the night breeze through the fir trees, the realization stole over her that they belonged together.

Just as their land lay side by side, a perfect alignment, so did their need for each other match as perfectly. Could she show him through the joining of their bodies that they should be joined in all ways?

Life could be so perfect for them...if only he would trust her...if only he would follow his heart...if only...

She clenched her hands together, fighting the need to walk around the small fire that separated them and sink into his arms.

What if he took her body but not her love?

Pain and doubt ate at her. His distrust and rejection of her had hurt her in ways she couldn't begin to recount. But if she didn't try, an opportunity might be lost forever—

His snort of laughter brought her tortured thinking to a halt. "Never mind," he taunted. "I'm not going to fall for your soft lies again. I want you, yes, but that's as far as it goes. If you issue an invitation, I'll take it, but it will be for pleasure only, nothing else."

"Sometimes passion can lead to other things." Her voice wavered slightly.

He rose and came around the glowing embers of the dying fire. Kneeling, he touched her mouth with one finger. "No way," he said huskily. "No promises. Nothing but *this*."

He bent and kissed her, his mouth incredibly passionate on hers. When he drew back, they were both breathing heavily.

"I want more," she told him. She lifted her lips to his.

He stood and backed away as if she were the bait in a trap for an unwary animal. "Yeah, you want the water and probably half my holdings, too. Sorry, you'll have to find another sucker."

She recoiled as if he'd slapped her. "Why?" she inquired coolly. "When you're so convenient?"

Leaving him with a thunderous expression, she went to her tent, undressed to her thermal underwear and went to sleep.

* * *

Beth groaned as she swung into the saddle. The leather was surely harder this morning than it had been yesterday. She turned her horse just as Keegan came alongside.

"I thought we'd leave the dogs on guard and the two of us would work the woods on the other side of the creek this morning."

She nodded.

"Watch the sky. There's a storm brewing in the west. It may come in by noon."

She nodded again.

He gave her a piercing study. "You should stay in camp and rest today," he said unexpectedly, his tone gruff.

Realizing he was worried about her did things to her heart that she hadn't the time or the energy to fight. She pulled on the reins. "Let's get on with it."

He let out an exasperated sigh behind her. She ignored it. They headed up the trail for the woods running to the north of the ravines they'd checked the day before. They found five cows in one area, three in another. By noon, they had twelve head.

"Take them back to the meadow. Hurry. The storm's coming up fast," he advised. "I'll check along the creek over here."

Scanning the sky, Beth decided he was right. The clouds were running before a swift wind out of the northwest now. Puffs of dust whirled away behind the small herd as she drove them down the winding trail off the ridge.

She found the dogs resting when she reached the meadow. One had his head down, sleeping, she assumed. The other lay about ten feet away, lying on a grassy knoll, his head up, on the alert for danger. Both animals bounded toward her when she whistled.

They circled around the cows she'd brought in, sniffing and checking them over. Satisfied, they drove the smaller group down to join the larger. That made twenty-nine. Twenty-eight to go.

Two more days should see them out of there.

She went to their camp, unsaddled and turned her mount into the meadow to graze. Gusts of wind swept down the ridge, forerunners of the coming tempest. She glanced worriedly at the sky. The black edge of the storm front loomed over the trees lining the ridge. Not long now. Another hour.

After retrieving a plastic rain fly from her supplies, she rigged a one-sided shelter over the firepit to keep it dry and give her and Keegan a place to sit, protected from the storm. She'd just finished when the first drops of rain hit.

She got rolls, cheese and dried fruit out for a quick lunch and suspended her bear bag from its limb again. Then she donned her poncho and crawled under the rain fly to wait for Keegan.

He wasn't long in coming. She heard the pound of galloping hooves before he came into sight. He leapt down, removed the saddle and freed his horse in quick, efficient moves. The horse joined her mare in the trees.

"You made it," Beth said. Her smile came naturally. She realized she couldn't stay angry with Keegan, no matter how mad he might make her at the moment. He had only to appear, and she softened at once. She understood his tough-mindedness. He'd had a hard life, after all. Hers had been a cinch in comparison.

"Did you find any more cattle?" She moved over, inviting him inside the shelter.

"A couple, that's all. The last ones are always the smartest about hiding out." He glanced at the sky once more before bringing his saddle inside and placing it next to hers. "I'd better cover my bedroll. A blowing rain will soak it."

"Put it inside my tent," she suggested.

He hesitated, then nodded. While he attended to it, she divided out their lunch, giving him larger portions than she took.

When Keegan returned and crawled under the shelter she'd made, he saw she'd laid out some food. Good. He was starved. He tossed his hat on the saddle horn.

Glancing at her rosy lips when she started on her cheese, he admitted he was hungry for her, more than just food. Her hair was long now, tossed by the wind into becoming tangles. Tendrils brushed against her cheeks and temples.

Black silk against white satin.

He longed to smooth it from her face, to push his fingers into the curls and cup her head, to kiss her until neither of them could breathe....

Picking up the roll, he bit into it. He ate with savage hunger. Anything to distract him from the woman beside him, he admitted. Too bad it wasn't working.

"I've been noticing how you run your cattle," she said. She turned to him with a thoughtful frown. "You stock a lot more to a pasture than I do, yet you apparently have plenty of grass."

"It's a new method we're experimenting with," he said. He had to clear the huskiness from his voice before he could explain. "We're trying to emulate nature."

"What do you mean?"

"We're working with the Ag Department at the university. They noticed that when buffalo graze, they stay in an area until the grass is eaten almost to the ground, then they move on. The land recovers. By the time the herd comes through again, the grass is knee-high, thicker and healthier than before. That's what we're doing—intensive grazing, then complete rest."

"So instead of keeping the cattle spread out over all the pastures, you move them around in herds?"

"Right."

"That makes sense."

"Glad you approve," he said dryly.

The rain hit. It came in a fury, all at once, like demons driven mad by the wind. He peered out from under the plastic cover. The sky was black and sullen. The clouds covered it from horizon to horizon.

"I moved the cows to the leeward side of the pasture. There's trees to shelter in and a rock ledge to one side. The dogs should be able to keep them in tight."

"Good." She yawned.

He glanced at her, realizing she must be tired. A fine tension hummed in him. "The afternoon is shot. Why don't you crawl into your tent and sleep?"

She look startled by the suggestion. "What about you?"

"What about me?" he asked warily.

To his surprise, she laughed. "Don't worry. I'm not going to pounce on you. I just thought you might need a nap, too. Your bedroll is in my tent."

He was so hard and aching by the time she finished speaking, he nearly groaned. Sweat broke out on his brow as fire swept through him.

"If I crawl into that tent, it won't be with sleep on my mind," he told her without pulling any punches.

A flush rose in her cheeks. "Mine, either," she admitted.

She met his challenging glare without flinching. A wave of uncertainty went through him. Was she...was she inviting him to make love to her?

He couldn't decide. She'd never looked at him in quite that way before—no anger, no defiance, no cynical sophistication, just a steady gaze that reached right into his soul...no, dammit, he wouldn't fall for her again. Not in a million years!

But if she wanted him...

Beth saw the conflicting thoughts go through Keegan's mind. A sharp ping of excitement coursed through her. All she had to do was reach out, and he'd come to her. She knew it. She also knew she didn't want him this way, with him wary of being used.

"I think I'll take you up on your suggestion," she said softly. Climbing out from under the shelter, she dashed to her tent, unzipped it and slipped inside. She undressed and snuggled into the sleeping bag. The storm was a cold one. The temperature had dropped ten or more degrees since morning.

An hour passed.

The storm abated to a whisper of rain. Then it came back in full fury. After ten minutes it quietened again. She was almost asleep when she heard the rasp of the zipper. Opening her eyes, she saw Keegan duck inside and fasten the zipper once more.

"It's damned cold," he said in a gruff tone, as if daring her to make something of his remark or his presence.

She smiled sleepily. "Make yourself comfortable."

He spread out his pad and smoothed out his sleeping bag. After removing his boots and rolling his jacket into a pillow, he lay down. She heard a soft rustle; then he tossed his jeans and shirt to the side of the tent.

With a satisfied murmur she went to sleep soundly.

The rain thrummed against the tent with a steady drone when she woke. Looking at her watch, she saw it was almost four. They'd slept for three hours. Keegan was still asleep.

She raised to her elbow and watched him for several minutes. She loved the hard planes of his face...the way his brows arched, thick and black, then winged out toward his temples...the thin line of his nose with the barely discernible angle that indicated it had been broken...the way the gray of his eyes changed from cool to hot...

He was watching her, his eyes slit open a fraction.

Her heart leapt around in her chest, then settled down to a loud, hard beat of longing. She removed one arm from the downy warmth and laid her hand along his jaw. He continued to stare at her without saying a word.

Then he turned his head and kissed the palm of her hand.

A thousand sparks leapt through her from that point of contact, igniting wild fires inside her. All thoughts of self-preservation fled. She leaned over and replaced her hand with her mouth. His lips opened and received her kiss.

With a groan he snaked a hand around her head and pulled her closer. The kiss deepened, becoming hungrier, gentler, more demanding, more giving.

She felt helpless against the passion that rose as suddenly as the storm outside, passion driven by the winds of love. She could no longer fight it. She moved closer.

His hand dipped inside her sleeping bag and found the soft knit of her thermals. Moving slowly over her, he also discovered how they fastened. He paused, then with a slight tug, he opened one snap, then another, and another. Reaching inside, he touched her flesh, then followed her bra strap to the hooks. He unfastened them with a quick twist of his fingers.

When he pushed the material up and out of his way, Beth sucked in her stomach as a spasm of sheer delight washed over her. He rose and bent over her, pushing her on her back. She ran her fingers into his dark hair when he kissed her breasts and held him to her. Love was a tenderness and a pain inside her.

"You make me ache," she murmured brokenly, unable to hold the words in. "And weak."

He lifted his head and stared into her eyes, seeing things she thought she should hide. But she couldn't.

"Yes," he ground out in a savage whisper.

But for all his fierceness, he was exquisitely tender when he ran a finger under her chin, caressing the sensitive flesh there. A quiver of need ran along nerve paths she didn't know she had.

She felt his breath on her lips and instinctively opened her mouth. He was lean and powerful, bending over her like that, and she was powerless to deny them this moment.

Inhaling deeply, she breathed the essence of him into her. He smelled of cologne and, to a lesser degree, of leather and their horses and, she thought, of the outdoors—a fresh, clean scent that tantalized her senses.

He traced a line up and down her neck. "Like satin," he said. "Black silk. White satin. All over."

She burned at his words. "You're like leather and rawhide. Hard, smooth, strong. Yet warm and . . . gentle . . . sometimes." She could hardly speak for the passion that raged through her.

"No, not gentle. Careful, yes, because I'm a man and I'm stronger than you, but not gentle," he denied.

Caressing him with both hands on each side of his beloved face, she shook her head. "You don't even know . . ."

"Tell me." His tone was harsh, demanding, hungry.

"When you touch me . . . it's heaven . . . and hell." She closed her eyes, shutting out everything but his hand and where he touched. Her throat. Her breasts. Her waist. Stroking down. Down. She held her breath.

"Yes. For me, too," he admitted.

She looked at him, into light, wintry eyes that promised such dark, hot delight. He caught her gaze with his. She was unable to hide her need or her love. It frightened her to need him this much. And to know he hated her.

Suddenly he smiled at her. Her heart reeled, and she was lost. She'd give him anything.

"Let's see what we can do," he said as if answering a request from her.

He half rose and examined both sleeping bags. She realized what he was checking. Heat rose to her face, but she didn't say a word.

"They zip together." He stopped and looked at her.

She nodded.

It took three minutes to zip the down-filled bags into one large sleeping compartment. When he lay beside her again, she realized there were only their thermals to keep them apart. When he tugged hers out of her waistband, she realized that soon even those would be gone.

"Don't look so worried," he muttered. "This isn't going to be anything you won't like."

"I know." She sat up enough to let him slip the top and her bra from her. Then the rest was gone. She helped him with his in the confined space.

"Now," he said in a hoarse whisper. He brought her into contact with him, flesh to flesh. There was violence in the movement, a hard, driving, pulsing need that brought them together in an explosion of desire. But there was caring, too.

Her breath was driven from her; then she gave a half sob, half moan as he slid his chest over hers.

"I won't hurt you," he said against her lips.

"You will. You just don't know all the ways."

He crushed his mouth against hers as if he didn't want to hear any more. The kiss was endless...endlessly deep...endlessly tormented....

She trembled uncontrollably and wrapped her arms around him as hard as she could.

He murmured words of need, even of endearment, to her, but nothing could soothe the painful need inside her. She writhed against him, wanting words of love, promises of forever. Tears seeped from the corners of her eyes as love swept over her, even more powerful than the night in her bed, creating the wildest yearning....

"Wait," he said, pulling back.

Their ragged breaths coupled with the soft fall of the rain were the only sounds. He reached for his jeans, then stopped.

"I don't have anything. I didn't plan on making love when I came up here. I figured that'd be the last thing we'd do."

For a second she pressed her lips together, then she said, "It's all right. I'm on the pill."

His eyes flicked to her.

"The doctor suggested them because of the pain each month," she added nervously.

"That night at your place, you were playing it safe..." His voice trailed off at the implication. The fire in his eyes cooled slightly. "I've learned to be careful, too. When I started out on the rodeo circuit, I was determined to make it to the top...and just as determined that no woman was going to trap me and tap into my winnings. I've always made sure I was covered."

He left the final decision up to her, not pushing for completion if she didn't want to give it. She believed him, but still she hesitated, knowing she should withdraw. When they weren't being lovers, he still thought of her as his enemy.

"Or," he added softly, "we can share pleasure without total contact." He waited.

She thought of all the things they could share . . . life and its pleasures, its troubles. "I want you." She laid a hand on his chest, let it trail downward.

He groaned and closed his eyes. "I've never had a woman bare. A first," he murmured in a strained voice. "Ah, Beth, take me in." He buried his face against her neck, his manner urgent. "Let me in."

"Yes. Oh, yes." She pulled him close, until they were joined completely.

Chapter Eleven

"Is it still raining?" Beth asked.

Keegan zipped down the nylon flap and peered through the net window. "Cats and dogs."

She found her flashlight and checked the time. "Almost ten. We didn't have any supper."

"I know. I'm starved. How about you?"

"Umm-hmm."

"Stay here," he advised when she stirred. "Dinner in ten minutes, madam." He executed a sideways bow from the waist.

In the faint light of her penlight, she watched while he pulled on his boots and jacket. Her eyes opened wider.

"Aren't you going to wear anything else?"

"No." He bent over and kissed her, surprising her.

"You'll freeze."

"You can warm me when I get back. Can I use your light?"

She handed it to him, and he was gone, leaving only a swirl of cold, rain-moistened air in the tent. She tucked her hands under her head and stared at the roof of the tent.

Physically, she was totally sated from their lovemaking. It acted on her mind like a drug, making her lethargic and slow. Or perhaps it was easier to drift than to think.

What was there to think about?

She had no more answers to the future now than she'd had a week or a month ago. She wanted to lie there, warm and drowsy, content and happy with the moment. Ah, but his lovemaking . . .

"Dinner," Keegan said, slipping under the storm fly of the tent, unzipping the opening and sitting down inside while he removed his boots with his feet still outside. He stuck his boots safely under the storm fly, then swung his legs in and zipped the flap closed. From his jacket, he removed cheese, rolls, trail mix and other goodies.

"A feast," she exclaimed.

His gaze roamed over her as she raised herself on one elbow. "We've had that. This is just to top us off."

He took off his jacket, careful of the raindrops clinging to it and folded it inside out. He set a bottle of filtered water between them.

"Champagne?" she inquired. She inspected the plastic bottle. "Hmm, a very good year."

"Right." He grinned at her, obviously pleased with her playful appreciation of his efforts.

She smiled at him. A shiver attacked her as the cold air caressed her bare torso. Keegan found her thermal top and helped her into it. He pulled his over his head and tucked his long legs into the sleeping bag.

"You're cold," she scolded as he touched his legs to hers.

"Warm me."

"I'm eating."

He swooped toward her and stole a kiss, then pulled back and started eating when she raised her face for more. "So eat."

They ate and drank their fill; then he lay on his back and pulled her against him, an arm under her head. She rested her leg on him and snuggled against his body, sharing their warmth.

"It's been several hours," he said.

Since they'd made love, she completed the thought. He caressed her shoulder, then slipped lower and stroked the side of her breast. The longing stirred again.

"I don't want . . . if you're sore . . ."

"No," she quickly said. "It's okay."

He looked relieved. His hands slipped to her waist. With little effort, he lifted her and put her on top of him.

"You don't weigh as much as a calf," he said with a scowl. "I was afraid I'd crush you in the heat of the moment."

She propped herself up with her elbows at either side of him. "I'm strong," she reminded him, grinning. "I can probably lick my weight in wildcats."

"You can probably lick me to a standstill," he murmured, his eyes going dark as the pupils widened. He rubbed his hands over her back and along her buttocks, made a return circuit up the side and started over again. "You make me weak with just a smile."

"It's the same for me."

"Is it?" he questioned.

"Yes." It hurt, she admitted, seeing the doubt in his eyes. "Do you think I'm . . . faking what I feel when we're together?"

He shook his head. "Not this." He touched her intimately, stealing her breath for a second. "But here . . ." He cupped his hand under her left breast over her heart. "I wonder what you feel inside."

"Would you believe me if I told you?"

"No."

His blunt denial tore at her control. Her composure trembled before she could steady it. Tears seeped into her eyes. Beneath her, she felt his chest rise in a long breath, then fall in a heavy sigh.

"I can't figure you out," he said. "For the life of me, I can't figure out what you want this time. Other than the water."

"Water," she repeated. "Like air, a necessity of life."

"Right." He shifted her slightly, then began a bold pattern of caresses that had them both panting in a minute.

"There are other things." She hesitated.

"Like what?" He looked into her eyes as he drove her insane with his erotic touches.

"Sharing," she whispered. "A home. A family."

"Like Kerrigan and Rachel."

"Yes." She felt suddenly desperate for those things.

"We'll never have what they have."

"Why?" She kissed the side of his mouth, experimented there with her tongue, checking the texture, the taste of him against the memories she'd stored. She felt his stomach muscles clench, then the unmistakable hardening of his body into raging desire.

"You demand too much. You'd take my soul if I let you."

He shifted them, rolling over until he was on top. He moved between her thighs and thrust against her, seeking and finding entry. For her, it was a meeting of the soul. For him? She couldn't tell.

A tiny light of hope flamed in her. He was having problems keeping the physical separate from the emotional.

Given time, she might win his trust again. Given time, even a mountain could be worn away.

"Wear your rain slicker," he advised.

The sky was overcast but not black as it had been the previous day. They set out at dawn after checking the herd in the meadow and feeding the dogs a hearty breakfast. Beth wanted to leave dry food out, but Keegan said the squirrels would get it.

She stared at his back as they rode up the ridge trail. Her imagination supplied vivid scenes that she couldn't suppress. She thought of them working together, building a future, experimenting with breeds and grazing patterns, respecting the wildlife that lived on the land.

A grain at a time, she reminded herself. She smiled defiantly at his back. Strong, solitary male. She'd show him.

They worked all morning, skipped lunch and worked through the afternoon. By then, they had all the cows rounded up but five.

"We'll check that last sector in the morning," he decided. "If we don't find them, we'll call it quits and drive the rest down to the chutes tomorrow afternoon."

"All right."

They headed back for the meadow. After taking care of the dogs, Beth went to their camp. Keegan had rubbed down their horses and was now watering them at the creek. When they finished drinking, he set them on hobbles and turned them loose.

Beth brought her ditty bag over, preparing to take a bath. The water was icy cold.

"You'll freeze," he called to her.

She looked around. He was smiling at her. A thrill went over her. She felt so helpless, loving him, wanting him. She returned his smile. "You can warm me up."

"I will," he promised, his voice going husky and deeper. Later, he did.

Beth sat on a knoll under a tree and watched the dogs circle the cattle. Keegan had insisted she stay and rest while he checked the last section for the missing cows. When he returned, they would drive the critters down the logging road to the holding pens.

They would finish two days earlier than expected.

Keegan returned before noon. He whistled and one of the dogs raced to join him, pushing the rest of the missing cows toward the herd. Keegan came to her.

He swung down and dropped the reins. "Hi," he said, giving her a slow once-over.

"Hi. Looks like you were successful."

"Yep, that's the last of the lot."

"I'm relieved," she admitted. "Now I won't have to pay for them."

"Short on money?"

"Isn't everybody?" she asked philosophically.

"No. Our offer is still open," he reminded her.

The warm, lazy feeling evaporated. She felt defeated. Two days of intimacy counted for nothing. He still wanted her ranch. He still wanted her gone. She must have been mad—thinking she could break down the barriers to his heart.

She stood and removed a couple of burrs from her jeans. "I need to get home. There's work to be done."

He stepped close, one hand going to her waist, the other under her chin to lift her head. She resisted.

"What?" he asked.

"We'd better hit the trail."

"I thought we'd rest a bit first," he murmured huskily.

Beth looked into his eyes and saw the desire. It just wasn't enough. "I'm tired," she said.

To her consternation, he smoothed the curls from her forehead, his gaze concerned. "You're one of the hardest-working people I ever met." There was a note of exasperated puzzlement in his tone. "Sometimes I don't understand you at all."

She went to her horse and mounted up. "I doubt if you ever will." But she smiled when she said it.

Keegan kept an eye on Beth as they pushed the cattle along the logging road. She puzzled him, angered him and drove him mad with desire at the same time. He wondered how much longer he could hold out against her.

Sometimes he thought he'd give her anything she wanted...if she would only stay. Then he would remember that this woman had tried to use his weakness for her once before.

He studied her straight, slender back as she rode near the lead cow. Something about her grabbed at his throat. She had the Ralston pride in spades. She was stubborn. She had a temper. Yet there was something...valiant about her. He had to admire her tenacity in trying to put her ranch to rights. It was a job even an experienced rancher would think twice about.

Hell, maybe he should marry her. Their land fitted together as neatly as her body fitted his. A prenuptial agreement would protect his investments. He wondered what she would say. If he asked.

They met up with Hank and a couple of the men at the holding pens, loading the last of the cows they'd brought down earlier. An early winter was predicted. He wanted the cattle out of the rough country by December.

"Yo," Hank called. "How'd it go?"

"We got 'em all," Keegan told him. "Thought you'd be through here by now."

"The truck was delayed due to the storm. The driver wouldn't risk getting stuck. We just started moving the critters yesterday."

"Actually, this works out better. You can get them all in this last load." Keegan turned to Beth. "We can ride on to the house. Call your dogs."

She called to the dogs to heel. They looked at the men as if they didn't trust the wranglers to do a good job, then padded over and took up positions on either side of Beth's mare. She nudged the mare with her knees, falling in behind Keegan with her little entourage of horses and dogs.

At the homeplace of the Sky Eagle ranch, she noticed all the activity. One man was moving a huge stack of hay with an automated bale lifter to a three-sided barn, obviously new. Two others were mucking out the stable. Keegan's twin was in a paddock with another man, working with a lame horse. Rachel and an old man were in the garden, looking at the last of the pumpkins.

A lump rose to Beth's throat. She thought of Skully, Ted, Jeff and herself—four of them to feed and take care of the herd during the winter and spring calving. A nervous spasm went down her back, like a thousand-legged bug crawling over her. Defeat felt just that close.

"Your place is so busy," she murmured, "so prosperous."

Keegan gave her a hard glance before reaching down to open the last gate that would admit them to the open quadrangle of well-kept lawn and driveway between the house and other buildings.

He would have to be blind not to see the envy in her eyes as she surveyed their operation. Was she using him again, trying to get him caught up in a blaze of passion so he'd forget the past and her treachery? He had news for her if that was her plan.

Rachel yelled a greeting and waved. She dashed out of the garden, stopped to close the gate, then stood under a tall pine and waited for them to tie up their horses.

"Come to the house," she invited both of them. "Wills and I have been baking pies all day. My folks are coming to visit this weekend." She was bursting from excitement. "Beth, you must come and have dinner with us Saturday night. My brother is coming, too, and I want you to meet him."

"Is he handsome?" Beth asked, laughing.

Keegan had a murderous thought as he swung down and gave his reins to one of the men from the stable. Maybe she was thinking of catching someone else if he wasn't going to fall for her again. Over his dead body. He'd keep her so lost in passion, she couldn't see her nose in front of her face, much less another man.

"Come on," he said, his throat tight as he thought of all the things he liked to do to her. She liked them, too. He held up his arms to help her dismount.

"I need to get home," she protested.

"Eat first. You could use a pound or two." He plucked her off the mare and set her on her feet. He tied her string of horses to a post and ordered the stable hand to water them. "Give them a bucket of oats, while you're at it," he added.

Taking Beth's arm, he guided her to Rachel. The three of them went toward the house. Kerrigan finished and bounded across the quadrangle, catching them just as they went into the kitchen.

The four of them washed up, then sat in the kitchen, eating warm pumpkin pie with whipped cream and discussing the cattle roundup and the winter to come.

"This last truckload will get all of our cows moved to the valley," Kerrigan said in satisfaction.

"Snow cows," Beth said.

"What?" Rachel asked.

"My father called the cows that are trucked to warmer locations during the winter *snow cows*. Like tourists who go south in the winter are called snowbirds," she explained.

"We move fifty miles, down into the Rogue Valley, a drop of over a thousand feet in altitude. Elmer trucks his cattle all the way to northern California. Your father didn't think much of the practice, I take it," Keegan put in with a wry expression.

"Well," Beth said, drawing the word out. "He thought it was a kind of sissy way to ranch."

"Sissy!" Keegan turned a mock scowl on her. "Moving several hundred head of dumb animals is not a sissy thing."

"Right," his brother agreed. "Stupid, maybe, but not sissy."

The four of them burst into laughter. A cry from the back of the house had Rachel on her feet. "Oh-oh, milk monster awakens."

She brought the baby to the table and nursed him while they finished their pie. When Beth got up to leave, Rachel reminded her of the dinner on Saturday night. "My brother loves Mexican food. I'm going to try out one of your mother's recipes on him. Come over about seven."

"I will. Thanks for the pie. It was delicious." Beth headed for the door. Keegan was there to open it for her. He walked out and saw her mounted.

"Shall I come over later?" he asked.

Her heart leapt to her throat. He gazed at her with hunger burning in his eyes, a low flame now, but she knew how that could change in an instant. "Yes," she whispered.

He smiled. The flames leapt a little higher in his eyes. Inside her, they burst into fireworks. She clicked to the mare and headed down the road. She'd have to go to the county road, then back up her drive since the horses couldn't get over the fence.

On the gravel drive, she set the mare at a ground-eating pace, eager to get home and get a hot shower and fresh clothes. It would be dark in another hour. She thought of Keegan.

Later.

She would wear that short black gown a friend had given her last Christmas as a joke. It was supposed to help her catch a man. Maybe it would work on a mule-headed rancher. She realized she hadn't given up on him yet.

At the end of the McPherson drive, she turned down the side of the road and entered the Ralston property. She automatically noted fences that needed repair as she approached her home. When she passed the path leading to the cemetery, she decided she would come out and sketch for a while after her bath.

She rode into the stable, where Ted and Jeff were tending the horses and feeding the orphan calves. "Hello," she called. "How's everything?"

"Fine with us," Ted assured her. "Skully's back is acting up, so he's at his place with a heating pad. He'll be okay, though."

"Good." She turned her animals over to Jeff, who was bending down and rubbing the blue heelers. The dogs quivered in delight at having their ears scratched. Smiling at him, she headed for the house. A lone figure waited on the porch.

She stopped on the steps, looking up at Keegan, who sat in the swing, rocking gently back and forth.

"It's later," he said, his eyes like hot flames licking over her.

Beth went to the double doors of her bedroom. She opened one and looked back over her shoulder. Keegan leapt from the swing in a rush. She ran, laughing, into the room, him hot on her trail.

When he paused long enough to close the door, she dashed into the bathroom and began to feverishly remove her clothing. She heard a thumping noise in the bedroom and peered around the door.

Keegan had his boots and shirt off. He was working at the fastenings of his pants. She tugged at her jeans, then realized she had to get her boots off. Sitting on the side of the bathtub, she tugged madly at them, then realized she was taking longer than if she proceeded at normal speed. She slowed down.

Keegan appeared in the doorway. He was magnificently naked. "Beat you," he said with a smug grin.

She pushed her pants down and stepped out of them. When she reached for her bra, other hands were there. He stripped her out of her underclothes with easy skill. Turning from his blatant arousal, she adjusted the flow of water and stepped into the shower. He joined her.

"Another first," he said.

"We've bathed together."

"At the warm springs, not here." His large hands rubbed slowly over her, spreading an erotic film of desire as well as lather over her skin.

He stood behind her, his taut body pressed to hers as he caressed her breasts and stomach. She rubbed against him like a cat, feeling voluptuously sensuous. Reaching back, she spread her fingers over his thighs and circled her fingers in delicate spirals over his hard flesh.

"I love the feel of you," she murmured. "The incredible hardness of your muscles, the shivery sensation of rubbing our bodies together."

She showed him, writhing slightly against him, feeling his chest hair on her back, brushing against him with her buttocks and luxuriating in the silky encounter of his body hair.

"You're so smooth," he said. He slowly skimmed his hands over her breasts, right down to her thighs. "Like satin. It's what I think of whenever I recall how you feel in my arms. About a hundred times a day," he added with a wry chuckle.

Keegan pushed her hair out of the way with his nose and kissed behind her ear. She arched her back, demanding more.

With a deft movement, he slipped his fingers over the soapy triangle at her legs. "And here, you're like silk."

He touched her intimately, wringing gasps of ecstasy from her. When she caught her breath and held it, he could take no more. He turned her around to face him. Sitting on the tiled shelf at the end of the tub, he pulled her onto his lap and brought her down on him. He closed his eyes as bliss ran like fire in his veins.

"Silk," he whispered. "Hot, wet silk."

"Is it just us?" she asked in wonder, her voice trembling. "Or is it this way for everybody?"

"I don't give a damn," he groaned.

He thrust powerfully into the warm, welcoming sheath, bare skin next to bare skin. The pleasure rushed through him, so strong he was like a tumbleweed caught in a gale, pushed in front of an invisible force that controlled him utterly.

"Wait," she said. She folded two washcloths and tucked them under her knees on the hard tiles; then she began to move with him, meeting thrust for thrust. Her head dropped back. Her eyes closed, and she caught her bottom lip between her teeth.

Seeing her response heightened his own. He was close to coming apart. Sliding one hand between them, he stroked her tender flesh until she cried out; then she caught her breath again and became very still. He felt the first undulations of her climax.

It was the end for him. Slipping both hands under her, he brought her hard against him, again and again, until he couldn't move at all. For another second he held her and rocked, very gently; then he collapsed against the wall, her on top of him, while they gulped deep, rasping breaths.

"The shower," she said after a while.

The water was getting cold. They finished washing and rinsed. After drying off, he looked at his clothes in distaste.

"I should have brought clean ones."

"You never sleep in anything, anyway," she said.

Keegan paused in surprise. He stepped into the doorway, still drying off with the towel and watched her search through a drawer. She pulled out a short black nightgown. A faint throb of sensual interest darted through him when she pulled it on. Glimpses of her body teased him through the soft gathers of black silky material.

"I've never see that before," he said.

She blushed when she realized he was watching; then she grabbed a robe, slipped on scuffs and padded from the room. In a minute, she was back, holding a dark blue velour robe. "Here. I don't think my father ever wore this. I gave it to him Christmas about three years ago."

Keegan put it on. It fit okay. Her father had been a tall man with a lean build, too.

"I can heat some soup for supper." She looked at him with a question in her eyes.

They would be expecting him at his house, but he was pretty sure Wills had seen him heading through the woods. If he stayed out all night, it was his business. "Fine."

He followed her into the kitchen. She removed a package of soup from the freezer and soon had it thawed and heated. It was homemade, he realized when she put a bowl in front of him. She set out crackers and sourdough rolls, then started a pot of coffee before taking her chair.

He had never eaten a meal in this house, but he'd thought of it. Once, when he was a teenager, before he and his brother left to make their fortunes on the rodeo circuit, he'd thought of it.

"You know, I used to think of this—of you and me here, eating together, living together—when I worked around the ranch and I'd see you and your parents doing things together. Your father used to smile then. I remember hearing him laugh."

Beth looked puzzled. "My parents? That would have been when I was a child."

"Yes. I was sixteen or seventeen. You were twelve or so."

She ate her soup, obviously deep in thought. She glanced at him across the table several times. He polished off the soup, had a second bowl, then used a roll to sop up the last drops. "That was one of the best meals I ever had," he said.

"Thanks." She studied him, then spoke what was on her mind. "I could have thought you wanted me in order to get my ranch," she said. "When we were together three years ago."

He frowned, feeling defensive the way he had all those years growing up on his grandfather's place. "What are you talking about?"

"My father'd had a heart attack. I was home, worried and distraught. The ranch had problems. You could have seen an opportunity to merge my land with yours by sweeping me off my feet, thinking my father would probably die soon."

The rest of the roll dropped into the empty bowl. "I never thought that. I'd never take advantage—"

"I know." She gave him a meaningful stare. "But it was suggested to me. I chose not to believe it, though. Do you know why?"

He had a feeling he was getting a lecture. "Why?"

"Because I believed in you and your love."

The light dawned. "You think I should have believed in yours, when you asked for the land next to the creek?"

She didn't answer.

"If I had, this place would have gone down faster. Your father was already ruining his range by overstocking. Extra water would have hastened that process. He'd have put on more cattle."

Beth gathered the used dishes and put them in the sink. She ran water over them and quickly washed them with a soapy sponge, then left them in the rack to dry. "Maybe with your advice, things would have improved."

"Would your father have listened to me?" He gave a snort of laughter to show his skepticism.

"Did you ever listen to me?" she asked.

"Why don't you just say it? This is really about us." He felt cornered, trapped into an admission he wasn't ready to make. She had used him and his fascination for her—he wasn't going to call it love—and it had backfired. Now she was trying to make him feel guilty.

"Are you trying to persuade me to let you at the water now?" he asked, pushing a cool smile to his lips.

She sighed, then did a strange thing—she smiled at him, a weary smile that tore right at his heart. "No. When we go to court, I'll get the land back."

So it was back to that. He might have known. The Ralstons were as stubborn as pit bulls and as devious as vipers. "Like hell you'll get it back." He headed for the door. It was only when the cold air hit him that he remembered he wore nothing but a velour robe. He slammed the door, anyway.

The lock turned in the slot behind him. He whirled around. She'd locked him out!

"I'll put your clothes on the side porch," she said through the glass. She walked out of the kitchen.

The wind played wanton games, sneaking under the robe and stroking him with icy fingers as he stomped around the porch to her bedroom. He found his clothing in a neat pile on the mat.

Cursing savagely, he pulled them on, tossed the robe on the swing and headed for home. Hell would freeze over before he chased after her again.

Chapter Twelve

"I'd been told by the protocol officer that I must accept whatever my hostess offered as refreshments," Rachel's mother said, telling of her early years as a diplomat's wife. "So when I was offered a cigarette, I thought I had to take it—"

"Mother doesn't smoke," Rachel put in with a grin.

Mrs. Barrett laughed in the attractive manner she had, making gentle fun of herself. "I didn't find out until later that women in that country didn't smoke, but my hostess had been told that American women did, so she was trying to be polite. She watched, in rather horrified fascination, as I lit up...and became horribly ill—"

"But not right off," her husband put in, giving his wife a teasing smile. "Dorothy gallantly puffed up a storm, according to the story that circulated among the embassy staff. She made it through the figs and sugared almonds and coffee, puffing all the while—"

"My hostess kept offering the cigarettes, and I kept smoking them," Dorothy took up the story. "When it was time to leave, I couldn't get up. I was so dizzy, I couldn't stand."

"So she sent me to get the security guard, who was waiting at the car," Rachel explained. "He carried her out. Mother smiled and waved and nodded graciously the whole time. Until we drove out of the compound and out of sight."

"Then she fainted dead away," Mr. Barrett said. "The driver and the guard thought she'd been poisoned or something. They rushed her back to the embassy and took her to the clinic, where the doctor pumped her stomach. Fortunately, before it became an international incident, Rachel piped up and told me 'Momma has been smoking.'"

His imitation of a very young, very disapproving Rachel caused a burst of laughter from their listeners.

Beth laughed, too. She let her gaze sweep around the group. Rachel's parents were delightful, at ease in a dinner setting as one would expect a diplomatic couple to be. The brother, Rafe, was chuckling, but the laughter didn't penetrate his eyes.

She remembered how he'd looked when she'd first arrived. He'd been holding his nephew, playing with him as easily as if he did that kind of thing every day. She knew from talking to Rachel that Rafe was a bachelor, that he'd also been in the foreign service, until a few years ago when he seemed to burn out.

There was something sad about him, Beth mused. It was as if he'd seen too much of the world—the bad parts, not the good ones. In an unguarded moment, while looking at the baby, she knew he'd seen babies crying, starving, dying. He'd glanced up, their eyes had met, and she'd seen the pain and the hidden anger at a world that let children suffer. Then he'd smiled and the impression had faded. Perhaps she'd only imagined it.

Looking at Rachel and Kerrigan, Beth's heart warmed. Like the Barretts, they, too, were a handsome couple. Their joy in each other was a tangible thing, suffusing the house with warmth.

Keegan stirred at her side. She glanced at him. He'd been icy with her all evening. Not obviously, though. He'd played the polite host, telling his share of amusing stories about rodeo days when Mrs. Barrett had indicated an interest in that phase of the twins' lives.

But Beth felt his cold anger each time he looked at her. It was like being hit by the chill November wind that blew in from the northwest. Winter was coming on strong, with rain in the valley and hail on the upper mountain peaks. Soon there would be snow.

"That was a wonderful meal," Rafe said, smiling at his sister. "You'll have to give me the recipe."

"It came from Beth. You'll have to ask her," Rachel advised.

Rafe turned his gaze to Beth. He had eyes like his sister's, gray and as clear as rain. He surveyed her dark hair, then her green eyes. "Your mother was Latino?"

"Half. My grandfather was from Mexico."

"But the eyes and skin..." His voice trailed off as his eyes skimmed over her very fair complexion with the natural blush.

"My father was a redheaded Irishman. I inherited his eyes and fair skin, but got my mother's black hair."

"A lovely combination," he murmured.

Their eyes met, and again she saw into him—a man who loved beauty but had seen too much ugliness. Her smile was sympathetic. "Thank you."

Keegan clenched his fist on his napkin. If Rachel's brother didn't quit looking at Beth like that, he was going to punch him. Yeah, right. That would be real smart. But he didn't like the way the guy smiled.

"Let's go into the living room for dessert," Rachel suggested. "Kerrigan has built us a fire. I love a fire on a cold night."

They stood when she did and filed out of the dining room.

"I'll help you," Beth volunteered.

Rafe stepped close to Beth. "So will I."

"I'm going to my room to freshen up," Mrs. Barrett decided. "I won't be a minute."

Her husband joined her.

Keegan stalked out of the dining room behind his brother. In the hall, Kerrigan slowed and glanced over his shoulder. He spoke in a barely audible voice. "Watch it, big brother. Rafe is my brother-in-law. If you start throwing punches because of a few appreciative glances at Beth, I'll have to defend him."

"Hell," Keegan said.

His twin grinned at him. "Yeah, life can be like that. You got it bad, man." He paused. "Why don't you marry her?"

Keegan muttered another expletive. "Why don't you mind your own business?"

Kerrigan held up both hands. "Just a suggestion." His face became serious. "If you married her, that would solve the water problem, wouldn't it? It would be in the family then."

They went into the living room. Keegan added another log to the fire and poked the logs until the flames leapt toward the chimney. The wind howled outside. A damned cold night.

"Hmm, that would be a good deal," Kerrigan continued. "Merge her land with ours. The Triple R would get access to the water, and we'd get access to the grazing rights."

Leasing grazing land in the national forest was impossible. The leases were valuable and passed down from one generation to the next like an inheritance. Their grandfather had cursed the Ralstons more than once because of that advantage.

Keegan grabbed his brother's suit lapel in an angry fist. "I'd never do anything so underhanded," he snarled.

His brother looked at him in surprise. "Hey," he said softly.

Keegan relaxed his hold. "Sorry." He ran a hand through his hair. "Beth accused me of doing something like that with her."

"When?"

"Last night."

"So that's why you came back early. We figured you would spend the night like you did the other time—" He stopped abruptly.

"You knew?" Keegan said.

"Did you think we wouldn't notice that you came in the back door for breakfast instead of from your room? Come on, brother. Rachel and I aren't stupid."

Keegan selected a chair and sat down, dropping forward to rest his forearms on his thighs as he gazed into the fire. "When the suit is settled, maybe I'll make an offer.... Hell, I don't know. It's all so complicated."

"She was the woman in your life three years ago, wasn't she? When I came home for Christmas the year you retired, I knew there'd been someone and that it had been pretty serious. You were quiet. Hurting inside. Grieving."

The brothers exchanged glances that spoke of years of silent communications. Last year, Keegan remembered, he'd used that same word to his twin. Grieving. A woman could do that to a man, make him grieve, make him hurt.

"Yeah."

"Marry her."

He shook his head. "Have you forgotten she has a lawsuit going against us? If she dropped it, I might—" He broke off.

"A test?" Kerrigan asked in a musing tone. A smile lit his face. "Just make sure you're not the one who fails."

Keegan shrugged impatiently. "After we win this suit, we can up our offer on her land. She'll be glad to sell before she goes under," he predicted.

Then he would decide what to do. Maybe he'd go to her, talk to her, see where they stood.

But not until they'd won the damned lawsuit!

Beth carefully stacked the dinner plates. Rafe collected the silverware and placed it in a plastic bowl. They were clearing the table, while Rachel prepared coffee and sliced the pie in the kitchen.

"Do you live at Moose Creek year-round?" she asked. Moose Creek was the name of an exclusive resort owned by Rachel and her brother, down near the Anderson ski area. Very posh, very "in" with the "in" crowd these days.

"Yes. I like the mountains."

"They're a good place to hide—" She realized what she was saying and stopped. A flush rose in her face. "I'm sorry. That was terribly rude of me."

"I think," he murmured, giving her a wry smile, "that you see too much."

"No, no," she protested. "It was just...when you were holding the baby earlier...there was a sadness."

"The babies of the world have a rough time," he commented. "There, that's all the knives, forks and spoons. Shall we see about that dessert?"

Beth recognized the change of subject as a close to the topic of his emotions. She smiled gratefully. Truth was, she hadn't been at her best so far that evening. She'd had little to add to the evening's conversation and had mostly listened, her mind wandering on its own tangents.

Rafe let her precede him into the kitchen. The pumpkin pie was ready. So was the coffee, elegantly served in a sterling silver service, loaded on a silver tray. Cups and spoons were on another tray.

"Take those first," Rachel directed, sprinkling nutmeg over the whipped-cream topping on the pie slices.

With Rafe carrying the heavier tray, Beth took the one with the cups and headed for the living room. The twins and the older couple were seated in front of the fireplace.

Keegan rose and took the tray from Beth when she came in. He noticed a blush lingered on her cheeks. What had they been talking about to bring the color to her face? He gave her a narrow-eyed scowl. Which she returned with an icy glare.

He thumped the tray on the coffee table. "Coffee?" he asked Mrs. Barrett. Anger swirled anew when Rafe and Beth left together, chatting about the pumpkins used in the pie. In a minute they were back, Rachel with them, with the plates of dessert. When everyone was seated, he noted that Rafe and Beth sat side by side on the sofa, their shoulders brushing as they ate.

Another hour passed.

"Well, I've got to go home," Beth announced, rising.

The men immediately rose, too.

"I'll walk you out," Keegan volunteered. He had a thing or two to say to her about charming Rachel's brother.

She smiled prettily. "Rafe has already volunteered."

Rachel's brother laid a hand on Beth's arm. "I need to move around and let some of that pie shake down." He smiled at Rachel. "You've turned into a darned fine cook. Who'd have thought it?"

Rachel wrinkled her nose at him. "A family never appreciates one's talents."

After saying good-night to everyone and hugging Rachel, Beth went to the front door. Rafe held her jacket for her. She'd worn a simple black wool suit with a green silk blouse. They went outside to her truck.

"If you have time for a vacation, give me a call," Rafe invited. He gave her his card. "Do you like to ski?"

"Yes, very much. But I'm kind of rusty."

"We'd take it easy. I'm strictly a recreational skier." He helped her into the truck with a hand on her arm. His touch was friendly but unobtrusive. It didn't singe her insides with longing.

"I...I probably won't," she said. "The ranch is short-handed right now. There's so much work." An apology was in her tone.

"I understand," he said.

She started the engine. He stepped back and closed the door. As she drove away from the house, she saw light spill onto the porch as someone came out of the house. A white shirt gleamed in the moonlight.

Keegan coming to check on her, she assumed. To make sure she wasn't seducing his guest? As if she needed more complications in her life.

In the rearview mirror, she saw Rafe join Keegan at the railing. Two hard men, she thought, hard to figure out, hard to love.

The courtroom was full, just as Beth had expected it to be. Ranchers had come for miles around to listen to the case, some out of simple curiosity, many concerned about the issue of water rights. Beth smiled at several men she knew. They gave her guarded nods in return.

She and Jack Norton took their places at the table assigned to them. It was only when she was seated that she dared look at the McPhersons. The twins were there with their lawyer.

Like her, they were dressed in conservative dark suits. Where the brothers wore white shirts with muted ties, she wore a softly draped silk blouse of pale peach with a single string of pearls.

Rachel was sitting behind the men on a courtroom bench. She gave Beth a big smile of encouragement. Rachel was the nicest person she had ever known, Beth decided, smiling back. She felt her lips tremble slightly.

Her eyes met Keegan's as she turned toward the front. His gaze was as piercing as ice shards. She clenched her hands and faced the front.

The bailiff entered from a side door. "All rise."

Everyone stood.

The judge swept into the rooms and took his seat. Judge Harvey was a new judge, one she didn't know. She sat down amid the general clatter of people settling themselves. The trial was on.

"Things are going well," Jack assured her at lunch.

She lowered the menu. "Are they?" Since she was the plaintiff, her side was presented first. Then the McPhersons got to defend their position. Like chess, she thought, each got a turn attacking the other.

Looking up, she stared straight into narrowed gray eyes. "Oh, no," she murmured.

Jack clucked sympathetically. "Sorry. I wasn't thinking. Their attorney eats here nearly every day. I should have realized it might bother you to have lunch with your adversaries, so to speak.''

''Not at all,'' Beth said coolly, deliberately turning her gaze from Keegan's icy glare. She smiled at Rachel, who was holding Kelly, feeling sadness well up inside.

The McPhersons were a solid team. With the three of them, the baby-sitter, their lawyer and his very attractive assistant, their table was full. She and Jack were the only two in their booth.

She felt the loneliness surrounding her like a vacuum. The long nights, spent mostly alone in her house with the November gales howling around the eaves, were the worst.

Nights are forever...

The wailing cry of a tormented love song sang through her mind. She could tell the songwriter about endless nights.

Keegan leaned close to the assistant attorney's blond hair and replied to a remark the woman had made. The assistant smiled at him in that way women did when they found a man interesting.

Beth wanted to go to him, nestle in his arms, be comforted. She wanted to drop the damned suit and be done with it.

She couldn't. Pride wouldn't let her give up.

Rachel came over to Beth's table, Kelly in her arms. Jack stood. The two women exchanged greetings. Beth introduced her attorney.

''This is so awkward,'' Rachel complained. She grinned. ''We all look like choir kids, our hair combed and slicked back, dressed in our Sunday best.''

Jack chuckled. ''In a divorce case last year, I used those very words to my client when it was time for the hearing. She showed up in her shortest skirt, tightest knit top and her longest eyelashes. Fortunately, a dress store was open in the mall, and we got her to switch to a dark blue suit.''

Beth managed a laugh. The baby craned his neck around at the sound, spied Beth and threw out his arms, lunging for her with a squeal of delight. She caught him as he fell toward her.

"Scamp," Rachel scolded. "He thinks everyone is ready to catch him like his daddy and his uncle."

The nickname tore at Beth's heart. "Scamp," she whispered, gazing into Kelly's eyes, which were blue, like his father's, with flecks of golden brown, like his mother's. Babies were intriguing combinations of their parents.

"Oh, there's our food," Rachel said. She reclaimed her son. "How do you feel about starting a quilt this winter? Think about it. Nice to meet you," she said to Jack as she left.

"Nice person," Jack said in admiration.

"Yes."

"Well, we have two more witnesses this afternoon, then they can present their side. Since the courthouse records were destroyed by fire and you both hold deeds to the land, this whole case depends on people's memory of your grandfather and the McPhersons' grandfather and what they thought the men would have done. The judge will have to decide who he believes."

"There's more of them to believe," she reminded him.

"The weight of the law will be on your side. Everyone knows Ralstons have held that land for generations. The McPhersons are newcomers by comparison."

Beth nodded. They ordered and ate quickly, then hurried back to the courtroom.

The afternoon witnesses were Skully and Ted. Jeff sat in the back of the courtroom, looking awed and nervous for the two old men who had raised him. They'd allowed him to miss a day of school.

Ted went on the witness stand first. Beth realized the two retired cowboys were her best weapons. They had known her grandfather personally, had worked alongside him in their younger days. Their adamant testimony that he would never have sold that land was convincing.

"Besides," Skully added during his time on the stand, "he couldn't have signed anything at that time. I was just remembering last night—he'd had a stroke and could hardly speak, much less write."

"My God," Jack muttered beside her. He leapt to his feet.

Both attorneys yelled motions over each other. The judge called them to the bench, where they conversed in low tones; then he declared a recess until the next morning.

Waiting for the crowd to clear out, Beth glanced at Keegan. He listened to his attorney, nodded, then looked at her. He was furious, she realized.

"We've got the case," Jack chortled, neatly arranging papers in his briefcase.

"What's going to happen?"

"Your family has used the same doctor for years. We have only to check his records and the hospital's to prove your granddad was incapacitated at the time. It's mostly a formality now. Everyone believed your hired hands."

"They're not—" she started, then stopped.

Beth considered Ted and Skully to be family, a part of the ranch and her life, but technically, she supposed they were hired hands. "I need to say goodbye to them. They have to get back to the ranch." She hurried out so she wouldn't come face-to-face with Keegan when his group left.

After seeing the old men and Jeff off, Beth went to her motel. It was one of the largest in Medford, convenient to the highway. Restless, she couldn't stay still long enough to read the novel she'd brought with her. Pulling on sweats and running shoes, she jogged down the side streets until she was breathless; then she walked until she was tired. It was twilight when she returned to the motel.

She rounded the corner, heading for her room, and crashed into a solid chest. "Oh, I'm sorry." She looked up at the tall man who steadied her with hands on her shoulders . . . and gasped.

"Are you staying here?" Keegan demanded, his hands tightening as he glared down at her.

"Yes."

He bit off one succinct curse and let her go. "I might have known. I'll move." He headed down the corridor.

"It doesn't bother me to have you here," she informed him. "After all, we're not sharing a room."

His head whipped around. For a long ten seconds, he didn't move, only looked at her with an unreadable expression. Then he pulled a key out of his pocket and entered a nearby room, closing the door behind him.

Beth continued to the stairs, went up them and to her room. She decided to order her dinner from room service. Even though she'd completely lost her appetite.

"I have the records," Jack told her, grinning in satisfaction. "It's an open-and-shut case."

"You went to the hospital?" Beth asked. She slipped past him and took her seat at the table.

"And the doctor. I can substantiate the degree of the stroke and the dates he was in the hospital before he died. He couldn't have signed any papers during that time."

"All rise," the bailiff intoned.

With the new evidence, the judge called them to his chambers. The attorneys looked over the evidence and presented opposing arguments about admitting it. The judge made his decision. It was over in fifteen minutes. The land belonged to the Ralstons.

She risked a glance at Keegan. And wished she hadn't.

He was looking straight at her, his face immobile. Only his eyes showed emotion. Cold, implacable fury. Whatever he might have felt for her at one time was gone. It was obvious he hated her now.

Chapter Thirteen

"Creek's up," Jeff said.

Beth peered out the barn door. The water lapped over the rounded stones at each side of the old wagon ford used by the early pioneers. "Umm-hmm."

It had rained every day since the trial. All the ponds had water in them, far from full, but enough to get them through the winter and into spring. Not enough for next summer, though.

She hadn't taken a tractor and ripped out the fence as Skully wanted to do. For one thing, they needed to get a fence up on the other side of the creek before they could let the cows down there for a drink. For another, it was too hard to work in the rain.

"Well, we're finished," Jeff announced.

Beth forced her attention to the task at hand. She and Jeff had taken care of feeding the livestock and checking over the cattle. They pulled on raincoats and headed for the house.

The wind cut right through her clothing, freezing cold, making her face and hands ache. It grabbed the door when she opened the latch and slammed the heavy oak into the kitchen wall. Jeff put his weight behind the door and closed it.

"Whew," he said.

"Amen," she replied. "I'm for a hot shower."

"Hurry," Skully advised. He was bent over the oven, peering at the turkey. "It's ready."

"Boy, it smells good." Jeff took a long sniff.

Beth hurried to her room, threw off her work clothes and turned on the shower. The caress of the warm water brought back memories she didn't want...Keegan's hands, roaming over her in gentle caresses...his lips, smiling sometimes, sometimes scowling, but always, when he touched her, exciting...his body, lean and hard, sharing pleasure so intense, so profound, the memory brought a surge of tears...Keegan's eyes, as gray and cold as the early winter storm. Hating her.

Quickly she finished washing, flicked off the water and began drying off, wanting to get out of the bedroom, away from all memory. But it was impossible.

The day of the trial had been the last time she'd seen Keegan. He'd left the area the next day, according to Rachel, who had called and invited Beth to Thanksgiving dinner at their house.

"We always have dinner here with our men," Beth had explained her polite refusal. Her men—Skully, Ted and Jeff.

"Bring them along. We'll have enough."

Rachel's laughter had enticed Beth to accept. It had been so long since she'd heard joy. Years, it seemed.

"Keegan won't be here," Rachel had continued in a quieter tone. "He's gone to Texas to look at some horses for our registered stock. He won't be back for a month, until just before Christmas."

It had been a temptation—to share the holiday in a close, loving family.

"Rachel, I can't," she'd finally said to her friend. "Not right now."

"I understand," Rachel had assured her, her sadness coming through the telephone. She'd switched to a lighter tone. "Don't eat too much turkey. Have a happy Thanksgiving."

"You, too," Beth had said.

Beth hung the towel over the rack and went into her bedroom. There, in that bed where she'd dreamed her girlish fantasies, he'd come to her, holding her, loving her, giving her hope. . . .

Warmth. Companionship. Fulfillment.

And he'd taken it all away with his distrust of her motives. Strange, she mused, both men—her father and Keegan—were gone from her life, but she still felt trapped between them, the way she'd been three years ago.

Love, she thought, the bitterness rising from some deep place within her. It could be a curse as much as a blessing.

She dressed carefully for the occasion, as her mother had taught her—a black wool skirt and a peach silk blouse with a pearl necklace and earrings, stockings and black patent leather pumps. A dusting of makeup, and she was ready.

Going into the dining room, she paused and watched Jeff set the long, formal table. Skully had already put on the Brussels cut-work-and-lace tablecloth. Her mother had believed in using the china and linens that filled the butler's pantry.

Beth wrote out place cards and stuck them in the slot on the tiny ceramic turkeys Jeff had set next to each plate. The large, matching turkey, which was a soup tureen, was in the center of the table. She peeked inside at the steaming soup. Their first course was ready to be served.

Skully stuck his head around the door. "Ready?"

"Yes," she and Jeff said in unison. Jeff selected a Mozart Symphony and turned the stereo on low. Beth went to the head of the table.

When they were seated and Beth, as tradition demanded of the last Ralston, had given the blessing, they began the feast.

"Remember the time Grandpa and Uncle Skully were mad about a card game and wouldn't speak to each other all during Thanksgiving dinner?" Jeff asked.

Beth roused from her gray mood and looked at the men around the table. They each wore a suit and tie. Ted's lovely white hair was short and waved back from his forehead. Skully's hair was pulled back in a braid and had a turkey feather stuck in it. Jeff had dark blond hair that covered his ears and curled around his collar. Skully had cut it for him.

A wave of affection swept over her. These men deserved her best. She smiled at Jeff. "I remember a time when my mom got mad at my father and made him a skillet of corn bread . . . from chicken feed."

"Did he eat it?" Jeff asked.

"With butter and three pieces of chicken," Skully interjected.

On this lighter note, they finished the meal. After the dishes were washed and the kitchen cleaned, Beth divided up the leftovers and sent some home with each man, double for Ted since Jeff lived with him.

Skully lingered after the other two departed. "How about a cup of coffee for the road?"

"Sure." She poured the coffee. They sat at the kitchen table. "I believe that was your best meal ever."

The old man smiled. She noted the lines on his face. The smile lines were much deeper than the frown lines. It was a nice legacy of his attitude toward life. She realized she was feeling very philosophical of late.

"You say that every year," he reminded her. He watched the steam rising from his cup for a minute. "Why don't you go to see him?" he asked suddenly.

She didn't bother to ask who. "I can't."

"Pride is a lonely bedfellow."

The desperate loneliness rose in her. "Did you ever love a woman, Skully? I mean, enough to want to marry her?"

"Yes."

A shudder went through Beth at the bleakness in the word. She wanted to ask what had happened, but it seemed too personal.

He answered as if she had. "I was poor, a cowboy without land of my own. I never wanted any, to tell you the truth. I liked what I was doing. Her father had a store. She wanted me to work there, become a tradesman. It would have been like prison."

"And you never found anyone else," Beth concluded.

Skully smiled, a nostalgic gleam appearing in his eyes. "I never said that. Your mother was a pretty special woman."

"Oh, Skully." She couldn't keep the pity from her voice.

"It wasn't a tragedy. I loved your father, too. He was only a few years younger than I was. For all his stubbornness, we were near as close as I am to my own brother." He grinned. "The three of us boys cut a swath through the gals in the county. Then your dad and Ted got married. Heck, I got the best of it. Ted's son was like my own. Then there was you, and later, Jeff came to live here when his folks died. I got the family with none of the problems."

"There's so few of us left," she said mournfully.

"Jeff will be going off to college in three years. He wants to be an engineer, build things." Skully sighed heavily. "You need to marry, gal. Get this place going again."

"It takes two."

"He's not far away," Skully reminded her. "And he's been here a couple of times."

Heat rushed into Beth's face.

"No need to get flustered. You two are right together. I saw it three years ago."

Looking into his eyes, Beth realized she had no secrets from Skully. "He hates me. Because of the land."

"Seems there must be more to it than that."

"He thinks I betrayed him, used him to get access to the water."

"You were caught in the middle." At her glance of surprise, Skully continued, "I heard your dad going on to you about it. He was sick, and you were afraid for him. He knew that. Only dishonest thing I ever saw him do, but things were pretty bad on the ranch then."

"Yes," she agreed. She drained her cup, set it aside.

His wise old eyes studied her. "Give him the land on the other side of the creek."

She stared at him, startled by the idea. "It might work," she said slowly. "If I show him I'm willing to share...if we could work together as neighbors..."

"That's the spirit." Skully stood and stretched. "Well, I need a nap after all that food and gabbing."

Beth smiled at him. He'd gotten her around to his way of thinking, and now he could go home. He'd done the same thing when she was a child, coaxing her into seeing her father in a new light when their stubborn natures had collided.

After helping him into his warm coat and hat, she stood at the door and watched him lean into the wind and dash for his small cottage. Sighing, she went to her room and changed to warm, knit pajamas. From there she drifted into the ranch office, which also served as a library.

She looked over the novels and histories of the West. Nothing grabbed her attention. She sat down in the big leather chair that had been used by generations of Ralstons as they worked on the ranch books. Idly she picked up the journal she'd been reading.

A daily record of ranch life, starting with her ancestress's diary when, as a bride, Elizabeth Myers Ralston had left her home in Massachusetts to come West with her husband.

Such courage, Beth thought. But they'd had love.

In fact, all her ancestors had been lucky, not only in love, but in life. The journal entries had very few tragedies to mar the fabric of their lives. Not that life had been easy. They'd worked hard, but mostly the writings were full of optimism and joy.

A bubble of hope rose in her, making her light-headed. If she showed her goodwill by giving back the land on the other side of the creek, Keegan would have to believe her good intentions.

Filled with determination for this new goal, she resumed her grandfather's journals. When she closed the last one, a pang of sadness echoed through her. She'd been about eight when he'd died. His handwriting had been shaky and almost illegible at the end, just before his stroke twenty years ago.

Each spring, before his last illness, he'd taken her for a walk to the orchard to look at the blossoms and assess the fall crop of fruit. He'd taken her opinion very seriously.

She wanted to pass that heritage on to her children. Hers and Keegan's. A shiver of apprehension went through her. What if Skully was wrong and she couldn't convince Keegan of her integrity?

The wind shrieked around the house, reminding her of Keegan's cold, stubborn heart.

"You can't do that," Jack advised her.

Beth watched the December sky from the warmth of Jack's office for a moment. Down here in the Rogue Valley, it was misting rain. At the higher elevation of the ranch, it was snowing a heavy, wet snow—a cold, miserable day wherever a person happened to be.

"Why not?" she asked, turning back to him.

"The land is too valuable. If you give it to McPherson, one of you will have to pay gift taxes on it."

"I can give it to the four of them—"

"Four owners for one parcel of land? Too complicated." Jack shook his head. "Their ranch is incorporated, so you can't give it to them through it. Besides, he'd refuse it, don't you think?"

"Probably," she agreed. "Well, it was a thought."

"A generous one."

"But stupid," she added on a rueful note.

Jack grinned. "Well, just complicated. The law, you know."

She understood. "The other thing is my shop and condo. Have you heard from the woman who leased them?"

"Yes. She was delighted at the chance to buy them. With the condo within walking distance of the shop, she says it's perfect. Here's her counteroffer."

Beth looked over the figures. "Fine. Better than I expected, to tell you the truth, given the state of the economy."

"I thought so, too. So, shall we proceed?"

"Yes."

When Beth walked out of the attorney's office a short time later, she felt both lighter and heavier. Lighter because she didn't have to worry about the business and condo in San Francisco anymore and because she'd have enough money to get the ranch on its feet; heavier because all her resources would be tied up in the ranch. It would either make or break her. Only time would tell.

The idea depressed her.

When she arrived back at the small town that served the ranchers and loggers in her area, she considered stopping at the diner for a late lunch. A muddy red pickup parked in front changed her mind. She pushed down on the gas pedal and left the town.

She wondered if Keegan had returned home after his buying trip. Her heart contracted painfully.

The rear wheels of the truck skidded on a slick curve, and she had to slow down. During the rest of the journey to her house, she had a lot of time to think. None of her thoughts were happy.

She reflected that she'd done her best for her father and for Keegan, considering the past. She'd tried to reconcile them and resolve the problem of the land next to the creek. She'd failed.

She had thought of her love as a bridge between the two hard-minded men in her life. She'd been confident that she would forge a compromise and that life would be wonderful for all of them as they worked together and loved each other. But she'd failed.

Her father had accused her of turning against her own family when she'd argued Keegan's side; Keegan had accused her of using passion to sway him when she spoke of her father's feelings. She'd failed in every attempt to bring them together.

Failure. Failure. Failure. The tires seemed to hiss the word at her as they sliced through the rain on the pavement.

God, she was in an awful mood.

At the ranch she dashed into the house, carrying the Christmas presents she'd bought for Skully, Ted and Jeff. She'd already sent cards to her friends in San Francisco and to the local people. She wished the holidays were over, but there was a week to go until Christmas.

A note from Skully was tacked on the corkboard. He informed her the chores were done and a pot of chili was on the stove.

Grateful, she changed to pajamas instead of work clothes, built a fire in the grate and ate in front of the leaping flames.

The wind swept down out of the mountains. Without it and the whisper of the fire, she would have eaten in utter silence. In her mind she reviewed the past three years, searching for clues, for things she could have done that would have made a difference.

She shook her head and sighed. She'd done her best. It was just that her father and Keegan hadn't listened.

It came to her that perhaps *they* had failed *her*.

Her roving thoughts came to an abrupt halt. For the first time, she acknowledged that perhaps *they* hadn't tried. What had either of them given back to her for all the love and worry she'd expended over them? They'd dug in their heels and refused to budge from their stances. And they'd each demanded her loyalty.

Neither of them had loved her enough to give an inch. It seemed a selfish thought, and yet... And yet it was true, she forced herself to admit. It was time she accepted the fact that neither man had loved her enough to put her happiness first.

The emptiness inside her spread until her soul existed in a void of total blackness.

"Abandon hope, all ye who enter here," she declaimed with a hand over her heart.

Mocking her self-pity didn't work, she found. The misery was too great. When the fire burned down, she went to bed and wished she didn't have to wake up. She'd never sunk quite that low in spirit. Before, she'd always had hope for a better tomorrow.

Beth shrugged out of her coat. She hung it and her knit hat on a hook, washed her hands, patted lotion on her cold face and walked briskly to the ranch office. She paid the bills, balanced the checking account and put the books away.

With a look of determination, she tackled the double set of oak filing cabinets set against the wall between two windows. It wasn't a day to be romping outdoors, but she hated paperwork. However, she'd vowed to clean out the files before the end of the year. She had the bottom two drawers to go.

Getting a large trash bag, she started by throwing out scads of outdated advice from magazines and brochures on cattle ranching. She kept the bulletins from the Oregon Cattlemen's Association for the past two years and tossed the rest. When she pulled the file stop forward, she saw some journals lying on the bottom of the cabinet.

"Father's journals," she exclaimed. She'd wondered where they were or if they existed. She knew her mom had kept the diary going before she died. Beth hadn't been sure her father had bothered.

She laid them on the desk—three hardcover ledgers with closely lined pages, filled with her father's writing.

Although she was anxious to read them, she virtuously finished the job she'd set for herself at the beginning of the month. This last task would see all the files and records updated and in order. Letters and business transactions, along with the journals, might make an interesting book. She would save those.

She decided to steep a pot of tea and have cinnamon toast before reading the ledgers. In the kitchen she put on the kettle to heat and spread margarine over bread slices. A knock on the door startled her. She put the knife down and opened the back door. Rachel was there. "Hi. Come in," Beth invited.

Rachel rushed in like a leaf blown by the wind. "Hello. Isn't this wind terrible?" she complained. "One of our big stacks of hay blew over this morning. The men are trying to move it next to the stable and cover it before the hay ruins."

"I wish them luck." Beth waved toward a chair. "Have a seat. I was just making toast and tea. Care to join me?"

"I'd love some."

They chatted about the weather and the problems it caused, while the bread toasted and filled the air with the scent of sugar, cinnamon and melted margarine.

"Come into the office. I made a fire," Beth said.

They took their plates and cups with them.

"Can you believe Christmas is less than a week away?" Rachel demanded when they were seated. Without waiting for an answer, she got to the point of her visit. "I came over to ask what you were doing tomorrow night. We're having some people over for eggnog."

Beth tried to think of an excuse that would seem plausible and not hurt Rachel's feelings.

"Keegan left for New York this morning."

"Oh."

Rachel set her cup down. She stared into the flames for a minute, a pensive expression coming over her face. "He's going to the opening of a show at the invitation of an actress he dated last year."

"Oh, yes, I remember seeing them on the news a couple of times," Beth said brightly. "He was at the ceremony when she won an award for a TV special."

"Beth—" Rachel stopped, then shook her head. "Men can be such...mules."

Beth searched inside herself. By force of will she had managed to keep the emotions at bay so that she felt nothing. She maintained the emptiness in light of this latest news.

"Amen to that," she said, laughing. It came out okay, she thought. Light. Uncaring.

Rachel gave her a probing glance. "He'll be back on Christmas Eve." She hesitated. "Why don't you join us for dinner? Just the four of us and a quiet evening."

Beth began shaking her head before Rachel finished. "Thanks, Rachel, but...no. I'd rather not."

"We can't be friends, can we?" Rachel burst out. "Damn Keegan and his pride!"

"It was never in the cards—the Ralstons and the Mc-Phersons." Beth felt a ping of sadness for the friendship that could never be, then it, too, was gone, and she was empty again.

"I'm only a McPherson by marriage," Rachel declared.

"Perhaps if we were to get together like this once in a while," Beth suggested. "Afternoon tea. Very posh and correct." She lifted her nose into the air.

"Yes, that would be fun."

"And you might bring that adorable son next time."

"I'll be hostess next week."

Beth thought of running into Keegan. Although she felt empty inside, it was a peaceful feeling. She was afraid to stir things up with a confrontation. "I'd rather have you come here. Would you mind?"

Rachel studied her for a minute. "No, of course not."

After her neighbor left, Beth stood at the window and watched the car move off into the rain. She thought of the home and family that waited at the end of the Sky Eagle road. For a second the blackness quivered, then it steadied, and she felt calm again.

She poured another cup of tea and returned to the office. There, she picked up a journal and began reading. Midway through the book, a slip of paper fell out.

Beth bent and picked it up off the floor. Uncurling from the chair, she built up the fire again and returned to her seat. With her feet tucked under her, she laid the journal in her lap and perused the note.

It was the carbon copy of a business form. The ink was very faint on the buff-colored paper. She turned the lamp up a notch and held the paper toward the light. As she picked out the words, her mouth dropped open in disbelief. It was a bill of sale . . . for the land along the creek.

Chapter Fourteen

"No," Beth said. "Oh, God, no."

She read the paper again. Her hand shook. The internal vacuum that had gotten her through each day shifted on its foundation. Emotions rushed in—disbelief, realization, anger and finally the blackest pit of all...despair.

She closed her eyes and sank back against the chair, her head too heavy to hold up. Her world crumpled silently around her, like ashes falling in a heap. Dear God, she felt like falling apart herself, just letting go and forgetting everything....

Except she couldn't. There were things to be done. She had to think. It was her responsibility to set the record straight.

Pushing the despair back, she sought the comfort of the emptiness again. She strived for calm, slowly driving out all emotion from the black pit until nothing was left but the dark.

Nothing.

At last she read the document again. All the implications of that one sheet of paper swarmed through her mind. Her father had lied. No, worse than that. He had committed a crime, an outright fraud. And she had believed him.

The emptiness wavered. Resentment flickered. And anger. She clung to the blank darkness until she could go on.

Ironically her father had spoken the truth when he'd insisted his father would never have sold that creek property to the McPhersons. Grandfather hadn't. Like Skully and Ted had said, he'd been too ill to sign anything. But her father hadn't been too ill.

She would have to turn the paper over to the court and correct the records. She read it once more. It was the end for her. She knew that. Without access to that water, her ranch was doomed.

A piece of paper. A single sheet of parchment.

She'd been clinging to the land, the only solid thing left in her world. It was all she had left of her life here, her heritage. She'd needed it to keep her going.

Because she'd already lost Keegan, she realized. And with losing him, she'd lost her future. The land was all she'd had.

And she didn't rightfully have that, either.

The log in the fireplace crackled and broke apart. The flames leapt greedily along the wood. Beth stared at the flames. She looked at the paper. It would burn fast, so fast . . . and no one would ever know . . . except her.

The ranch was all she had. The water was necessary to keep it going. Keegan had so much—land, water, family, the actress.

He had so much and she had so little. He didn't need the water. She did. He didn't know what it was to fail.

He'd never been trapped inside the black pit.

She clutched the chair and closed her eyes against the allure of the flames. They danced behind her eyelids. She thrust herself up, surging to her feet, knowing she should flee.

But the temptation was strong.

The fire beckoned with the promise of consuming all in its flickering, intricate dervish. It danced and danced before her. . . .

Beth walked into Jack's office at nine the next morning. She had already talked to him at his home. He'd told her to bring the paper in. Without a word she laid the copy of the bill of sale on his desk.

"The original is probably somewhere in the Sky Eagle's records," she said when Jack looked up after reading the document.

"Are we sure this is authentic?" he asked.

She nodded. "I am. I . . . recognized the writing immediately."

The irony of that statement struck her. The handwriting had belonged to her father. He'd forged her grandfather's name.

She'd figured out why. The ranch had been in trouble even in her grandfather's day. Her father had been running things on his own for almost a year since her grandfather's stroke and he had desperately needed money.

The twins' grandfather had wanted the land by the creek, so her father had forged the name and sold the land, using the money to put the ranch back on its feet. He'd succeeded in keeping it going for seventeen years before he went into debt again. The long drought had been the breaking point.

Anyway, the reason for the forgery wasn't the main issue. The land had been sold, money had exchanged hands, and the honor of the Ralstons was at stake. The land had to be returned to its rightful owners.

"I want you to do whatever is necessary to get the land turned over to the Sky Eagle ranch." She smiled. "It will make a nice Christmas present, don't you think?"

Jack gave her a stern glance. "We need to study this, make sure it's authentic. I'll call in a handwriting expert—"

"No," she said firmly. "I'll vouch for it. It's real. There're a couple of other things I want you to do." She took a list from her purse and began going over the items one by one.

When she finished, her attorney studied her a long moment. "You've made up your mind, haven't you?"

"Yes," she said, "I have."

The letter arrived on Christmas Eve. Keegan stopped by the mailbox at the end of the ranch road before going on to the house.

He should have been glad to be home. He was tired. He'd been to every play and every party in New York for the past two weeks. He hadn't been to bed at all the previous night and he'd taken the first flight out that morning. But no surge of joy heralded his arrival on the land he'd grown to love.

The ranch reminded him of too many disappointments in his life. Hell, admit it, it reminded him of Beth.

Feeling grim as death, he flicked through the mail. What was this? A letter from Jack Norton. Beth's attorney.

What the hell? He tore open the letter and unfolded the piece of creamy-colored bond paper. He read through the brief message twice before he believed it. If the offer still stood, the letter informed them, his client had decided to accept it.

Beth was selling out.

He stepped on the gas and headed for the house. Maybe Kerrigan and Rachel could tell him what was going on.

Keegan saw his brother dash from the stable when he drove up. They met at the back of the truck. Kerrigan grabbed his suitcase and hefted it over the railing.

"About time, big brother," he said and clapped an arm around Keegan's shoulders in an affectionate hug. "Come on in. Rachel is baking cookies. We can sample a dozen or two."

When Keegan opened the kitchen door, the scent of sugar and spices assailed him with a sense of homecoming. He hadn't let himself acknowledge how much he'd missed this place during the month he'd been gone.

Rachel exclaimed in delight and danced over to give him a kiss and a big hug. "I was beginning to think we'd have to arm the men and send them after you," she scolded after their greeting.

"No way. I'd walk from New York for a taste of your Christmas cookies." He laid the mail on the counter, except for the letter from Beth's attorney.

"Sit down and help yourselves." She waved toward the platter of homemade goodies on the table. "There's fresh coffee, too."

Kerrigan poured coffee for the three of them.

"Where's the monster?" Keegan asked.

"Asleep, thank goodness." Rachel brushed a strand of hair from her eyes. "He loves the tree, although he seems to think he's a present, too. He wants to nest under it. I have to watch him every second when he's up. He's walking now," she added offhandedly.

Keegan grinned. "Takes after his uncle," he declared. He turned to his twin. "We got a strange letter. From Jack

Norton. He says Beth wants to sell her place. You know what's going on?''

Kerrigan and Rachel exchanged glances. Their smiles dried up. Keegan braced himself for unpleasant news.

''We tried to call you,'' Rachel began.

''If you'd ever returned our calls, you'd know there's been some rather startling happenings around here,'' his brother said, frowning at him.

Keegan stirred uncomfortably at the reprimand. He hadn't called because he'd been trying like hell to forget this corner of the world and Beth's underhanded winning of the case. Saving that bit about her grandfather's stroke until last had been a ploy to sway the court. One thing he knew— *his* grandfather hadn't lied. Whatever else the old man had done, he'd never lied.

''The land by the creek has been returned to us,'' Kerrigan announced.

That didn't make an ounce of sense. ''What are you talking about?''

''It's true,'' Rachel put in. The timer went off on the stove. She darted across the room to take care of the baking.

Keegan stared at his brother. He started to speak and found his throat had closed up. ''What happened?'' he asked hoarsely.

''Beth found a copy of the bill of sale. She took it to Jack Norton. Norton contacted our attorney, and they showed it to the judge. The land is ours now, free and clear, no controversy.''

Keegan was flummoxed at the news. ''Ours,'' he repeated, trying to grasp some truth that persisted in evading him. ''She gave it back, just like that?''

''Just like that,'' Rachel assured him. She gave him a rather hard look over her shoulder.

"You say she wants to sell?" Kerrigan asked, puzzled. "Have you seen her?"

Keegan handed over the letter. Kerrigan read it. Rachel put in a new batch of cookies, then came over and read the letter. When she put it down, she had tears in her eyes.

She looked at Keegan. "Well, this should make you happy."

"Rachel," Kerrigan said in tones Keegan had never heard him use to his wife.

"I'm sorry," she said, "but Beth is my friend." She left the kitchen abruptly.

"Rachel blames me for Beth's decision to leave," Keegan concluded. A weight settled on his chest. He clenched his fist, wanting to get the hell out of there and ride...where? Not to the Triple R. Beth would probably shoot him on sight.

His twin shrugged helplessly. "Before she found the bill of sale, Beth tried to give the land on this side of the creek to Kelly, to be held in trust with us as guardians. We refused, of course, but Rachel saw it as a heroic effort at peace between the ranches. She thinks Beth loves you and that if you'd tried harder, you two could have worked things out."

The cookie Keegan had eaten felt like granite dust in his stomach. He pushed the chair back and paced the room. "I've got to get out of here," he muttered. "I've got to...think." He started down the hall.

"Are we still on for the Triple R?" Kerrigan called.

He stopped and looked back. "Buy it," he said grimly.

Going to his room, he changed and headed for the stable. A short time later he headed for the hills on his favorite stallion, a pack horse following behind them.

He reached the line shack near the eagle's gorge late in the afternoon. He unpacked and stowed his gear inside.

Then he went for a walk along the ridge. He spied the nest where the eagles had raised their young the year before.

Last year's fire had blackened the ground, but he found a clean boulder to perch on. He gazed at the distant peaks. Here, where no one would bother him, he could look at himself.

He didn't like what he saw—a man hardened by life, a man who wouldn't listen to the truth, no matter how earnestly it was spoken, a man who'd taken a woman's love and returned it with distrust and scorn, not once but twice.

Beth.

She must hate him now. He put a hand over his eyes, but he was helpless against the despair that attacked him.

Beth.

She'd wanted peace between the two men in her life. He and her father had torn her to pieces in their war with each other.

Beth.

She'd given him her love. She'd assumed his love was as great and pure as hers. But it wasn't. His love had made demands and conceded nothing. The only thing he'd given her had been an impossible choice.

Beth.

She could have destroyed that paper. So simple. The flare of a match and it would have been gone. But she hadn't. Knowing that to turn it in would cost her everything, yet she hadn't.

Beth.

He looked into his soul and wondered if he would have been that honorable.

Beth, he whispered silently in his heart.

But there was no answer.

He stayed on the mountain for two weeks.

* * *

"It's five after three," Beth said. "Where are they?"

The woman handling the closing of the sale looked up from her stack of papers. "You don't have to wait," she said. "I'll forward the check to you."

"I want it now. Everything's arranged." She wanted her money so she could leave. She had five days after the closing to get the movers in and clear out of the house. The packing was done. The furniture would be loaded onto the van in two days. She'd stay at the house until then and follow her stuff to Seattle.

She had decided to try a new city and make a new life. She'd found a Victorian mansion at a good location. There she would open her flower shop, plus she planned to rent space to artisans to make and sell their products. That should be fun ... well, interesting. She no longer expected more of life.

She sighed and forced all thoughts at bay. The door opened. She whipped around. Keegan entered. He was alone. She had assumed their attorney would handle the transaction.

"Mr. McPherson?" the woman with the title company asked.

"Yes. Keegan McPherson."

"And your...uh, brother?"

"I can sign for him."

"Then we can begin. You have a cashier's check?"

He nodded.

Beth felt the emptiness inside her contract, as if his presence crowded her internal space as it did the room. She held on to the darkness, needing the calm that came with it.

He was dressed in a well-fitted suit of dark blue with a light blue shirt. His gray eyes took on slate blue tones. She realized he was watching her. She looked away.

Without another word, he began reading over the papers. When he finished, he laid them on the polished desk.

"Do you have any questions?" the title officer asked.

"Where's the lease for the grazing rights?"

The woman's blank expression clearly indicated her answer.

He turned to Beth. "Didn't you renew the lease for the year?"

"Yes." A niggle of uneasiness riffled through her. What was he getting at? She held on to her poise, not allowing even anger to intrude on her inner silence. Life was easier without emotions.

"I want it, too."

"You'll have to talk to the forest service. The quarter isn't up until the end of March. The lease is paid through then."

"Good. When it's transferred, I'll sign the papers." He stood up.

"What?" This was some trick. Perhaps he thought she would come down in price. Anger reared. She tamped it down. "I have no control over the lease. You'll have to apply—"

"The ranch can't sustain a working herd without the extra land. The lease has to go with it or it's no deal." He headed for the door and walked out.

Beth stared at the woman across the desk, whose mouth was open in a frankly puzzled manner. The anger resurrected itself. Anger was good, she decided. She could handle it.

"Damn him!" she muttered, grabbed her purse and took off.

She caught him at his truck. "Just a minute," she ordered through clenched teeth. She grabbed the truck door before he could close it. "You can't walk out like that."

"I just did." His eyes challenged her. "I think we should reconsider the offer—"

"It's the same offer you made in August," she snapped. "The situation has changed since then."

For the life of her, she couldn't figure him out. There was a watchful quality to his gaze, as if he were trying to see beneath the surface of her thoughts. She stepped away from the truck, afraid of standing too close, of getting hurt...no, she wouldn't let that happen.

"Do you think I'm still trying to trick you?" she asked, ice shards of control in every word.

A flicker of some emotion went through him. "No," he said. "I don't think that."

He stared straight ahead, his hands gripped around the steering wheel. He looked so...sad...almost defeated, as if he'd suffered some terrible grief. It was nothing to her, she reminded herself. Hold the cold, the anger, the darkness.

"If you're waiting until I go bankrupt, it'll be a while," she informed him, letting the emptiness wash over her. "I'll sell to the foreign conglomerate then," she threatened, knowing she wouldn't.

He must have known it, too, for he didn't turn on her in anger. He simply swung around and faced her. A smile— again she had the impression of sadness—played at the edges of his mouth. "No, you won't," he said quietly, with absolute certainty.

There was no reasoning with him. She spun on one foot, got in the ranch truck and started the engine.

"I'll see you later," he called before she could drive off.

Keegan followed her the whole way from Medford, through the ranching town and over the county roads until he turned off at his drive. Beth breathed a sigh of relief.

At her house she wandered through the rooms like a ghost. Boxes were everywhere. She picked up the old leather art portfolio that had belonged to her grandmother. Looking at her drawings, she thought how silly she'd been to imagine she could come back and life would suddenly be perfect.

Grabbing all the sketches, she tossed them into a trash can. Restless, she took her pencil case and sketch pad, pulled on her heavy coat and headed for the cemetery. There, seated on the marble slab, she tried to draw, but her heart wasn't in it.

A stillness spread over her. Not even the wind blew. She studied her father's grave. He was at peace now, the thought came to her. A line from Hamlet flitted through her mind. "...And choirs of angels sing thee to thy rest." Her father would never have been able to rest with deceit hanging over his spirit. Now he could.

It's finished, she thought, the problems between the Ralstons and the McPhersons. Finished.

She watched clouds form over the mountain peaks to the north. A thunderstorm. Or snow.

Lost in reverie, she stayed there while the storm built. When the lightning started, she went to the house.

Inside she sat in the increasing gloom, her mind strangely blank, and surveyed the sky from the big window in the office. The call of an owl barely registered on her consciousness.

A minute passed. The owl called again. A tremor ran over her. Perhaps the lightning had disturbed it.

When the call came a third time, she could no longer ignore it. Slowly she got to her feet and went out on the porch. She stood by the railing, one hand clasped around the fluted post holding the roof, and surveyed the woods.

In the deepening gloom of the storm and the coming twilight, a man's distinct shape materialized against the trees. Keegan stepped on the boulder and leapt the fence. He crossed the yard and stood at the bottom of the steps. He'd changed to jeans and a white shirt and wore a down parka against the cold.

"No," she said, denying any feeling his presence stirred. She wanted to stay blank inside...safe.

Anguish crossed his handsome features. "Beth..."

She wrapped her arms across her waist. "Leave me alone, Keegan. I've done all I can to make things right."

"Don't you think I know that?" he ground out. He gripped the banister until his knuckles turned white.

"I'll be leaving in a couple of days—"

"No." He bounded up the steps and stood beside her. He gripped her shoulders. "No," he said again, a fierce whisper.

"Let me go." The emptiness inside her wavered, began to shred at the edges, as if he touched her there, too.

"Never."

She stared into his icy gray eyes. There was no coldness in them. "I...I don't understand."

"I've been a fool," he admitted in a low, strained voice. "If you hate me, tell me and I'll leave. But I hope you don't." He lifted one hand and smoothed the blowing tendrils from her face, his touch so gentle, so very gentle.

"What are you saying?" Her throat was so tight she could only whisper the question.

"I want you to stay."

"I...I can't." A rent appeared in the emptiness. She tried to hold it together.

"I want to start again. With a clean slate. With nothing between us but what we feel for each other."

He closed his eyes, but not before she'd seen the pain in them. When he looked at her again, he didn't try to hide his feelings. He dropped to his knees and wrapped his arms around her thighs. He pressed his face to her abdomen.

"Keegan," she said, confused. The emptiness trembled and tumbled away, leaving her vulnerable and afraid. Feelings rushed in. She touched his shoulder, concern for him eating at her, overriding her sense of self-preservation.

"I'll crawl," he said. "I'm that desperate."

She tugged at him, wanting him on his feet. She'd rather hear him rail at her than see him like this . . . anguished and defeated. She couldn't bear it. "Don't. Please don't."

He stood, dropping his arms at his side. "I've lost you, haven't I? You were everything good in my life, and I didn't see it." He stopped; then he laughed, briefly, bitterly. "Well, no one likes to see a grown man cry."

With one more longing look at her, he turned and gripped the banister. She saw him avert his face and swipe at his eyes as he paused on the step below her. An ache pierced her heart.

"I . . . I wouldn't mind," she said shakily. "I might cry with you."

He spun around, his eyes level with hers.

"It's supposed to be therapeutic . . . to have a good cry." She gave him a half smile, then stared at him solemnly.

"Don't tease," he requested hoarsely. "I know I deserve whatever hell you want to put me through, but not now. My control isn't all that steady."

She identified the emotion in his eyes. Pain. Yes. Regret. That, too. And . . . what else? "Keegan, you have to tell me. I can't go on instinct anymore. What do you want from me?"

"Your love," he answered promptly. "Like you gave it before. Openly. Completely."

"Then you believe I didn't try to sway you with passion?" Her voice shook uncontrollably. If he couldn't give her his trust, she couldn't accept his love.

"Yes." He was adamant, his gaze dead level. "I was wrong. I see that...now." He reached for her, stopped himself and clenched his fists at his side. "I love you," he said, low and desperate. "I've never stopped. I'll love you forever. Oh, God, Beth, tell me to get out or take me in."

She didn't think. She didn't consider the consequences. She simply reached out and clasped him to her, holding him, feeling his warmth surround her, feeling his arms draw her closer, so tight they could hardly breathe, feeling his lips on hers.

Feeling...

He bent suddenly and lifted her. He carried her to her bedroom door. There he stopped. "May I?"

It touched her to hear him ask permission to enter her home, to see him somehow humbled by his need of her—this hard-minded man who'd won her so completely three years ago.

"Yes."

Inside he set her down. They each let their coats fall to the floor, their eyes locked on each other.

"I love you," he said.

Outside, the first drops of sleety rain began to fall. She opened her mouth, but no words came.

"It's all right," he whispered. "You don't have to say it. If you'll give me a chance, I'll earn your love again."

A light blinked on inside her, dispelling any lingering traces of darkness. "No, you don't have to." But the words were hard to say. It was like taking a giant leap and not being sure where she would land. But she did it. "I love you, too."

He caught her to him. A tremor ran over his lean, hard frame. "Ah, Beth, I was afraid I'd never hear you say that again." He held her face up to his.

The kiss was endless, reaching right down inside her, healing the last of the old wounds. Then his hands roved over her, gently, skillfully, thoroughly, until they were both undressed.

He pulled the covers back and laid her in bed. Then there was only the hunger and the love, all around them, inside and outside, everywhere. It filled all the empty places.

"I'll have to unpack," she murmured a long time later.

"I'll help you. We'll move my things over here." He paused and looked at her.

"Yes." She touched him tenderly.

"Will you let me buy into your operation?"

"Yes. Why didn't you take it this afternoon?"

A smile, slightly sardonic, directed at himself, appeared on his face. "I couldn't. This was your land, your heritage. I couldn't take it from you. If you'll let me share it, I'll be content."

"I wanted to give the land by the creek back to you. Before I found the bill of sale."

"I know. Rachel and Kerrigan told me. They've agreed to sell the land on this side to me. Then I'll give it to you."

She was surprised. "Why?"

"Don't ask stupid questions," he ordered gruffly.

"Because you love me," she concluded, knowing it was true. She sighed as pure happiness rushed over her.

He gathered her close and whispered in her ear. "More than the land, and God knows I love that." He touched her face with fingers that were exquisitely gentle. ''More than life itself.''

It was all she could have ever hoped for.

* * * * *

Silhouette

SPECIAL EDITION®

**It takes a very
special man to win**

That

SPECIAL
Woman!

She's friend, wife, mother—she's you! And beside each Special
Woman stands a wonderfully special man. It's a celebration of
our heroines—and the men who become part of their lives.

Look for these exciting titles from Silhouette Special Edition:

August   MORE THAN HE BARGAINED FOR by Carole Halston
Heroine: Avery Payton—a woman struggling for independence
falls for the man next door.

September   A HUSBAND TO REMEMBER by Lisa Jackson
Heroine: Nikki Carrothers—a woman without memories meets the
man she should never have forgotten...her husband.

October   ON HER OWN by Pat Warren
Heroine: Sara Shepard—a woman returns to her hometown and
confronts the hero of her childhood dreams.

November   GRAND PRIZE WINNER! by Tracy Sinclair
Heroine: Kelley McCormick—a woman takes the trip of a lifetime
and wins the greatest prize of all...love!

December   POINT OF DEPARTURE by Lindsay McKenna
(Women of Glory)
Heroine: Lt. Callie Donovan—a woman takes on the system and
must accept the help of a kind and sexy stranger.

Don't miss THAT SPECIAL WOMAN! each month—from some
of your special authors! Only from Silhouette Special Edition!

TSW3

Silhouette®

SPECIAL EDITION™®

WILD RIVER TRILOGY

by Laurie Paige

Come meet the wild McPherson men and see how these three sexy
bachelors are tamed!

In HOME FOR A WILD HEART (SE #828) you got to know
Kerrigan McPherson. Now meet the rest of the family:

A PLACE FOR EAGLES, September 1993—
Keegan McPherson gets the surprise of his life.

THE WAY OF A MAN, November 1993—
Paul McPherson finally meets his match.

Don't miss any of these exciting titles—only for our readers and only
from Silhouette Special Edition!

Silhouette

SPECIAL EDITION®

*From this
day
forward*

**Coming in September,
the second book in an exciting trilogy by**

Debbie Macomber
BRIDE WANTED

Advertising for a bride on a billboard may have been brazen, but it got
Chase Goodman what he wanted—beautiful Lesley Campbell. And
now he wanted much more....

FROM THIS DAY FORWARD—Three couples marry first
and find love later in this heartwarming trilogy.

Look for
MARRIAGE WANTED (SE #842) in October.
Only from Silhouette Special Edition.

Silhouette Books has done it again!

Opening night in October has never been as exciting! Come watch as the curtain rises and romance flourishes when the stars of tomorrow make their debuts today!

Revel in Jodi O'Donnell's STILL SWEET ON HIM—
Silhouette Romance #969
...as Callie Farrell's renovation of the family homestead leads her straight into the arms of teenage crush Drew Barnett!

Tingle with Carol Devine's BEAUTY AND THE BEASTMASTER—
Silhouette Desire #816
...as legal eagle Amanda Tarkington is carried off by wrestler Bram Masterson!

Thrill to Elyn Day's A BED OF ROSES—
Silhouette Special Edition #846
...as Dana Whitaker's body and soul are healed by sexy physical therapist Michael Gordon!

Believe when Kylie Brant's McLAIN'S LAW —
Silhouette Intimate Moments #528
...takes you into detective Connor McLain's life as he falls for psychic—and suspect—Michele Easton!

Catch the classics of tomorrow—*premiering* today—
only from ❤. *Silhouette*

Silhouette Books
is proud to present
our best authors,
their best books...
and the best in
your reading pleasure!

Throughout 1993, look for exciting
books by these top names in
contemporary romance:

DIANA PALMER—
Fire and Ice in June

ELIZABETH LOWELL—
Fever in July

CATHERINE COULTER—
Afterglow in August

LINDA HOWARD—
Come Lie With Me in September

When it comes to passion,
we wrote the book.

BOBT2

TAKE A WALK ON THE
DARK SIDE OF LOVE WITH

Silhouette®

SHADOWS '93

October is the shivery season, when chill winds blow and
shadows walk the night. Come along with us into a haunting
world where love and danger go hand in hand, where
passions will thrill you and dangers will chill you. Silhouette's
second annual collection from the dark side of love brings
you three perfectly haunting tales from three of our most
bewitching authors:

Kathleen Korbel
Carla Cassidy
Lori Herter

Haunting a store near you this October.

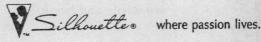

Only from   *Silhouette*®   where passion lives.

SHAD93